THE SOUL SUMMONER

Book One

ELICIA HYDER

Inkwell & Quill, LLC

Inkwell & Quill, LLC

Cover by Christian Bentulan

For More Information:
www.eliciahyder.com

The Soul Summoner is for my kids...
in hopes that it pays for college.

ACKNOWLEDGMENTS

Special Thanks to everyone who made this book possible:

To Dr. Gopal Kunta and his staff (Hi, Rena!) - Thanks for keeping me alive to see this thing published.

To my family and friends who nursed me back to health this year.

Chris for being my in-house specialist in all things police and military related. I love you.

Matt Nichols at Mr. Maple in Flat Rock, NC for teaching me about trees.

Jane M. Wallace, BSN RN for checking my medical ramblings.

All my favorite Asheville businesses and beers mentioned in this book and the city itself for being as rad as it is.

MY AWESOME LAUNCH TEAM - I would be nowhere without you! (Alphabetically):

Nikki Allen, Elsbeth Balas, Tracie Bechard, Cindy Brown, Tiffany Cagle, R.K. Close, Erica, May Freighter, Venice Gilmore, Lina Hanson, Ashley Huttinger, Susan Huttinger, Kristin Jacques, Ara James, Tango Jordan, Juliet Lyons, Chuck Mason, Sal Mason, Tammy Oja, Wendy Pyatt, Lucy Rhodes, Megan Robinson, Melody Shalurne, Vandi Shelton, Ana Simons, Stephanie Smith, Heather Grace Stewart, Leigh W. Stuart, Jen Wander Woman, Shanna Whitten, Russ Williams, Stephanie Williams, Bridgett Wilson, Natalie Wolicki, Ann Writes

The Soul Summoner Series Order

Book 1 - **The Soul Summoner**
Book 2 - **The Siren**
Book 3 - **The Angel of Death**
Book 4 - **The Taken**
Book 5 - **The Sacrifice**
Book 6 - **The Regular Guy**
Book 7 - **The Soul Destroyer**
Book 8 - **The Guardian**
Book 9 - **The Daughter of Zion**

Standalones:
The Detective
The Mercenary
The Archangel

CHAPTER ONE

Her hazel eyes were judging me again. *God, I wish I could read minds instead.*

Adrianne spun her fork into her spaghetti, letting the tines scrape against the china. I cringed from the sound. She pointed her forkful of noodles at my face. "I think you're a witch."

I laughed to cover my nerves. "You've said that before." Under the white tablecloth, I crossed my fingers and prayed we would breeze through this conversation one more time.

A small, teasing smile played at the corner of her painted lips. "I really think you are."

I shook my head. "I'm not a witch."

She shrugged. "You might be a witch."

I picked up my white wine. "I wish I had a dollar for every time I've heard that. I could pay off my student loans." With one deep gulp, I finished off the glass.

She swallowed the bite in her mouth and leaned toward me. "Come on. I might die if I don't get to see him tonight! Do you really want that kind of guilt on your hands?"

I rolled my eyes. "You're so dramatic."

She placed her fork beside her plate and reached over to squeeze my hand. "Please try."

My shoulders caved. "OK." I shoved my chair back a few inches and crossed my legs on top of my seat. I closed my eyes, shook my long brown hair off my shoulders, and blew out a deep slow breath as I made circular O's with my fingertips. Slowly, my hands floated down till they rested on my knees. I began to moan. "Ohhhhhmmmm..."

Adrianne threw her napkin at me, drawing the attention of the surrounding guests at Alejandro's Italian Bistro. "Be serious!"

I dropped my feet to the floor and laughed as I scooted closer to the table. "*You* be serious," I said. "You know that's not how it works."

She laughed. "You don't even know how it works!" She flattened her palms on the tablecloth. "Here, I'll make it easy. Repeat after me. Billy Stewart, Billy Stewart, Billy Stewart," she chanted.

I groaned and closed my eyes. "Billy Stewart, Billy Stewart, Billy Stewart."

She broke out in giggles and covered her mouth. "You're such a freak!"

I raised an eyebrow. "You call me that a lot."

"You know I'm only joking. Sort of."

Adrianne Marx had been my best friend since the fifth grade, but sometimes I still had trouble deciphering when she was joking and when she was being serious.

I picked up my fork again and pointed it at her. "It's not gonna happen, so don't get too excited."

She let out a deep breath. "I'm not."

I smirked. "Whatever."

Our waiter, who had been the topic of our conversation before Adrianne began gushing about her new crush on Billy Stewart, appeared at our table.

"Can I get you ladies anything else?" His Southern drawl was so smooth I had nicknamed him Elvis over dinner. He was a little older than the two of us, maybe twenty-three, and he had a sweet, genuine smile. His hair was almost black, and his eyes were the color of sparkling sapphires. I had drunk enough water that night to float the Titanic just so I could watch him refill my glass.

I looked at his name tag. "Luke, do I look like a witch?"

His mouth fell open. "Uh, I don't think so?" His response was more of a question than an answer.

Across the table, Adrianne was twisting strands of her auburn ponytail around her finger. I nodded toward Luke. "See, he doesn't think I'm a witch."

Luke lowered his voice and leaned one hand on our table. "You're too pretty to be a witch," he added, with a wink.

I smiled with satisfaction.

Adrianne laughed and pushed her plate away from her. "Don't be fooled, Luke. She has powers you can't even dream of."

He looked down at me and smiled. "Oh really?" He leaned down and lowered his voice. "How about you let me take care of this for you"—he dangled our bill in front of my face—"and later, when I get off, I can hear all about your powers?"

Heat rose in my cheeks as I took the check from his hand, and when I pulled a pen from his waistband apron, his breath caught in his chest. I flashed my best sultry smile up at him and scribbled my name and phone number on the back of the bill. I stood up, letting my hand linger in his as I gave him the check. "I'm in town on a break from college for the weekend, so let me know when you get off."

He smiled and backed away from the table. "I will"—he looked down at the paper—"Sloan."

I took a deep breath to calm the butterflies in my stomach as Adrianne followed me toward the front door. She nudged me with her elbow. "You should win some kind of award for being able to pick up guys," she said as we passed through the small rush of dinner customers coming in.

I shrugged my shoulders and glanced back at her with a mischievous grin. "Maybe it's part of my gift."

"Witch," she muttered.

The icy chill of winter nipped at my face as I pushed the glass door open. When we walked out onto the sidewalk, I stopped so suddenly that Adrianne tripped over my legs and tumbled to the concrete.

Billy Stewart was waiting at a red light in front of the restaurant.

Adrianne might never have even noticed Billy's official game warden truck at the stoplight had my mouth not been hanging open when she struggled to her feet. She was cursing me under her breath as her eyes followed the direction of my dumbfounded gaze across the dark parking lot. When her eyes landed on the green and gold truck, she fell back a step.

Her fingers, still coated in gravel dust, dug into my arm. "Is that...?"

I turned my horrified eyes to meet hers when traffic started moving again.

Frantically, she waved her finger in the direction of the traffic light. "That was Billy Stewart!" She was so excited that her voice cracked.

"Yeah, it was." Mortification settled over me, and I pressed my eyes closed, hoping to wake from a bad dream. When I focused on Adrianne again, I realized she had taken a pretty nasty fall. Her blue jeans were torn and her right knee was bloody. "Oh geez, I'm so sorry."

She looked at me, her eyes wild with a clear mix of anxiety and amusement. She glanced down at the gash on her knee. "Can you heal me too?" Her question had a touch of maniacal laughter.

I shoved her shoulder. "Shut up." I tugged her toward the

restaurant's entrance. "Let's go to the bathroom and get you cleaned up."

Once we were behind the closed door of the ladies room, Adrianne's curious eyes turned toward me again. She hiked her leg up on the counter beside the sink. "What the hell just happened out there?"

I ran some cold water over a paper towel and handed it to her "I need a drink." I splashed my face with cold water and, for a moment, considered drowning myself in the sink.

She pointed at me as she dabbed the oozing blood off her kneecap. "You and me both, sister. You've got some major explaining to do."

Alejandro's had a small bar near the front door where I had never seen anyone actually sit. When we pulled out two empty bar stools, the slightly balding bartender looked at us like we might be lost. His eyebrows rose in question as he mindlessly polished water spots off of a wine glass.

"I think I'm going to need a Jack and Coke," Adrianne announced.

I held up two fingers. "Make that two."

"IDs?" he asked.

Getting carded was one of the best things about being twenty-one. Any other time, I would have whipped out my finally-legal identification with a smile plastered on my face. But in that moment, fear of what the next conversation might bring loomed over me like a black storm cloud that was ready to drop a funnel.

I had already learned the hard way not to talk about these things.

People are scared of what they can't comprehend, and the last thing I wanted was for Adrianne to be afraid of me. Despite my unnatural propensity toward popularity, Adrianne was one of the only real friends I had.

I knew the jabs she made about me being a witch were all in jest, but there was a part of her that had been genuinely curious about me since we were kids. Adrianne, above anyone else, had the most cause to be suspicious of the odd 'coincidences' that were happening more and more frequently around me.

Summoning Billy Stewart had been a complete accident. God knows I had tried my whole life to summon all sorts of people—my birth mother and Johnny Depp to name a couple—without any success at all. Sitting next to Adrianne at the bar, I knew from the look in her eyes that seeing Billy at that stoplight solidified to her what I already knew to be true: I was different. Very different.

Swiveling her chair around to face me, she pointed to the dining table we had just vacated. "OK, I was kidding about Billy at dinner. That was some serious David Copperfield shit you just pulled out there, Sloan. Totally creepy."

I groaned and dropped my face into my hands. "I know."

An arm came to rest behind my back, and Luke appeared between our seats with a tantalizing grin that would normally make me swoon. "Did you miss me that much?" he asked.

Adrianne pointed a well-manicured fingernail at him. "Not now, Elvis," she said without taking her eyes off me.

Stunned, Luke took a few steps back.

I offered him an apologetic wink. "We need a minute."

He nodded awkwardly, stuffed his hands into his pockets, and left us alone.

When he was gone, I turned back to Adrianne. "I don't suppose you could be convinced this was all a really big coincidence?"

"Sloan, when we ran into my Gran after you said you needed to pick up some canned green beans from her, that was a coincidence. When we were talking about going to Matt Sheridan's keg party and we ran into him at the beer store, that was a coincidence. When you said you hoped Shannon Green would get syphilis and we saw her walking out of the Health Department, maybe even that was a coincidence." We both laughed.

She tapped her nails against the bar top. "Billy Stewart is supposed to be working on the backside of a mountain right now,

Sloan. He shouldn't be anywhere near the city. I was joking and trying to get you to make him magically appear…and then *you did.* That's not a coincidence."

I groaned.

She lowered her voice and leaned into me. "What are you not telling me? Did you make that happen or not?"

It was too late to try and recover with a lie. I had no other choice but to tell her the truth. My legs were shaking under the table and a trickle of sweat ran down my spine. "I'm not a hundred percent certain, but yes. I think so."

She sucked in a deep breath and blew it out slowly. Her eyes were wide and looking everywhere but into mine. "I'm going to be honest. You're kinda freaking me out a little bit right now."

I nodded and pinched the bridge of my nose. "I know. I wish I had a grand explanation, but I've never had anyone explain it to me either."

I felt her hand squeeze mine. "I love you, so let me have it. Tell me everything."

My stomach felt like an elevator free falling through the shaft. "You're going to think I'm crazy."

"Sloan, I think we bypassed crazy about twenty minutes ago," she said with a genuine chuckle.

The bartender placed our drinks in front of us, and I wrapped my fingers around the short tumbler. Adrianne drained half of her whiskey in one swallow.

I took a deep breath. I let my thoughts roll around for a moment in my head, and I tried to choose my words carefully so I didn't sound as nuts as I felt. Finally, I looked at her and lowered my voice. "You know when you're out and you see someone you really feel like you know, but you can't remember how or who they are?"

She nodded. "Sure."

I paused for a moment. "I feel that way around *everyone*. Like I already know them."

Her face contorted with confusion. She tried to laugh it off without success. "Well, I've always said you've never met a stranger."

I looked at her seriously. "I haven't *ever* met a stranger, Adrianne."

She cleared her throat. "I really don't understand what you're talking about."

Sadly, I didn't understand what I was talking about either.

"I see people I've never met and feel like I've known them forever. I can even just see a picture of someone and know if they are alive or dead and what kind of person they are. I don't know their names or anything specific, but I have a weird sense about them before ever talking to them. It's like I recognize their soul."

She let my words sink in for a moment. "Like the time you told me not to go out with the exchange student in the eleventh grade, and then he date-raped that cheerleader?"

"Yes. I knew he had a lot of evil in him," I said.

"And you get these 'vibes' from everyone?" she asked.

I nodded. "Absolutely everyone."

"So that's why you're so good with people…why you can talk to anyone and everyone at any time?"

I nodded again. "It's easy to befriend people when it feels like you've known them for years, and I seem to be somewhat of a people-magnet."

She interrupted me. "But what does that have to do with Billy Stewart showing up here tonight?"

"There's more."

She sat back, exasperated. "Of course there is."

"I think it's somehow related. People are naturally drawn to me, and somehow I can manipulate that."

Her eyes widened. "You can control people?" Her voice was almost a whisper.

"I don't think I would call it *controlling* people…" My voice trailed off as I sorted through my thoughts. "I know things about people, and sometimes when I talk about someone, it's like I can summon them to me."

She laughed, but it was clear she didn't think it was funny. "Come on, Sloan. Really?"

"Just think about it." I looked at her over the rim of my tumbler and sipped my drink.

She was quiet for a while. There were a thousand odd events she could have been replaying in her mind. Like, the time I said I wanted Jason Ward to ask me to the homecoming dance, and he was waiting by my locker after class. Or, when I told her I had a bad feeling about our gym teacher, and we found out on Monday he had died of a heart attack over the weekend. Finally, she looked at me again. "You know I wouldn't believe a word of this if I hadn't known you for so long."

I nodded. "I don't believe it most of the time myself."

"When you say you 'know' people. What do you know? Like, do you know that guy?" She pointed at the bartender.

I laughed. "No. It's just a sense I get. I can tell you he's an OK guy, but I'm not a mind reader."

She drummed her long nails on the countertop. "So you're psychic?"

"No, I don't think so. I just seem to be able to read people really well."

She leaned toward me and dramatically fanned her fingers like a magician. "And make people suddenly appear!"

"Shhhh!" I looked cautiously around.

Luke, who was waiting nearby, caught my eye and started in our direction.

Adrianne extended her long arm to stop him. "Not so fast, you little eager beaver."

I laughed, and the tension finally started to drain from my shoulders. After a moment, I gripped her arm. "You're not gonna get all freaked out on me now, are you? I haven't told anyone about this since I was old enough to know better."

Her head snapped back with surprise. "Old enough to know better?"

I ran my fingers across the faint scar just above my right eyebrow. "Kids can be pretty cruel when they find out you're different. When I was eight and we still lived in Florida, one of them threw a big rock at me during recess."

She gasped. "That's horrible!"

I nodded. "After that, Mom and Dad decided it would be best to move."

"So they know about what you can do?" she asked.

I shook my head. "Not exactly. Whatever is wrong with me can't be explained by science, so I think it scares them to talk about it. They haven't brought it up once since we moved here." I touched my scar again. "And seven stitches in the face taught me to keep my mouth shut."

She squeezed my hand, her eyes no longer judgmental. "Well, I'm not going to freak out, and I'm not going to tell anyone."

I sighed. "Thank you."

She grinned over the top of her glass. "No one would believe me anyway."

"I know."

Suddenly, she perked up with a wild smile. "What about Brad Pitt?"

I raised my eyebrows. "What about him?"

"Can you get him here?"

I laughed. "That's not the way it works!"

She crossed her arms over her chest. "How do you know?"

I smiled. "Because I've already tried."

CHAPTER TWO

It had been several years since that night when I finally told Adrianne the truth about me. She had spent that entire weekend hounding me with ridiculous questions:

Can you read people's minds?

If you can sense bad people, why did you let me date Bobby?

How do you get people to come when you call their name?

ARE YOU a witch??

I couldn't blame her. Adrianne knew about as much as I did about whatever powers or abilities I possessed. After that weekend, however, she calmed down, and our friendship returned to being as it had been before I told her—maybe even better.

I finished college that year at the University of North Carolina at Chapel Hill and graduated with a degree in public relations much to the dismay of my father. He was a geriatrics physician who had wanted me to follow in the family footsteps of a long line of doctors in the Jordan family history. Specifically he wanted me to become an obstetrician so we could, as he would like to joke, 'bookend the family practice with one doctor to bring 'em into this world and another doctor to take 'em out!' He was a funny man, my dad.

It had been my mother's idea for me to put my impeccable people skills to use and pursue a career in public relations. I had interned with the Buncombe County media department during college, and when I graduated they offered me a full-time job in the communications office. After two years, I had been promoted to Public Information Officer, which was a fancy title for a publicist. It hadn't proven to be the most glamorous job in the world, but it was fairly easy, close to home, and it paid really well.

Settling in Asheville after college made sense. Most of my life had been centered around that weird little town. Asheville had somehow slid straight from the 70's into the new millennium, pausing in the time shift only long enough to pick up a few Goth kids from the 90's. It was the only city I knew of where one could pay homage to a war memorial, open an investment account, befriend a vampire, visit a fine art gallery, and pick up a new bong —all on the same street. In 2000, Rolling Stone magazine christened Asheville as 'America's New Freak Capital' which reaffirmed my decision to put down permanent roots there.

Over the years, I got better at using my ability and at hiding it. Talking about someone and having them make an appearance had almost become routine. I still couldn't summon just anyone at will, but I had noticed that if I was talking about someone and picturing them in my mind at the same time, they were much more likely to show up. It still hadn't proven true with Johnny Depp or Brad Pitt, however.

The leaves had just begun their colorful transformation in the fall when my workday began at the sheriff's office rather than at my office in the county building. I was to attend the swearing in of two new deputies at nine in the morning and prepare a press release. Before I left my house, I checked my purse to make sure I had remembered to bring my Xanax. I took a half of one as a preemptive strike against the anxiety attack I knew was coming. The sheriff was headquartered at the county jail. I hated going to the jail. A place packed with that many bad people was a panic incubator for a girl like me.

I arrived on time and checked my reflection in the glass doors as I approached the sheriff's office entrance. My white blouse was tucked in all the way around, and my black slacks weren't showing any panty lines. I reached for the door handle, but before I could pull on it, the sheriff himself swung it open and stepped aside for me to enter.

The lobby was full, and I suspected the entire bunch had just watched me check out my own ass in the mirrored glass. "Wonderful," I muttered.

"Nice to see you, Ms. Jordan," Sheriff Davis said with a grin.

I shook his extended hand. "You too, sir."

"We were about to head to my conference room," he said.

I nodded, ducking my head with embarrassment as I fell in line with the group.

As we shuffled through the lobby, the nerve endings at the base of my neck began to tingle. I sucked in a sharp breath and held it. On the count of three, I blew it out slowly and reminded myself that the walls weren't really humming with evil. It was only my imagination. I needed to think about something else. Anything else.

My eyes scanned the room of county officials before landing on the two new officers who were being deputized. One, in particular, was certainly an adequate distraction. He was about my age and a little taller than me in the heels I was wearing. He had short blond hair, and his black police uniform fit so well over his sculpted torso that I would've believed it had been custom made had I not known the county was too cheap for such a luxury. A polished brass name tag was pinned to his chest that I had to squint to read. "N. McNamara" could have been Mr. January on the Buncombe County Hot Cop Calendar if one existed.

"Good morning, Sloan," a familiar, squeaky voice said behind me, snapping me out of my hormone infused daze.

Mary Travers, a petite woman with mousy brown hair and a face smushed like a Pug's, was shuffling to match my stride. I smiled down at her. I liked Mary a lot. She was old enough to be my mother and was one of the most genuinely kind people I'd ever encountered. As the county manager, Mary was also my boss.

"Hey, Mary. How are you today?" I asked.

She pushed her bifocals up the bridge of her stubby nose. "Busy as a bee." She looked up at me. "Are we going to be ready to have the newsletter out by Friday?"

"I'm confident I'll have it done by Thursday," I answered with a smile.

She hugged the armload of file folders she was carrying. "And you'll take the pictures today and get the statement posted on the website and on the Facebook and Twitter thing?"

"Yes, ma'am. I've got it all under control."

She patted my arm like a grandmother praising a child. "Good girl."

The whole group was coming to a slow stop at the locked, heavy metal door to get inside the heart of the facility. All of the doors were secured electronically and were only able to be opened by whoever was running the master control desk. I suspected, given our halted status, that Virginia Claybrooks was working master control.

The sheriff rang the buzzer for a second time, impatiently trying to see through the double-sided mirror beside the door. There was no answer. He pressed the buzzer again.

A loud woman belted over the loudspeaker. "Who keeps blowin' up my door? I'll get to you when I get to you! I've only got two hands, ya know?"

Yep. It was Ms. Claybrooks.

The sheriff let out an exasperated sigh. "Ms. Claybrooks, it's Sheriff Davis. Can you please open the door?"

"Uh...Oh, oh," she stammered over the loudspeaker. Her voice shifted from shrill and threatening to syrupy sweet. "Sheriff, you shoulda said somethin'. C'mon in."

He closed his eyes and silently shook his head as the door slid open. "Thank you, Ms. Claybrooks," he said to her as we passed by her office door.

She stood up and gave him a small wave and a wide, toothy smile.

Ms. Claybrooks, a black lady from southern Georgia, was barely five feet tall and almost as wide. Her bosom was narrowly confined to the sheriff's office button-up shirt she was stuffed into. She wore bright red lipstick and a short bobbed wig. I would guess she was in her mid-fifties. Ms. Claybrooks was one of my favorite people on the planet and almost made it worthwhile for me to face my fears and visit the sheriff's office more often.

She peeked around the corner as the group of us filed in. "Dang, Sheriff Davis! How many people you bringin' through my door today?"

He didn't answer.

I smiled at her. "Hey, Ms. Claybrooks."

Her face shifted into a tilted look of confusion. She planted her feet and put her hand on her wide hip. "How 'you know my name? Do I know you?"

"Everyone knows your name," Mary added with a sweet smile.

"Well, hi there, Mary!" Ms. Claybrooks cheered. "Let's do lunch soon, m'kay?"

Mary nodded and waved to her. "Maybe later this week!"

Ms. Claybrooks swung around into her office and plopped down in the master control chair before picking up her radio and barking into it again. "I told you to hold your damn horses!" she shouted at another unfortunate soul.

I giggled. "I absolutely love that woman."

Mary nodded. "She definitely brightens the mood around this dreary place."

That was the truest statement I had heard all week, but dreary wasn't the word I would've chosen. Before I started to obsess over the heebie jeebies that were creeping in on me, I changed the subject. I leaned down so only Mary could hear me as we filed into the conference room. "Did everyone see me looking at my backside in the window?"

She nodded and chuckled silently. "Everybody."

I groaned.

The swearing in ceremony consisted of oaths, pictures, and paperwork. The hot Mr. January officer was from Raleigh, and he was a detective with an impressive resume. His name was Nathan McNamara. Unfortunately, hanging around to meet him after the ceremony would require spending more time at the jail than I was willing to, no matter how good he looked in his uniform.

Mary insisted on us getting an early lunch together before returning to our office, so she rode with me down the street to the Tupelo Honey Cafe.

"It was a good ceremony today," I said as we sat down at a wooden table that overlooked the street.

She shrugged her shoulders. "Wasn't much of a ceremony if you ask me." She opened up the brunch menu and adjusted her glasses as she carefully scanned the page. "What do you like here?"

"The craft martinis," I replied.

She laughed.

"What do you think about the new officers?" I asked.

"They seem satisfactory," she said, void of any emotion.

I pushed my menu away from me and folded my hands together on the table. "Just satisfactory?"

"Well, the one was really handsome." She was grinning behind her menu.

I perked up. "The cute blond one from Raleigh?"

She pursed her lips and shook her head. "No. The older one who came here from Knoxville. He was a fox."

In my opinion, with his red hair and ultra long nose, he could have been a fox—an actual fox—maybe in a previous lifetime. I grimaced. "No. I meant Detective McNamara. I wouldn't mind getting on a first name basis with him."

She smiled. "Oh, to be young. You never told me what is good to eat here," she said, signaling the end of our boy talk.

My shoulders sank, and I looked out of the window to the busy downtown street. "The goat cheese grits are amazing."

It had been over a year and a half since I had been in an actual relationship with a man. Getting dates wasn't a problem because I enjoyed meeting new people. The problem was my ability to see the grime on the souls of everyone I went out with. That, and the constant worry that men were simply attracted to me because of my power. The longest romance I had ever entertained was with Luke Burcham, the waiter from Alejandro's. Our relationship lasted long distance for a total of three and a half months while I was in college. Elvis broke up with me because he felt like I was hiding something from him. If he only knew.

After lunch, I returned to my office in the Buncombe County building. It was a cozy space with calming gray walls and black and white photos of places I had never visited. The large window behind my desk framed the view of the national forest that was beginning to pop with the colors of autumn. Asheville tourism advice was one of my biggest responsibilities as nature lovers from all over the country flocked to the colorful North Carolina mountains in the fall.

For a few hours, I worked on the county e-mail newsletter before remembering the unedited photos on my camera from that morning. As I ejected the memory card, it catapulted from its slot into the furthest corner under my desk. After an unsuccessful attempt to retrieve it blindly with my toes, I crawled under my desk.

There was a knock at my door.

Startled, I smacked my skull against the underside of my keyboard tray.

When I popped my head up after scrambling backward on my hands and knees, Detective Nathan McNamara was wide-eyed and standing in my doorway with his hand still posed in the knocking position.

"I'm sorry." He cautiously stepped into the room and looked around. "I didn't mean to frighten you. Are you Ms. Jordan?"

In an instant, I forgot about my possible skull fracture and broke out in an involuntary smile. I stood up and extended my hand. "Call me Sloan," I answered as he squeezed my hand. "You're Detective McNamara, correct?"

He shook his head. "Just Nathan or Nate, please."

I smiled again and motioned to the two empty chairs in front of my desk. "Nathan, what can I do for you?"

He had changed out of his formal uniform and was wearing a black polo shirt and black tactical cargos. He wore an olive drab ball cap with a grayscale American flag patch on the front. He had a badge pinned to his belt that I couldn't even look at for fear of getting too distracted. It was the first time I had seen him up close. His eyes were the color of cold gray steel. I had to remind myself he was talking to me and I probably should pay attention so I could respond.

"I have a press release about a missing person." He handed me a sheet of paper before settling into a chair.

Blame it on the tantalizing belt or the eyes, but after glancing at the middle-aged man's photo, without thinking I blurted out "he's dead" as mindlessly as I would've said "thank you" or "yes, I'll go out with you!"

His eyes widened. "Excuse me?" He drew out each syllable.

I slowly sank down behind my desk and cleared my throat as I scrambled for a recovery. "It's just my guess." I shrugged my shoulders like it was no big deal that I had just sounded at best calloused and uncaring, or at worst—crazy.

He studied my face until I thought my heart would pound out of my chest. I couldn't even bring myself to look him in the eye.

Forcing a smile, I placed the sheet carefully in front of my computer screen. "I'll take care of it right away." I hoped he would leave so I could have a proper meltdown, but he looked too puzzled to move. I decided to change the subject. "How did you get stuck bringing me press releases on your first day?"

His shoulders relaxed. "Rookie grunt work, I guess. I think some people aren't too happy that I lateraled straight over to detective."

My heart rate was beginning to slow to normal. "Probably not. Welcome to the department, by the way. You're from Raleigh, right?"

"Yes, ma'am. Technically, I'm from—"

I cut him off, laughing and waving my hand in his direction. "Watch it with the 'ma'am' stuff. I'm pretty sure you're older than me, and I would rather be unprofessional than feel old."

He laughed. "Sorry. I transferred here from Raleigh, but I grew up closer to Durham."

"No kidding?" I asked. "I went to college at UNC."

He reclined in the seat and grimaced. "Ahhh...I'm a State fan."

I crossed my fingers like the letter X. "Boo." I leaned against my desk and frowned. "Oh, that's so sad. I thought I was really going to like you!"

He laughed. "Sucks for me, I guess."

Grinning, I folded my hands in my lap. "Too bad."

Nathan rose from his seat. "Well, I've injured you, insulted you, and I like NC State. I'd better take off before you hate me any more than you already do."

"I'm glad you stopped by, Nathan," I said.

He smiled and I felt a little dizzy. "Me too." He paused at the door. "I'll see you around, Sloan."

I thought about telling him to just fax over missing persons' reports in the future, but I just nodded and enjoyed watching him leave. Interdepartmental efficiency be damned; I wasn't going to let a fax machine stand in the way of another possible visit from Detective McNamara.

When he was gone, I dropped my forehead onto my desk and groaned. After a moment of sulking and one hell of a scolding internal monologue, I typed out the pointless press release.

The cops weren't looking for a person anymore. They were looking for a corpse.

After work, I drove to my parents' mountainside chalet for dinner like I did almost every Monday night.

Robert and Audrey Jordan were actually my adoptive parents but few people knew it. Audrey had been a twenty-two year old nursing student in Florida when she found me wrapped in a pink blanket on a park bench outside of the hospital where she worked. I was only a couple of days old. Even though she was unmarried and only working as an intern, she fought the courts for custody of me and won. My adoption was finalized shortly after she married the man who would become my dad. She had often joked that Robert only married her because he loved me so much, but I knew that wasn't true. They never had any other children.

Even though they were amazing parents, I often wondered if their love for me was completely real, or if it was some kind of supernatural manipulation that obligated them to me.

"Knock knock!" I called as I pushed the front door open.

Mom was in the kitchen with her hands covered in flour. "Hey honey," she called over her shoulder. My mother was about a foot shorter than me and almost too thin. She had cropped brown hair that was showing more gray every time I saw her. However, even at fifty, she still jogged three miles every day and taught yoga at the local senior center.

"Where's Dad?" I jerked my thumb in the direction of the driveway. "His car isn't here."

"Oh, he's running late at the office. He'll be home soon," she said.

I sat down on a stool at the kitchen breakfast bar. "Can I help with anything?" I already knew what her answer would be.

She shook her head. "Nope. I'm almost done. How was work today?"

I recalled the look on Detective McNamara's face and slumped in my seat. I groaned and dropped my face into my hands. "Ugh. I made an idiot out of myself twice today."

She chuckled. "What did you do?"

"Well, I had to go the sheriff's office this morning for a meeting, and before I walked inside I checked myself out very thoroughly in the reflection of the mirrored glass. Little did I know that half the county was in the lobby watching me check my butt for panty lines."

She covered her mouth with her hand and laughed.

I cringed. "And I said something really stupid to this cute new detective at work."

"Oh really?" Her voice slid up an octave. She was clearly more interested in the cute guy than me embarrassing myself. My mother wanted grandkids.

I sighed. "Yeah. I probably blew my chances with him."

Her laugh was full of sarcasm. "You know better than that."

With Nathan McNamara, I wasn't so sure. He had seen a bit of my circus freak side that day.

"Do you like him?" she asked, recalling my attention to the conversation.

I drew circles with my finger on the countertop. "Well, he's really, really attractive and he seems like a pretty good guy, but I only met him today, so I don't know yet."

She nodded and motioned toward the television in the den behind me. "Honey, can you turn on the news?"

I got up and found the remote on the coffee table. I switched on the TV and surfed to the local news station. On the screen, a man in a ridiculous blue suit was waving his arms and pacing around a used car lot. "Commercials." I sat back down at the counter.

"I want to see the weather. I've put together a running group for tomorrow morning," she said. "You should join us."

I laughed. "No thanks."

She leaned over the counter and squeezed my forearm. "Chasing boys around the office isn't exercise, Sloan."

I felt an uneasy nudge in the back of my brain. It was a twinge akin to having a tiny pebble trapped under the lining of a tennis shoe. I pulled away and looked at my mom. There were lines I had never noticed before at the creases of her eyes.

"Are you feeling all right?" I asked.

She looked at me curiously and laughed. "I'd be better if I knew my daughter was taking better care of herself."

The door from the garage opened, and my dad walked in pulling his rolling briefcase behind him. He was thin and wiry like my mother. His brown hair was graying around the ears, but it was still thick with a distinctive wave toward the back. He had the lightest blue eyes I had ever seen. My father could have been a movie star. "Hey, sweetheart," he said when he saw me.

"Hey, Daddy." I smiled over at him. "How was work?"

"Exhausting." He groaned and parked his briefcase by the wall. "I had one patient break a hip in my waiting room, and another dementia patient wandered into my office and fell asleep on my sofa."

I laughed.

He sighed. "I should've gone into pediatrics."

My mother helped him pull his coat off and laughed as she folded it over her arm. "Then you could've had babies spitting up on your sport coat and toddlers peeing in your office."

He gave her a soft peck on the lips. "I missed you today." My mother was still a nurse, and she worked in my dad's office.

She patted his chest. "I'm sorry, honey. I don't know what I was thinking. I completely planned my days wrong this week and forgot you said you needed me today. I hope you weren't too shorthanded."

The sound of the news station anchorwoman caught my attention. *"Breaking news in Buncombe County..."*

Dad gave me a side hug. "How was your day, Sloan?"

I held up my hand to silence him and then grabbed the remote. I turned up the volume on the television. "Just a sec, Dad."

The man's photo from the press release was splashed across the screen. *"The body of missing BB&C executive Byron Milstaf was found today at his sister's lake home in Tuxedo, North Carolina. Milstaf has been missing since Saturday from his home in Asheville. Police say it was an apparent suicide, and no foul play is suspected. In other news..."*

"Are you all right?" My dad was peering down at me. "Did you know that man?"

I looked out the window toward the mountains. "Sort of."

A few times during the week, I had briefly considered making up an excuse to visit the sheriff's office so I could bump into Detective McNamara again. However, those urges were overridden by my fear of the jail. I had also considered phoning in some sort of detective-necessary issue but couldn't justify missing pens from the supply closet as a reason to call the police. So I was pleasantly surprised when I came into work the following Monday to find Nathan leaning against my office door with a stack of paperwork in his hand.

"Good morning, Detective. Are they still sticking you with the office grunt work?" I batted my eyelashes up at him as I fumbled for the key to my office.

"No," he said. "I came on my own. I was hoping to talk to you."

When the door was opened, he followed me inside and closed the door behind us. I eyed him suspiciously as I walked around my desk and placed my briefcase on the floor. He wore black cargos and a dark gray t-shirt with his badge on a chain around his neck. His American flag ball cap was pulled down low over his eyes. He wasn't doing office work that day. His rigid stance made me a little nervous.

"Talk to me about what?" I sat down in my chair and pressed the power button on my computer.

He folded his arms across his chest, tucking the papers against his side. "How did you know that Byron Milstaf was dead?"

It was my hope to never revisit that conversation.

I turned my palms up. "I told you. It was a guess."

He shook his head. "I don't believe that. I'm an interview and interrogation specialist. I know when people are lying."

Laughing, I cocked my head to the side. "Are you planning on interrogating me, Nathan?"

A muscle worked in his jaw. "No, ma'am. I would just appreciate you telling me the truth."

I pointed to the chairs and narrowed my eyes. "Have a seat, Detective." Any flirtatious desire was suddenly quelled.

My icy tone caused his eyebrows to lift. He sat in the chair and rested the ankle of his tactical boot on top of his knee. His stare was expectant, and his perfect lips were shut.

Leaning forward, I rested my elbows on the desk. "First of all, I don't appreciate being clotheslined at my office door with accusations about being dishonest. I especially don't like it when it comes from a detective who is apparently suspicious about a deceased victim. Don't barge in here and shut my door and demand answers from me without telling me why you're here." I splayed my palms face down and leaned toward him. "I may be young and I may be a woman, but I'm not going to be bullied by anyone. Not even you."

For a moment, he was speechless.

His tense shoulders relaxed a bit. He leaned forward and dropped his stack of papers on my desk. On the top was a report sheet with a photo stapled to it. It was a picture of a child, a little girl. She had blond ringlets and a bright, cheerful smile. Her eyes were captivating; one was blue and one was bright green. My stomach twisted in knots.

"What is this?" I looked at him instead of at the photograph.

He tapped his finger on the picture. "This is Kayleigh Marie Neeland. Last night, there was a raid on a suspected meth operation in Leicester. Her mom's boyfriend, Ray Whitmore, panicked when the cops busted down the door. He grabbed Kayleigh and held a Taurus 9mm to her head, using her as a shield to escape. At 3:19 this morning, we found his abandoned car in Haywood County with blood on the back seat."

I was horrified but determined to keep a clear head. I sat back in my chair and turned my hands up in question. "What do you want from me?"

I could tell he wasn't sure exactly what he expected to find out in my office, but it was obvious this wasn't an excuse for a social call. "I guess I want your opinion," he replied.

I pushed the papers toward him. "My opinion is that you should do your job, Detective McNamara, and stop wasting your time in the office of the department publicist."

He let out a frustrated huff and stood up so fast his chair threatened to topple backwards. He reached into the velcro pocket on his thigh and slammed down a business card before picking up the stack of papers. He cut his eyes at me. "Kayleigh is about to turn six. For her birthday she wants a Prince Charming to go with the Sleeping Beauty doll she got from her Nana at Christmas. She hasn't put down that doll all year until she dropped it in the driveway as she was being dragged away. If you think of anything, Sloan, give me a call." Without waiting for a response, he turned on his heel and stormed out of my office.

I picked up his business card and flicked it against my fingertips as my brain scrambled to make sense of what had just happened. Why had he come to my office that morning? What did he think I might know? The bigger question was, what was I going to do?

Kayleigh Neeland was still alive and I knew it.

CHAPTER THREE

Adrianne agreed to meet me for lunch on her break from her job at the Merrimon Avenue Salon. My head was throbbing as I sat in the corner booth waiting for her at the Mellow Mushroom. She walked in with fresh new highlights and pink high heels that were so tall I wasn't sure how she cleared the doorway without ducking. She slid into the bench across from me and pushed her sunglasses up on top of her head. "Hey weirdo," she said with a wink.

I forced a smile and rubbed my temples. "Do you have anything for a headache?"

She retrieved a bottle of ibuprofen from her purse and slid it across the table toward me. "You all right?"

I grimaced. "Rough day."

She glanced down at her silver watch. "It's only eleven."

I closed my eyes and pinched the bridge of my nose. "I know."

The waiter appeared and took her drink order. When he was gone, she scanned the menu and then looked up at me. "What's up? You sounded really stressed on the phone."

I sighed. "I've got a big problem at work." She waited expectantly, and I leaned on my elbow to support my throbbing head.

"There's this new guy, a detective, at the department. I sort of slipped up the other day and told him I knew that a missing person was dead."

She straightened in her seat. "Who was dead?"

"Some random guy he wanted me to do a press release about."

"How did you know he was dead?"

I just glared at her with a raised eyebrow.

"Oh."

"Well, I played it off, and he hasn't said another word about it until today. He met me at my office this morning asking questions," I said.

Her lips sank into a frown. "Uh oh."

The waiter returned with her water and we ordered a pizza to share.

"What did he want to know?" she asked.

I thought that was obvious. "Well, the guy turned up dead in another county, and the detective wanted to know how I knew."

"And what did you say?"

"I played dumb. I insisted it was a guess," I said.

She shifted uneasily in her seat. "Does he think you were involved? Like, are you a suspect or something?"

I shook my head. "No. It was a suicide, but he suspects something because he came to my office asking me about a little girl who was kidnapped at gunpoint. They think she might be dead."

"Is she dead?"

"No."

She raised an eyebrow. "Do you know where she is?"

I shook my head. "It doesn't really work like that. I can't find people."

"But people can find you," she said. "What's her name?"

"Kayleigh Neeland." I knew what Adrianne was trying to do. She wanted to see if I could summon the girl. "I don't think I can summon someone I don't know. If I could, I would have found my birth mom years ago."

"I heard about that kid on the news this morning. What are you going to do? Are you going to tell him you know she's alive?" Adrianne was mindlessly tearing her straw paper to bits.

I had been asking myself the same question all morning. "It's only going to make him ask more questions that I can't answer. Adrianne, I think I have seriously screwed up my perfect job."

She thought about it for a second. "Or maybe you've found a way to really do your job well." She lowered her voice. "Sloan, what's the purpose of being...whatever you are, if you're not supposed to use it to help people?"

"This isn't exactly the kind of news people process well. I can't even get my parents to believe me. You know that, Adrianne."

She nodded. "But what do you do? Keep your mouth shut when you're the only person who knows this little girl is still alive?"

I squeezed my eyes closed. "That's why I have a headache."

Her eyebrows scrunched together. "Not to sound like a bitch or anything, Sloan, but I think you're being pretty selfish. This is a little kid we're talking about. You have the power to help her, but you're worried what questions about you that it might raise."

She was right.

"I know. It's completely selfish. There's just going to be a whole lot of blowback from this that I'm not sure I'm ready to deal with," I said.

She smirked. "Poor you." She leaned forward. "Are you ready to deal with the guilt you're going to feel if that little girl winds up dead, and you didn't say anything?"

I hated it when Adrianne was right.

After lunch I took the rest of the day off and went home to the stillness of my house. I stretched out on my white sofa that was trendy and stylish but absolutely uncomfortable. In an attempt to relax, I kicked off my black heels and covered my eyes with my forearm.

The details of Kayleigh's abduction replayed over and over in my mind. I envisioned that Sleeping Beauty doll discarded in the driveway and realized Nathan McNamara was a better manipulator than I could ever be. I picked up my cell phone, punched in his phone number, and sent a one line text message.

She's alive. - Sloan

A reply came less than ten seconds later. *Where are you?*

When I didn't respond, he tried to call me.

I hit ignore and tapped out another message. *I can't help you any more than that. I promise, that's all I know.*

I hadn't lied to Adrianne. I had no way of finding the girl even if I wanted to. I wasn't omniscient, and I couldn't see anything that a detective couldn't. The only thing I had to offer was more confusion, and that was exactly the reason I chose to stay out of the affairs of others. I wasn't hero material.

The little bit of help I could offer obviously wasn't enough for the good detective. Twenty minutes later, my doorbell rang.

The hardwood floor was cold against my bare feet as I trudged across the room to the entrance foyer. I pulled open the front door and leaned my head against it. "You looked up my home address?"

"Can I come in?" Nathan's ball cap was still pulled low over his eyes, but I could still see they were bloodshot from stress and lack of sleep.

Rolling my eyes, I stepped out of his way. "Be my guest."

This wasn't exactly what I had in mind when I dreamed of Nathan McNamara's first invitation into my house. I felt like a criminal watching him wipe his boots on my welcome mat. "Nathan, I told you I can't help you with anything else. All I know is that, yes, Kayleigh is still alive."

He followed me to the couch and sat down next to me. "Do you know where she is?"

I folded my arms across my chest and narrowed my eyes. "Do you not understand the version of English that I speak?"

He tightened his hand into a fist, clenched his jaw, and

squeezed his eyes closed for a split second before throwing both hands in the air in frustration. "Can you not, for one second, put yourself in my shoes here?" He was almost shouting.

"You?" I spat at him. "You keep pushing and prying into things that aren't any of your business!"

He jabbed his thumb into the center of his chest. "This is my job!"

I held my hands up. "I'm not your witness! I'm not involved in this thing at all, and I don't want to be! You're pinning all your hopes and dreams of finding this kid on a feeling I have that I can't explain to myself, much less to you or a judge or the freaking media!" Tears were beginning to prickle my eyes.

He dropped his head and took a few deep breaths before he finally placed his hand on my knee. He blew out a slow sigh. "I'm sorry."

Nervously raking all my fingers through my hair, I tried to exhale all of the anxiety and adrenaline that was pumping through my veins. After a few beats of awkward silence, I looked over at him. His head was down, but his face was bent toward me.

"I'm sorry too," I whispered.

He placed his hand on my back for a second and then stood. "I appreciate you letting me know, Sloan."

I nodded, and he backed out of the room. When I heard the front door open, despite my better judgement, I called out to him. "Wait."

I turned around, and he looked over his shoulder. He closed the door.

"Just wait." I dropped my face into my hands, and when I looked up again, he was seated on my coffee table in front of me. "I don't know where she is. It's just a feeling I get. I know she's alive."

He leaned forward, resting his elbows on his knees. "What do you mean, it's a feeling? Do you get feelings about everyone?"

I nodded. "Yes."

"Is it just a dead or alive thing or what?"

I sighed. "It's more than that. I know things about people."

His face was inscrutable. "What do you know?"

"Like, I know you're a pretty decent guy who has lived a clean life. However, I have another feeling that I may regret ever having met you."

He thought for a moment. "What if you talked to Kayleigh's mother? Would you know if she was lying to me?"

I raised an eyebrow. "I thought you were the interrogation specialist? I thought you could tell when people are lying?"

His head tilted to the side. "Will you help me?"

"I will talk to the mother, but that's it." I pointed my finger at him. "I mean it, Nathan."

He quickly stood so I wouldn't have a chance to change my mind. He pulled his keys out of his pocket. "I'll drive."

In the passenger's seat of Nathan's county-issued tan SUV, I wondered what on earth I was getting myself into. I could see before me the proverbial can of worms that was about to be cracked wide open. My entire life, I had dedicated myself to trying to be like everyone else, and there I was headed at forty-five miles per hour toward never being normal again.

Nathan was angled back in his seat with one hand on the steering wheel. "Thanks for doing this." He slowly merged onto the interstate.

I just nodded.

He looked over his shoulder at me. "You know I'm going to have a hell of a lot of questions when this is all over with."

My index fingernail was bloody from my nervous chewing. "Why did you come to my office this morning?"

After a few quiet seconds, I cut my eyes over at him. He was grinning. "I guess I just had a *feeling*."

"Jerk."

He laughed.

Desperate for a new topic of conversation, I forced a change of subject. "What's your story, Nathan? How did you wind up here? Why Asheville?"

He sucked in a deep breath. "My girlfriend lives here."

The day kept getting better and better.

Nodding, I prayed he wouldn't continue. He did.

"She's a reporter for WKNC."

"Of course she is," I grumbled under my breath. I probably knew his girlfriend through work.

He leaned his ear toward me. "What'd you say?"

I examined my bloody fingernail again. "I didn't say anything."

"What about you?" he asked. "Have you always lived here?"

I nodded. "Other than college and the time I spent being probed by the aliens on the mothership, yes."

He laughed again.

"I actually grew up about five minutes away from here. If you ever visit the Grove Park Inn, you will pass my parents' house on the way up the mountain," I said.

He took the exit onto College Street. "I hear that hotel is really nice."

Sitting up straight, I looked out my window. "Where are we going?"

"The jail. The mom was arrested last night during the raid," he said.

I dropped my face into the palm of my hand and groaned.

"Is that a problem?"

I forced a smile. "Nope."

He pointed at me. "You're lying."

I shuddered. "I hate the jail. It gives me the creeps."

He focused on the road ahead. "I won't let anything get to you."

His words would have made me feel all warm and tingly inside, had the thoughts of prison rapists and murderers—and his reporter girlfriend—not squelched the moment. I waved my hands in the air and rolled my eyes. "Yay."

He chuckled and playfully shoved me in the shoulder.

We pulled into the parking lot in front of the drab green building, and I contorted my shoulders to try to relieve some of the tension that was building in my spine. I reached for my purse, pulled out my prescription bottle, and popped half of a chalky tablet under my tongue.

He looked at me surprised. "What are you taking?"

"Xanax, nosy," I said.

"You should probably leave your purse in here," he said.

I had never actually been in the guts of the jail side of the building. For a moment I considered taking the other half of my anxiety pill, but I was afraid I might end up drooling on his leather seat during the drive home. We parked in a parking spot that was labeled with his name, and I shoved my purse under my seat.

I matched Nathan step for step as we approached the front door. He paused and looked at me when we reached the landing at the top of the stairs. I looked around in confusion. "What are you doing?"

He motioned toward the door. "I wasn't sure if you needed to check out your ass in the window or not."

Smacking him hard in the chest, I genuinely laughed for the first time all day.

When we entered, the lobby was empty. We walked up to the sliding door and he pressed the buzzer. No response. He shook his head and pressed the buzzer again, this time letting his finger linger on the button.

"Press that button again!" Ms. Claybrooks yelled over the speaker. "Press it again! I'll come atch'you with razor blades and lemon juice!"

His wide eyes spun around to meet mine. I covered my mouth to keep from laughing too loudly. He pointed at the door. "Is she always like this?"

I nodded. "Every time I've ever been here."

"Razor blades and lemon juice?" He chuckled. "What the hell?"

"Who's callin'?" she finally barked over the intercom.

"Detective McNamara," he answered.

"Do I know you?"

He rested his hand on his hip and sighed. "Ms. Claybrooks, I've been here for a few weeks now."

"Ohhhhh," she purred. "You're one of the new boys, huh? Are you the red head or the cute little blond boy?"

He laughed and dropped his head. "I guess I'm the cute little blond boy."

"You come on in, cutie pie." The door slid open.

Laughing, I squeezed his arm. "I love her so much."

My heart was pounding as I followed him through a maze of concrete walls and metal doors. Just when I was certain I would never find my way out, we entered a small office, and he dropped his keys on the desk. "You OK?" he asked.

I imagined that my face was white, and I could feel sweat beading across my forehead. "Yeah, I'm good. Let's get this over with."

He picked up the phone and pressed a few buttons. "This is Detective McNamara. I need Rebecca Neeland in CID." He hung up the phone and pulled his shirt up over his waistband. I darted my eyes away as he unholstered his handgun.

I caught my reflection in the glass of a framed certificate on his wall. I smoothed my hair down and swiped some smudged mascara out from under my eyes. "What's CID?"

"Criminal Investigations Division." He pulled open the bottom drawer of the desk. "Do you have anything in your pockets I should lock up? Pens, knives, scissors, fingernail file?"

I ran my hands over the smooth fabric of my black, slim-line skirt. "Nope, I think I left all of my knives and nail files in my other skirt."

He chuckled.

We left the office and walked down to another room. I recognized it as an interrogation room from television, except the mirrored glass was a disappointingly small window instead of the whole wall. I guessed the Buncombe County jail didn't have the budget Hollywood did. I looked around at the bleak gray walls and shuddered.

"How do you want to do this?" he asked.

"Can I talk to her alone?"

He shook his head. "Absolutely not."

I scrunched up my nose. "Well, can you at least try to not be so intimidating? Maybe smile a little bit?"

"I smile," he argued.

"Not when you're in interrogator mode. I saw *that guy* this morning, remember?" I gestured toward him and tried hard not to roll my eyes.

He smiled and nodded his head.

I took a step in his direction and lowered my voice so no one else could hear. "Nathan, please keep in mind that I really don't know exactly what I'm doing here, so please don't put too much hope in this."

He squeezed my shoulder. "We have over two dozen officers knocking down doors as we speak. We are doing everything we can on our end. This woman was really uncooperative when we brought her in, and she was tweaked out of her mind on crystal meth. I appreciate you just trying to help."

"Have you told anyone about our conversations today?" I asked.

"Not a soul."

I relaxed a little.

There was a knock on the doorframe, and we both turned around. A bedraggled woman, about my age, was being led into the room by a female deputy. It was obvious Rebecca Neeland was, at one time, a stunning girl. She had thick, naturally high-lighted blond hair and striking green eyes. But her hair was weighed down with straggly dead ends, and her eyes were cloaked in dark circles. Her full lips were dry and cracked, and her sallow skin was thin, blistered, and stretched over high cheekbones and a perfectly shaped button nose. She scowled at us before casting her gaze at the tile floor beneath her orange sandals.

"Thank you, Deputy," Nathan said. "I'll take it from here."

"I'll be outside," the deputy answered. She pulled the door closed behind her as she stepped into the hallway.

"Have a seat, Rebecca." He motioned toward the armless chair at the table. "I'm Detective McNamara and this is Ms. Jordan. Can I get you something to drink? Some water or—"

She cut him off. "No. What do you want?" she snapped. "Have you found my baby yet?"

I studied her face. Rebecca Neeland wasn't a victim, but she wasn't necessarily a villain either. She had certainly made some bad choices, and I couldn't tell if she would ever right her path or not, but she wasn't evil. I slipped into the seat across from her. "Hey. Is it Rebecca? Or Becky maybe?"

Her eyes darted to the table. "Becca," she muttered.

"Hey, Becca. I'm Sloan," I said.

"Who are you?" she asked.

I laughed. "I'm nobody."

She glanced skeptically down at my white buttoned blouse and cocked her head to the side. "You don't look like nobody."

"Well, I'm not a cop. Or a lawyer." I turned my palms face-up on the table. "I'm actually a publicist."

Her eyebrows scrunched together. "A publicist?"

"Yeah, I work with news people and stuff. It's very boring," I said.

"What are you doin' here? Am I gonna be on TV or somethin'?" she asked.

I shook my head. "No. I just want to help. My buddy, Nathan, over there came by my office this morning with this picture of Kayleigh, and it broke my heart. She's really cute." I pushed the photograph of her daughter in her direction.

Her eyes teared up, and she quickly swiped at them with the sleeve of her orange jumpsuit.

I placed my hand on top of hers. "Do you have any idea where we can look for her?"

She jerked her hand away. "I already told 'em, I don't know where Ray went."

"How long have you and Ray been together?" I asked.

"Since I moved here from Greensboro. What's it matter?" she snipped.

I shrugged my shoulders. "Just curious because if my friend up and disappeared right now, I would have a good idea where to go looking for him, and we haven't been together that long." I lowered my voice and cut my eyes at her with mock sympathy. "Does Ray keep secrets from you?"

She scowled. "Ray don't keep nothin' from me."

"But, obviously, you must not know him very well." I took a deep breath. "Or, Ray doesn't trust you to keep quiet, and he doesn't tell you everything."

She tapped her finger against the table. "Ray knows I can keep my mouth shut."

"So you do know where he goes?"

"Of course I do!"

My eyes widened. So did hers.

I lowered my voice again. "Rebecca, I'm not a legal genius here, but I'm pretty sure if you don't tell us what you know, then you're going to make things a lot worse for yourself in here. You'll get a lot more time stacked up on you in this hell hole, and you'll lose your daughter, maybe forever."

She just stared at me.

I tapped my chest. "I'm going to go and get Kayleigh. I'm not going to arrest Ray. I just want to make sure your little girl is safe."

Her eyes widened with curiosity. "You're going to go get her?"

I nodded. "Yes. Me. I'm going to go."

She shifted in her seat. Her eyes darted nervously around the room before settling on the picture of Kayleigh. She leaned forward. "There's an abandoned house at the end of the road on Clarksdale. Ray goes there sometimes," she whispered.

I smiled. "Thank you."

I looked over my shoulder to where Nathan was leaned against the wall with his mouth hanging open. I pushed my chair back and stood up. "Let's go."

Rebecca jumped out of her chair. "But you said you was gonna go! Not him!"

I nodded and held my hands up in defense. "I said I was going to get Kayleigh and not arrest Ray. That's the truth. I'm just a publicist."

She shouted a few obscenities, and the deputy outside rushed in as Nathan and I walked out of the room.

"How did you do that?" he asked as he jerked his radio off of his tactical belt.

It was hard to keep up with his pace; I was practically jogging in my heels. "I guess I know how to talk to people."

He was on his radio the whole way out to the car. When I ran over to the passenger's side and grabbed the door handle, he stopped and pointed at me over the hood of the vehicle. "Oh, no. You're not going."

"Oh yes I am! You're not leaving me here!" I shouted. "There's not enough Xanax in the world, buddy."

He must have accurately assumed it would be pointless to try and argue with me, so he got in and started the SUV. I buckled my seatbelt as he peeled out of the parking lot with his blue lights flashing. "When we get there you have to stay in the damn car."

I held my hands up in resignation. "Oh, I don't want to be a hero. I'll stay."

It was a short drive through an older residential part of town. The houses along Clarksdale were sixties style homes that looked as though they hadn't been cared for since the sixties. The house at the end was a foreclosure covered in graffiti and no trespassing signs. Given the state of the area, it was doubtful that any of the neighboring residents would have noticed—or, much less, reported—any unusual activity at the end of the street.

Two other patrol cars had beaten us there by seconds. There were police officers in the street with their weapons drawn, slowly approaching the house. Nathan practically leapt from the car before he even slid the transmission into park.

I watched in silence as Nathan directed the officers around the sides and back of the house. After a few minutes, he kicked in the front door. My knuckles went white as I clenched the dashboard looking for any sign of activity from within the dilapidated home. After a few minutes, a news van from Channel 2 and two other police officers pulled in behind us. I rolled my window down enough to hear what was being said. I could hear over the radio someone's voice requesting a body bag.

An over-groomed female reporter from News Channel 2 was swatting her brown bangs out of her eyes as the cameraman was getting his equipment ready. After a moment of straightening her suit, she began her spiel. "We are here at the scene of the possible location of missing five-year-old, Kayleigh Neeland. Kayleigh was abducted by her mother's boyfriend during a meth lab raid last night in Leicester. Information from an unidentified source has led officers to this address on Clarksdale Avenue in West Asheville..." She paused, and I turned to see Nathan standing in the doorway with his hands up.

"She's not here!" he called to me.

The reporter strained to see who he was talking to. I wanted to cower down and throw a blanket or something over my head, but I knew it was too late for that. I pushed my door open. "Is it safe for me to get out?" I yelled.

He nodded and I crossed the lawn. He met me in the tall grass and lowered his voice. "Ray is dead inside. It looks like someone got to him before we did. Kayleigh isn't here," he said. "We searched the entire house."

I shook my head. "She's not dead."

He shielded me with his arm, moving me away from the crowd that was growing in front of the house. "I'm running out of ideas here, Sloan."

"Take me inside. I want to check," I said.

He narrowed his eyes. "That's not a good idea."

"Do you have a better one?" I asked.

He jerked his head toward the house and put his hand on the small of my back. "Come on."

I followed him in the front door, and the stench almost knocked me to my knees. The room was sour with mildew, and the walls had gaping holes where the wiring had been stripped out. Melted puddles of wax from half-burnt candles were cemented into the dingy, torn carpet and trash was everywhere. A mattress was beneath the window and stained with...I didn't even want to know what. In the doorway of the kitchen was a body that I assumed belonged to the recently departed Ray Whitmore. His eyes were open and covered in a milky film.

Oddly, dead bodies didn't bother me. Dead bodies were just discarded shells. I would forever be more fearful of the living than the dead.

A familiar sensation came over me, and I carefully scanned the room again. "We're not alone, Nathan."

His gun was drawn. "She's here?"

"Someone is." I stumbled over a pile of trash. "I can feel it."

My eyes searched the room for any sign that a child had ever been there. I shuddered at such a thought. "Come on, Kayleigh, where are you?" I mumbled.

Nathan's head jerked up. "Did you hear that?"

I was completely clueless. "Hear what?"

Then I heard it. A very faint sliding sound was over our heads. "Nathan, she's in the attic!"

We both began scanning the crumbling popcorn ceiling for an opening. I stepped over a pile of beer cans and rags and peeked around the doorway to the hall. "It's in here!" I lunged forward to grasp the string to the attic pull-down door.

Nathan clotheslined me with his forearm. "No. Let me."

He pulled on the string, lowering the stairs to the floor. Once it was open, we could hear a muffled whimper. With his flashlight in one hand and his gun in the other, he carefully maneuvered his way up the ladder.

I chewed on my nails. "Be careful."

"Oh, God," he said once his head was through to the attic. "Sloan, I'm going to need you up here to hold the flashlight."

I hoisted myself up the rickety steps, and when my eyes adjusted to the dim light above, I saw her. Kayleigh Neeland was curled up on her side in her Dora the Explorer pajamas. Her ankles and wrists were tied together with what looked to be fishing line. A wide piece of duct tape covered her mouth. She had soiled herself, and her face was covered in dried blood from a cut across her tiny forehead. Her exhausted eyes were terrified. It was all I could do to not scream at the horror.

Nathan passed me his flashlight and tucked his gun into his holster. He held out his hands for her to see. "Kayleigh, I'm not going to hurt you. I'm a policeman, and I'm here to help you." She blinked her eyes at him. "I need to get my knife so I can cut those ties off of your hands, OK? But I promise I won't hurt you."

Slowly, he pulled out a tactical knife and carefully cut the line holding her hands together. As gently as he could, he peeled away the strands that had sliced into her delicate skin. She cried out in pain as he freed her bloody hands.

"I'm so sorry," he said over and over, his voice quavering as he tried to maintain his composure.

Even from a few feet away with hardly any light, I could see Kayleigh was trembling. He severed the lines around her feet and, though she was weak, she scrambled toward him. Nathan sat all the way down and scooped her up in his lap. Gently, he rocked her and smoothed her matted blond hair. "Shh...it's all over." He kissed the top of her head. "Shhh."

When she saw me standing halfway up the ladder, she stretched out her arms. I thrust the flashlight at Nathan and reached for her. Carefully, I lifted her up, and she clung to me like I was a lone buoy afloat in the wide ocean.

"Nathan, get the tape off." I turned around so he could work the tape on her mouth over my shoulder. After a moment and a few whimpers, he wadded up the duct tape and tossed it on the floor with the rest of the trash. She buried her face in my shoulder.

Two officers had appeared at the bottom of the steps. "Hand her down, ma'am," one of them said.

I shook my head. "No. Just help me get down without falling."

"Get the paramedics in here!" Nathan shouted.

When I finally descended the ladder, I sat down against the steps with her still in my arms. "We've got you. You're safe now. You don't have to be afraid anymore." Tears streamed down my cheeks.

"Don't let me go," she whispered.

CHAPTER FOUR

As promised, I didn't let Kayleigh go. I rode with her to the hospital and tried to help the police shield her from the crowd of media when we got out of the ambulance. I knew some of the reporters from my work at the county office, so everyone knew my name by the time we arrived.

"Sloan Jordan, what is your involvement here?"

"Are you related to the victim?"

"How did you help the police find Kayleigh?"

Their shouts and questions rattled around in my skull as we fought our way through the ambulance bay doors.

A team of emergency room staff ushered us straight to triage when we entered, and I held her hand as they surveyed her injuries. A nurse, who reminded me a lot of my mother, carefully cleaned her face exposing a lot of bruising and swelling around the site of the large gash in her forehead. "Sweetie, do you remember how this happened?" she asked.

Kayleigh shook her head. Her eyes were leaking uncontrollable tears, but she wasn't audibly crying.

The nurse looked up at me. "My guess is she was knocked unconscious."

I cringed.

I wasn't sure how much time had passed when Nathan eventually came through the door carrying a bundle in his arms, but I was half asleep in the chair next to Kayleigh's bed. After being poked, prodded, x-rayed, and questioned, she was finally sleeping somewhat peacefully.

"Hey," he said. He knelt down beside me and placed his hand on my forearm. "How's she doing?"

I leaned out of the way so he could see the bruising for himself as Kayleigh slept. His jaw tightened, and he let out a slow puff of air. "Her grandparents were notified and they just got here from Greensboro. They are on their way back here now," he said.

I sighed. "That's good. She's been asking me to call her Nana, and I didn't know what to tell her."

He turned his attention to me. "How are you holding up? I brought you a sweatshirt from my car. It's not exactly clean, but I figured you might want to change." He shook the sweatshirt out straight in front of him.

I offered him a weak smile. "You have no idea how grateful I am." I looked down at my dingy blouse; it had been white when I left my house that morning.

Just then, a couple in their late sixties came in with a doctor. "Oh, my sweet baby!" the woman exclaimed as she rushed to the bedside.

Kayleigh's eyes fluttered open and then darted around the room in confusion. I reached for her hand. When her eyes settled on the couple rushing toward her, Kayleigh scrambled up in the bed and reached out for the woman. "Nana!"

The grandfather was in tears, but he stopped to shake Nathan's hand. "Thank you, Detective. Thank you."

Nathan just nodded.

When the grandmother finally released the child, she grabbed me around the neck and squeezed me so tight I thought she might cut off the circulation to my head. "Thank you so much," she cried. "God bless you."

When she finally released me, I stepped closer to Kayleigh's bedside and surveyed her tiny, battered face. "Hey Kayleigh, is it OK if I step out for a little bit now that your Nana is here?"

She nodded.

I leaned down and pressed a kiss to the top her head. I gently raked my fingers through her blond curls. "I promise I'll check on you in a little bit, OK?"

"OK," she whispered.

I felt Nathan's hand at the small of my back as he turned me toward the door. Once we were around the corner, out of sight, I crumbled. Uncontrollable sobs, that I'd been holding in for hours, erupted without warning so violently that I doubled over and had to grasp my knees. Nathan's arms wrapped around me, and his fingers tangled in my hair as he pulled my head to his chest. I could feel his warm breath on my neck as he breathed. "Shhhh..."

When I regained my composure, I pulled away and looked at him. I was still gripping his forearms for support. "I'm sorry."

He cupped my face in his hands and swiped away what I was sure was a mess of mascara with his thumbs. "Are you kidding? There is absolutely no reason for you to be apologizing. I couldn't have done this without you. You saved that little girl's life."

I took a deep breath and let it out slowly. "What do we do now?"

He handed me the sweatshirt and pointed to the bathroom behind us. "First, you change."

In the bathroom, I scrubbed my hands clean and splashed my face with cold water a few times. I unbuttoned my blouse and, though it was probably washable, shoved it in the wastebasket. I washed my hands again before pulling the black hooded sweatshirt, with the letters S.W.A.T. across the back, over my head. The strong smell of Nathan's cologne and sweat about made my eyes roll backward. It was the only pleasant feeling I had experienced all day. I combed my fingers through my hair and retied my mangled ponytail before leaving the bathroom.

Nathan was leaned against the wall making notes in a small black notebook. He looked me up and down. "Did you forget your shirt?"

I shook my head. "I trashed it. I'm never wearing that thing again."

He nodded. "Come on, let's try and sneak out of here and find some food. I don't know about you, but I'm starving."

I pointed toward the entrance to the emergency room. "I assume the waiting room is full of reporters?"

"Yep. You definitely don't want to go out there." He held the door at the end of the hall open for me.

I hugged my arms to my chest as we passed down the fluorescent lit hallway that reeked of antiseptic and sickness. "What are they saying?" I asked.

He looked over at me with an expression that made it clear he was worried I might either cry or punch him in the face. "They're talking about you quite a bit. Apparently, News Channel 2 is replaying some video of you carrying Kayleigh out of the house. Everyone wants to know why you were there."

I sighed. "Honestly, right now I don't even care. I'm just glad it's over."

As we followed the signs to the hospital cafeteria, his cell phone rang. I realized my purse, along with my wallet and phone, was still under the seat of his car. If my mother had seen the news she was probably frantic with worry. My voicemail inbox was probably full.

As Nathan talked, I couldn't help but listen in on his conversation. "Hey. Yeah, it's over. The guy was dead when we got there, and we found the little girl in the attic." He paused for a few seconds and then looked over at me. "Yeah, she works in public relations for the county. I just, uh, happened to be in her office when I got the call, and she wanted to tag along."

I rolled my eyes. "You're a terrible liar."

He ignored me. "Yeah, I'm going to have a late night. A ton of paperwork, ya know," he continued. "I'll grab dinner on my own. Probably at the office. I'll try and call you later if it's not too late." He paused and listened again. "Yeah, me too. Bye."

I tsked my tongue against the roof of my mouth. "Lying to your girlfriend already? That's not a good sign."

"What was I supposed to tell her? That you're psychic or something?" he asked.

"Then we would both sound crazy," I said.

We finally reached the bustling cafeteria. The smell reminded me of elementary school lunch trays and cartons of milk. He stopped at the vending machine and looked at me. "You hungry?"

"No, but I would love a Diet Coke if you could spot me the change. My purse is still in your car," I said.

"I'm sorry. I meant to grab it for you and I totally forgot. I can run out and get it if you want," he said.

I waved my hand. "I'll get it when we leave. I don't have the headspace to deal with the phone calls right now anyway."

He fed a dollar bill into the drink machine. "I'm pretty sure a Diet Coke is the least I can do for you."

When he handed me my drink, I watched him buy a bag of Skittles, a Snickers bar, and pack of Nerds. I looked at his toned physique and then cocked my head sideways. "I had you pegged for a health nut or something."

He shrugged. "I'm a candy freak. I just have to run twice as far."

I laughed.

He motioned to an empty table near the door and we sat down. He ripped open the wrapper around the Snickers bar. "It's question time."

I pointed at him. "No questions."

He leaned forward. "Sloan, I have to come up with some really brilliant reason why you are on that police report from today. You've got to give me something."

I rested my elbows on the table and propped my chin up in my hands. I studied his face for a moment. "Give me a serious answer as to why you came to my office asking me about Kayleigh."

He thought for a second, biding his time by chewing on a bite of his candy bar. He squinted his eyes enough to indicate he was seriously attempting to answer my question. "There was something about the way you said 'he's dead' when you saw that missing person's report on Milstaf. I am always analyzing how people phrase things, their body language, and the inflection in their voice to judge if they are being honest or not. You might as well have been telling me the sun was shining outside. You weren't speculating—you *knew*." He sat back in his seat. "It stuck with me."

After a moment of staring at him and racking my brain for what to say next, I sighed and turned my palms up. "I don't know how I know these things. I just do."

"Are you ever wrong?"

"Not in twenty-seven years," I answered.

I could almost hear the gears turning in his mind. "Can you tell with everyone? Like, I have a sister. Is she alive or dead?" he asked.

I shrugged. "I would have to see a photograph of her."

He seemed to be making mental notes as I talked. He drummed his fingers on the table. "You also knew we weren't alone in that house. You knew Kayleigh was there."

"No. I knew *someone* was there. We got lucky that it was Kayleigh."

He thought it over. "How? Is it like hearing a heartbeat?"

"It's more like feeling a pulse," I explained.

That seemed to make sense to him. "Could it have been a rat? Or a dog?"

"No. I only feel humans. Animals must operate on a different system than we do," I said.

"Is that all you can do?" he asked. I glanced up at the ceiling, and he pointed at me again. "You're about to tell me a lie," he said.

"Quit using your interrogation crap on me!"

He laughed. "Tell me the truth. I swear it won't leave this table."

There was a boulder of anxiety forming in the pit of my stomach. He kept staring at me, waiting for an answer I didn't want to give. I opened my mouth and closed it several times before finally being able to form words. "I seem to be able to call people to me, like, subconsciously."

He closed his eyes and turned his ear toward me, like he was certain he had misheard something. "What?"

I thought for a second. "You know when we were in the house and you heard Kayleigh move in the attic?" He nodded. I looked at him seriously. "I had just said her name out loud."

"And you think you made me find her?"

I shook my head. "No. I made her be found."

He just stared at me without chewing the bite in his mouth. Finally, he started laughing. "Ha, you're good. That's pretty funny. You almost had me."

I wasn't laughing.

In slow motion, I could see the humor dripping from his face and fear surfacing underneath. I sank down in my chair, bracing for the blowback.

"You're not joking are you?" he asked a moment later.

I shook my head again.

He shifted uneasily in his seat. "How do you do it?"

"No idea," I said. "I just have this sense about other people. Like, I already know them before I meet them and somehow they are drawn to me like magnets."

"And no one knows you can do this? That you can make people magically appear by talking about them?" His eyes were wide with disbelief.

"Well, my best friend knows and now you know," I said.

He swallowed a bite. "Your parents?"

"Oh no. My dad's a doctor and my mother is a nurse. I'm pretty sure they would have me committed."

"Huh," he mumbled. He finished off his candy bar and chewed in silence for what felt like an eternity.

The tension was killing me. "Are you going to freak out?"

His eyes settled on me again. "No," he said. "I'm not going to freak out. This is nuts though."

"I know."

He grabbed his Skittles and Nerds and tucked them into his jacket pocket. "We should probably head back to the emergency room. I know you want to check on the girl before I take you home, and we've got to deal with the media sooner or later."

"What are you going to put in your report?" I cringed as I waited for his answer.

He pressed his eyes closed. "That I knew this thing would be a media nightmare, so I thought it would be smart to bring PR along."

I turned toward him and frowned, putting my hand on my hip. "You didn't need to know my secret to come up with that explanation."

He smiled and gave me a mischievous wink. "I know."

I punched him in the shoulder.

Nathan had already briefed Sheriff Davis about my presence at the scene, and the sheriff was in the lobby with the media when we returned to that side of the hospital. He had assumed I already had a speech prepared for him for the ten o'clock news. I didn't, but I faked it pretty well as I went over his notes with him. When he finished detailing the events for the broadcast, the female reporter I had seen at the house on Clarksdale, raised her hand with a question.

When she was acknowledged, she looked at me. I looked down at my ragged outfit as several news cameras panned in my direction. "Sloan Jordan was at the scene today and was videoed carrying Kayleigh Neeland from the house. What was Ms. Jordan's involvement with this case?"

The sheriff was a little surprised by the question, but he

handled it like a true politician. "Ms. Jordan, as you know, is the county's publicist, and she was there for the sake of the media when our officers needed help with the frightened child. That was Ms. Jordan's only involvement."

I wish.

It was after dark when Nathan finally pulled up to the curb in front of my house. To my surprise, he turned off the engine and walked with me to the door. I put my keys in the lock and turned the handle. "Do you want to come in? I've got coffee...and Jack Daniels," I added with an exhausted laugh.

He smiled. "No. I'd better get home. I can't thank you enough for today, Sloan."

I shook my head. "Stop thanking me. She's safe and that's all that matters."

He nodded.

"I can change out of your shirt if you'll give me a minute," I offered.

He tugged on the hem. "Just keep it for a while. I'll get it from you soon."

His smooth voice gave me chills.

He lingered for a moment. I wondered if he was thinking of changing his mind about my invitation inside. Finally, he turned toward my steps. "I'll see you at work."

"Goodnight, Nathan."

CHAPTER FIVE

I slept in the next morning and called out of work for the day. When I finally talked myself into getting out of bed, I returned all of the missed calls from my mother, my dad, and Adrianne. My parents wanted to check on me after being put through such a traumatic ordeal. Adrianne wanted to know what the hell I was thinking appearing on the news in a black hoodie and no makeup.

I was still wearing the hoodie when my doorbell rang just before noon. I had taken a shower before bed, but couldn't help myself when I thought of how nice it would be to fall asleep to the smell of that shirt. I cursed the decision when I opened the door to Nathan standing there holding a to-go bag from Tupelo Honey.

He looked me up and down and smiled. I died a little on the inside.

I leaned against the door. "What are you doing here?"

He stepped inside and laughed. "I guess I didn't come by to get my shirt back."

I rolled my eyes and closed the door behind him.

"I went by your office, but you weren't there. Your boss said you had taken a comp day, so I decided to bring you lunch. She suggested goat cheese grits." He held up the plastic bag.

I laughed and accepted it. "Thanks. Come sit down." I returned to my spot on the couch and pulled my fleece blanket up over my bare legs.

He sat on the loveseat catty-cornered to the couch and laid a thick file folder on the coffee table. I looked at it and then at him. My eyes widened and I shook my head. "Oh no," I said. "I'm not doing anymore police work. Do you hear me? I am not going to be your secret, silent partner helping you crack cold-cases and solve murder mysteries."

He laughed and flipped the folder open. "It's not that, I promise."

I relaxed a little and pulled the plastic bowl of steaming grits out of the bag. He had also gotten me some type of sandwich.

Nathan passed me a worn 8x10 photograph of a football player and a cheerleader. The number fifty-four was printed on his jersey and drawn on the girl's cheek in blue paint and glitter. The football player with the tousled blond hair and crooked smile was a younger, less stern version of Nathan. The girl on his arm held a bouquet of red roses and had a blue ribbon tied in her long, dark hair. She was strikingly beautiful.

She was also dead.

I tapped my finger on the picture and looked up at him. "Who is this girl?"

"My little sister, Ashley."

I deflated a little. "How did she die?"

He took a deep breath and leaned his elbows on his knees. He cast his gaze to the carpet. He had been forewarned about my ability, but that hadn't lessened the shock of it.

After a moment, he sat back against the seat. "She went missing two weeks after this photo was taken after a different football game." He looked at the picture for a moment before tucking it back into the folder. "I didn't know until just now that she was really dead."

Gasping with shock and trying to swallow wasn't a good combination. I sucked a spoonful of grits down my throat, then coughed and sprayed them all over my lap. I yanked a napkin out of the paper bag, wiped my mouth, and put the food on the coffee table. I covered his hands with my own. "I'm sorry, Nathan. I really had no idea. I assumed—"

He cut me off with a wave of his hand. "It's OK. I've believed she was dead for a very long time now, but they never found her body."

I gulped and slowly retreated to my side of the sofa. "Is this why you went into police work?"

He forced a smile, but it was full of pain. "I was planning to be an engineer."

"What happened to her?"

He laid his head back and stared at the ceiling. "She was a junior in high school when she disappeared. I was a senior and the captain of the football team. Ashley was a cheerleader. She was supposed to ride with me to a party after a game we won, but our coach took an extra-long time during the end of the game meeting. I couldn't find her when we broke out. I assumed she had ridden with some of her friends, but she never showed up at the party. The last time anyone saw her, she was putting her gym bag in the back seat of my car in the parking lot."

"So instead of becoming an engineer, you became a cop," I said.

He nodded. "When I got out of high school, I did my two years at the community college studying criminal justice and enrolled in the police academy."

"So you could protect people?"

He shook his head. "No. So I could find the person who took my sister."

I hugged my knees to my chest and tugged the blanket down over my feet. "And nothing ever turned up?"

He sat forward again and reached for the folder. "Not on my sister's case." He pulled out more photographs. "There have been eleven disappearances very similar to hers since then. All of them happened in different cities between Asheville and Raleigh."

I sat up and looked at the faces of the girls smiling up from their pictures.

I looked up at him. "You think they are related?"

He shrugged. "If not, it's a pretty big coincidence."

My skin began to crawl. I really hated the word 'coincidence'. "Why are you telling me all of this?" I asked.

He leaned toward me. "Because you can help me."

"No offense, Nathan, I realize this is your sister we are talking about, but you just promised me that you're not trying to pull me into criminal investigation," I reminded him.

"I know, I lied to get you to listen to me," he admitted. "Sloan, what if this is a serial killer?"

I pushed the photos toward him. "Then I really don't want anything at all to do with it!"

"Can you just tell me if they are alive or dead?" He picked up the photos and moved to the seat next to me before fanning them out on the coffee table. "That's all I'm asking for."

I cut my eyes at him for several moments before begrudgingly leaning forward and taking a closer look. My eyes moved slowly from face to face until I settled on one that was very familiar. I tapped her picture. "I went to school with this girl." I said. "I remember Adrianne telling me about someone we went to school with who disappeared while I was away at college."

He nodded his head. "Leslie Ann Bryson. She disappeared in 2009 after getting off work at Chili's Bar and Grill."

I shuddered. "Are there any more girls from around here?"

He shook his head and pulled out a legal sized sheet of ledger paper. It was a timeline. A map was glued to the bottom of the sheet with red "X" marks and numbers scrawled on it. There had been two disappearances in Raleigh, two in Greensboro, two in

Hickory, two around Winston-Salem, two around Statesville, and Leslie Ann Bryson in Asheville.

A light bulb flickered on in my brain.

I pointed at him. "You didn't move here for your girlfriend," I said. "You moved here because you believe the next victim is going to be from around here!"

He just stared at me.

I raised an eyebrow. "Why isn't this the FBI's problem?"

He closed the folder. "Well, the FBI just recently started looking into this as these cases being possibly related."

I closed my eyes and pressed my palms over them in frustration. "Nathan, why the hell did you have to come to Asheville? My life was so much less complicated before you showed up! Do you even have a girlfriend?"

"Yes. I didn't lie about that."

I smirked and shoved him hard in the shoulder. "Does she know you're using her as an alibi to be some kind of vigilante with a badge?"

"I'm not using her," he argued. "And I did move here for her. I don't know the next abduction will happen here. I don't even know if these crimes were all committed by the same person."

I pointed at him. "But you suspect it and you are using her. And now, you're trying to use me." I got to my feet and began to stalk across the room.

He followed and grabbed me around the waist before I could throw the front door open and insist that he leave. He pulled me against his body and rested the side of his face against my hair. "Sloan, I'm just asking you to think about it," he said quietly in my ear.

His pheromones were making my head foggy and I suspected he knew it. I wrenched his arm off of my mid-section and pulled on the front door handle. "Go away, Nathan," I said as I pointed to the street.

His shoulders slumped and he moved toward the door.

"Wait," I said.

Out of the corner of my eye, I saw his shoulders straighten and his eyes widen with hope. I returned to the living room, gathered up his files, and closed the folder. I rejoined him at the door and shoved the folder into his chest, forcing him backward over the threshold.

"Now, go away." I slammed the door in his face and tumbled the deadbolt.

Surprisingly, I didn't see Nathan at all the rest of the week. I thought for sure he would be waiting at my office door when I arrived for work the morning after I expelled him from my house, but he wasn't. He didn't call or text either. Not that I was disappointed.

On Friday after work, I met Adrianne at 12 Bones Smokehouse for dinner and drinks. She was waiting at the bar and flirting with the bartender when I arrived. Like me, it seemed Adrianne would be eternally single, but it wasn't for lack of suitors. Adrianne became more and more exotic with age. I felt sloppy in my work blouse, black pants, and heels next to her mile-long legs and eyelet lace party dress.

I slid onto the barstool next to her. "I hate you."

She laughed and tossed her hair over her shoulder. "What did I do?"

"Look at you." I motioned to her evening outfit. "I look like I came from a meeting with the school board."

She nudged me with her elbow. "*Did* you come from a meeting with the school board?"

"No. That was on Monday."

We both laughed.

The bartender walked toward us. "What are you drinking tonight, Sloan?"

"Beer," I answered. "Rebel IPA if you've got it on tap this week. Thanks, Gary."

He nodded and turned away.

"Drinking the hard stuff tonight?" She traced her finger around the rim of her martini and waited expectantly for a reason.

I groaned. "It's been a week from hell."

"I figured as much. I haven't heard from you in days," she said.

I sighed as the bartender placed the frothy amber liquid in front of me. "I know. I'm sorry. I've been so swamped and so stressed out."

She lifted the skewered olive from her glass and popped it between her cherry lips. "Why? What's going on?"

I took a long swig of ice cold beer. "So, obviously, I helped the detective find that little kid. Then, the very next day, he showed up at my house with this huge folder full of a bunch of missing girls. He wants me to help him with the case. He thinks it might be a serial killer."

She blinked in disbelief. "He wants you to investigate a serial killer?"

I gripped the frosty glass. "Pretty much."

"What did you tell him?"

I laughed and took another long drink. "Oh, I kicked him out of my house."

She nodded. "Good girl. You don't need to get involved in that stuff."

I dropped my face into my hands and whined. "But he makes it so hard! I'm so freaking attracted to this man it's infuriating. And"—I gripped her arm—"one of the victims is his sister. His *sister*, Adrianne!"

She raised an eyebrow and turned toward me on her seat. "You didn't tell me you had a thing for him."

I dropped my face into my hands again. "I don't want to have a thing for him, but I *sooooo* do."

"What's his name?" she asked.

I straightened and looked at her. "Detective Nathan McNamara," I said. "Even his stupid name is sexy."

She laughed and her eyes widened. "Oh yeah. He's the blond guy who was standing next to you on the news."

I sighed. "Yes."

"He is hot. *Super* hot." She sipped her drink. "Are you sleeping with him?"

"No!"

She shrugged her shoulders and laughed. "I would be."

"This has been the worst week ever." I groaned as I raked my fingers through my hair.

"So the hot cop wants you to hunt down a serial killer," she said. "How would you even do that?"

I shook my head. "I *can't* do that."

"Are you sure? You didn't think you could find that little girl either, but you did. Maybe you can find a serial killer too and you just don't know it," she said.

I pointed at her. "Just two seconds ago, you told me to stay away from it."

She shrugged. "That was before I knew all the facts."

"There is another fact." I tilted my glass toward her. "Remember that girl from our school who went missing a few years ago?"

Her eyebrows lifted. "She's one of them?"

I nodded.

"Is she dead?"

I leaned my elbows on the bar top and cradled my face in my hands. "Adrianne, they're all dead."

She shifted uncomfortably on her barstool. "That's big."

"I know," I said.

"What are you going to do?"

I shook my head. "Nothing. I'm not going to do anything. I'm going to drink my beer and enjoy my peaceful, quiet little life."

She laughed and drained the last of her martini. "Finish your beer. We're getting out of here."

"Where are we going?" I looked at my watch. It wasn't even eight o'clock.

She pointed to my outfit. "We are going to your house so you can change into proper Friday night clothes, and then we are going out."

"We are out, and I need to get some food in my stomach," I argued.

She shook her head and signaled the bartender for our check. "No, ma'am. We are going out and getting your mind off of dead girls, serial killers, and the hot detective."

After several wardrobe changes and having my hair yanked and pulled till my scalp nearly bled, we arrived at The Social Lounge. It was the closest thing Asheville had to a swanky, upscale bar. My dress, which looked like a black satin garbage bag cinched at the waist with a jeweled belt, kept sneaking its way up my backside. Adrianne had given me the dress two birthdays prior, and it had hung in my closet ever since. My heels were too tall and my makeup was too thick, but my hair did look amazing. Sometimes it was a really good thing to have a top hair stylist for a best friend.

We made our way up to the rooftop and navigated through what appeared to be Manhattan transplants until we found two empty bar stools at the bar. When our drinks were delivered, I looked at my Rebel IPA and at her martini and scowled. "I don't see the difference here as opposed to an hour ago when we were paying a lot less for the same drinks, and I was a *lot* more comfortable."

She winked at me over the rim of her glass as she tilted it up to her glossy lips. "You look so good now our drinks might end up being free." She nodded toward the other side of the bar. "Those guys are cute."

I followed the path of her eyes. At the far left end of the bar, two thirty-something-year-old frat boys were speaking in hushed tones as they stared at us—no, as they stared at Adrianne. One was tall and wiry with blond hair and a chiseled face. The other was shorter with dark, wavy hair and overly perfect teeth. He gave me the creeps.

I shook my head. "No. Absolutely not."

She rolled her eyes. "They're cute, and they look like they could afford to pay our tab at the end of the night." She smiled over at them.

I sighed and drank my beer.

"I'll have what she's having," a voice said to the bartender from behind me. I saw Adrianne's eyes widen and then dart away. "A beer girl, huh?" Nathan wedged his body between my chair and the older man seated next to me.

I covered my eyes with my hand. "Seriously?"

"You called him here," Adrianne teased as she nudged me with her elbow.

His lips spread into a wide smile. "You were talking about me, huh?"

I smirked. "Oh, it wasn't flattering." I drained half of my glass before putting it down.

He leaned down close to my ear. "I'm kinda surprised I haven't heard from you this week."

His voice disturbed the butterflies that had taken up residence in my stomach since he had moved to town, but I refused to let him know it.

I glanced up at him. "Was I not clear enough for you the other day when I slammed my front door in your face?"

The bartender placed a beer in front of Nathan. "Do you want to start a tab?"

Nathan shook his head and put a twenty dollar bill on the counter. "No thanks. Take care of these three drinks and keep the change."

"I'm not inviting you to join us," I told him.

He shook his head. "I wasn't expecting you to."

Adrianne reached across me and offered him her hand. "I'm Adrianne. Sloan's best friend. You're Detective McNamara."

"Just Nathan or Nate," he said as he shook her hand. "It's nice to meet you."

"You can join us," she said with a smile. "My invitation."

He laughed and looked at me. "As tempting as that sounds, I can't. Thank you though." He looked back and waved to someone. I knew it was his girlfriend before I even turned around.

Shannon Green, the girl I had wished syphilis on in high school, was walking toward us when I spun around in my chair.

I looked at Adrianne. "Is this really happening right now?"

"Sloan?" Shannon hesitated as she approached.

Nathan's eyes darted between us. "You two know each other?"

I laughed and crossed my legs. "Oh yes. We know each other very well." I pointed at her. "This is your girlfriend?"

"Uh oh," I heard Adrianne mumble next to me.

"Yes," Shannon answered, so bubbly I wanted to smack her. She draped her arms around Nathan's neck and leaned her body into his. "Isn't he wonderful?"

"He's actually a pain in the ass." I looked at him. "I thought you said your girlfriend was a reporter?"

Shannon tossed her hair over her shoulder. "I am a reporter."

Adrianne laughed. "You're the traffic girl!"

Shannon put her hand on her hip. "I'm not *just* the traffic girl!" she protested. She started counting on her fingers. "I have to put together news stories, and interview people, and lots of stuff."

Adrianne nodded, sarcasm dripping from her eyes. "I'm sure that it's very challenging to keep up with the traffic of the Asheville metropolis."

Shannon wanted to speak, but her mouth couldn't find any words. Her eyes darted from Adrianne to me and then back at Nathan. He was doing his best to try and look offended on her behalf, but he wasn't very successful. Finally, Shannon turned and stalked off.

I chuckled quietly to myself and turned around in my seat. I picked up what was left of my beer and tipped it toward Nathan. "Thanks for the drink, Detective."

When they were gone, Adrianne gripped my bicep so hard she left fingerprints. "Hold up. Wait a second. He's dating Shannon Green? Out of all the women in this city, *that's* his girlfriend?" She was laughing so hard she doubled over in her seat.

"Apparently so." I sighed and shook my head.

Tears leaked from her eyes as she slapped the bar and laughed next to me. "How does this stuff happen to you? That's the funniest thing I've ever seen in my life!"

I buried my face in my hands and couldn't help but laugh. "I have the worst luck in the history of the world." I finished off my glass and held it up so the bartender would see I desperately needed another one.

Adrianne draped her arm across my shoulders. "Well, look on the bright side," she said. "You finally have an opportunity for payback. Now you have the chance to hook up with *her* boyfriend."

"When you said, 'you're the traffic girl' I about died," I said, trying to control my giggles.

She made a serious face with overly pouty lips. "She really is a serious news reporter."

I nodded and grinned at her over my glass. "I know I couldn't get to work without her in the mornings."

The laughter erupted all over again.

"What's so funny?" someone asked from behind.

"I'm afraid to even turn around," I grumbled.

It was the two guys from the other end of the bar. Between their heads, I caught Nathan watching from across the room. I turned a sultry smile toward the blond guy, since he seemed to be less creepy than the guy with the offensively white teeth. "Hi there," I purred.

He leaned toward me. "Can we buy you ladies a round?"

Nathan was still watching.

"Absolutely."

I woke up the next morning to the sound of the phone ringing. I looked at the caller ID. It was my dad. I pressed the answer button and rubbed my tired eyes. "Hello?"

"Hey, sweetheart. Did I wake you?" he asked.

I yawned. "Yeah. I had a bit of a late night last night. What's up?"

"Mom wanted me to call and tell you that she made biscuits and gravy for breakfast and that you should come over since you missed dinner this week," he said.

I groaned. "What time is it?"

"It's after nine."

"I'll be there soon if I can drag myself out of bed. Don't let breakfast get cold if it takes me a little bit. Go ahead and eat without me," I said.

"OK. Be careful. Love you," he said.

"Love you too, Dad." I disconnected the call and looked at notifications screen on my phone. I had a text message from Nathan that I had missed about an hour before.

Did you make it home OK last night?

I decided to let him wonder and didn't respond.

The smell of sausage billowed out of the front door when I walked into my parents' house. My stomach immediately rumbled. "Oh my gosh, it smells like heaven in here," I said as I walked into the kitchen.

Dad was at the breakfast bar with a cup of coffee and the

newspaper. Mom was in her housecoat and slippers at the stove. I kissed him on the cheek. "Morning, Daddy."

He looked up from his paper. "Morning, sleepyhead."

Mom turned around with a coffee mug in her hand. "The coffee's fresh." She kissed my cheek as she handed me the empty mug.

I shuffled toward the coffee pot, filled my cup full, and pulled up a seat next to my father. He was reading the obituaries. "Are you looking for a hole in your patient load?" I asked.

"Sloan," he scolded. "That's not funny."

I winked at him. "It's a little funny."

He just grinned.

"How was your week?" I tilted the steaming cup of life-giving caffeine up to my lips.

He turned in his seat toward me. "Not as interesting as yours, I hear," he said. "You've been on the news all week."

"Still?" I asked.

Mom turned around and pointed a spatula at me. "Your Aunt Betty saw the broadcast all the way up in Lexington."

I sipped my coffee. "Really? I can't believe people are still talking about it."

Dad looked curiously over at me. "One reporter said that she heard you say the girl wasn't dead before anyone even knew she was in the house."

I rolled my eyes. "That's crazy. How would I know that?"

He was eyeing me with blatant skepticism.

I shrugged my shoulders. "There was a lot of commotion. She probably misheard something."

I could tell my father didn't believe me, but he didn't push the subject. My parents enjoyed their state of voluntary ignorance concerning the oddities that always seemed to follow me. If they didn't bring it up, they knew I wouldn't, and our mutual silence on the matter would allow them to keep on believing there wasn't anything medically or psychologically unsound about their only child.

"The detective who was at the hospital with you and the sheriff, is he the one you told me about the other day?" Mom asked.

I nodded. "That would be him."

A small, teasing, smile played at the corners of her lips. "He's very handsome."

My father perked up. "Are you dating someone?"

I laughed. "No."

My mother turned with her hand on her hip. "Why is that funny?"

I shrugged. "I just haven't met anyone worth dating."

"What's wrong with the detective?" she asked.

"A lot," I said. "And he has a girlfriend. Guess who it is. Shannon Green."

My mother gasped and her mouth fell open. "No!"

I cupped the warm mug with both hands. "Yep."

"The traffic girl?" my dad asked.

"That's the one," I replied.

"What's wrong with the traffic girl?" he asked, confused. "I thought the two of you were friends."

"*Were*," Mom said. "Till that hussy went and stole Sloan's boyfriend. You don't remember? Sloan cried for a month."

I groaned. "Let's not relive it, Mom."

"Well, sweetie, you can do better," she assured me. "You don't want any guy who would stoop to so low of a standard."

I nodded and rolled my eyes. "I know." I looked at Dad, desperate to change the subject. "Tell me about your week."

He thought for a moment. "Well, it doesn't compare with finding a missing little girl, but I did find another missing Alzheimer's patient of mine serenading people on the elevator with *Your Mama Don't Dance and Your Daddy Don't Rock and Roll*."

I almost spat out my coffee. "That's pitiful!"

He nodded. "And pretty humorous. Especially when she got me to sing it with her on our ride back up." He smiled. "I think God has to allow us a little laughter because it's such an awful disease."

I sighed. "Your job is never boring, is it?"

He shook his head. "Never."

I looked over at Mom. "Speaking of missing people, weren't you friends with that Bryson woman whose daughter disappeared a few years ago?"

She thought for a moment. "I worked with her at the hospital, but she ended up quitting. She was really devastated after her daughter went missing."

"They never found out what happened to her?" I asked.

She shook her head. "No. The Brysons spent all their savings on private investigators and everything. I don't suppose anything ever turned up. I can't imagine something happening and not knowing whether your child is alive or dead. It's turned their whole family upside down, I think."

"That's so sad," I said.

"What brought that up?" Dad asked.

"Someone at work mentioned the case. They thought I might have heard of it," I said. "No real reason."

"I know it made me want to hold on to you a little tighter," Mom said to me. "And you were off at college. I was sick over it."

I shuddered and stood up from my seat. "Dad, can I use your computer?" I asked. "I need to check my email."

"Sure, it's turned on in my office." He motioned toward the steps that led to the second floor.

"Make it fast," Mom called after me. "Breakfast will be ready in two minutes."

Dad's office always reminded me of something out of a Norman Rockwell painting. The shelves were covered with medical books, papers were neatly arranged on the desk, and the brown shutters were always halfway open because he liked to see the birds outside his window. I sat down at his computer and clicked on the Internet icon. I wasn't sure what I hoped to accomplish, but I typed "Leslie Bryson Asheville Disappearance" into the search bar and clicked on the first article.

For the longest time, I sat and stared at her picture. I was pretty sure she and I had shared a class—maybe art or Spanish. Finally, I skimmed the article. Her family had offered a huge reward for her return, but the police never found anything. I looked at the photo of her mother holding a "Bring Leslie Home" sign. I thought of my own mother and nearly burst into tears.

"Sloan, the biscuits are done!" Mom called from the bottom of the stairs.

I closed the browser window and stood up. "Coming!"

When I pulled up in front of my house, there was a family waiting on my porch. I parked and got out of my car and recognized them immediately when the little girl ran down my steps toward me. Kayleigh Neeland looked like a completely different child wearing a pink dress, sparkly shoes, and carrying her Sleeping Beauty doll by the hand.

I teared up as I dropped my keys on the sidewalk and knelt down to her level. She threw her little arms around my neck.

"What a wonderful surprise!" I squealed as I hugged her. After a moment, I pulled away to see the bruising had almost completely faded, and the stitches had been removed from her forehead. "You look so pretty, Kayleigh."

She swayed back and forth, the thick tulle under her skirt giving off a light swooshing sound as she batted her eyelashes. "Do you like my dress? My Nana made it for me."

I had to wipe tears from my eyes. "I love it. You look like a princess!" I kissed her tiny cheek.

Her grandparents made their way down the steps to meet me. I stood up and Kayleigh clung to my leg. Her Nana reached out to hug me. "Ms. Jordan, I can't thank you enough for what you did for my grandbaby."

I ran my fingers through Kayleigh's blond curls. "I'm so thankful for a happy ending."

"So are we," the woman's husband added. He pointed to the door. "We rang the bell, but no one answered. Kayleigh wouldn't let us leave so we waited for a few minutes to see if you came home."

I laughed. "I'm so glad you did!"

Kayleigh tugged on the leg of my sweatpants. "Miss Sloan, I got you a present." She looked up at her grandmother. "Give it to her, Nana."

Her grandmother held out a small box and a folded sheet of pink construction paper.

I knelt down next to Kayleigh again and opened the paper to a crayon drawing inside. I smiled at her. "Did you make me a card too?"

She nodded with a bright smile.

It was a picture of two figures holding hands. "Is this you?" I asked, pointing to the smaller figure in a pink dress who had one blue eye and one green eye.

She nodded furiously again. She pointed to the other figure. "And that's you!"

I looked at it sideways. "Do I have wings?" I asked, laughing.

"Yes! 'Cause you're an angel and angels have wings!" she said.

I had to sit all the way down on my backside. She fell into my lap, and I tried desperately to choke back huge, bear-sized sobs. I hugged her around the shoulders.

She pried the small box from my hands. "Here, I'll open it for you!"

After a moment of fighting with the tape and ripping the pink wrapping paper, she wrenched open the box displaying a small, silver angel pin. She thrust it toward my face. "It's an angel, just like you!"

I covered my face with my hand and tried to regain my composure. "I love it," I cried.

"Now, you can wear it and think of me!" She blinked her bright blue and green eyes up at me.

I kissed the top of her head. "I will wear it every single day," I wept. I hugged her tight again. "Thank you so much."

Her grandfather offered me a hand up. Once I was on my feet, I straightened my outfit and hugged both of them again. "Thank you for coming to see me," I said. "You've made my whole year."

"The gratitude is all ours. You gave us our whole world back," he said.

I wiped my nose with the back of my hand and looked down at Kayleigh again. "I hope you'll come see me again soon."

Her eyes widened. "I'll try, but I gotta go to kindergarten, Nana says, in a few days, so I might get kinda busy."

More tears spilled onto my cheeks. "You'll be great."

"I know," she said with more confidence than I had ever had.

When they were gone, I sank to the steps of my front porch. Holding my angel pin in one hand and my cell phone in the other, I typed out a message to Nathan. *Bring your folder. I'll be home all day.*

My phone buzzed before I made it to the front door. *I'll come by and pick you up.*

CHAPTER SIX

"WHERE ARE WE going?" I asked as I buckled my seatbelt. "Don't you dare say the jail."

Nathan pulled away from the curb. "My place."

Normally an answer like that would take my breath in a good way. This time, I choked on the air. "Is Shannon going to be there?"

"She's at her house. I don't live with Shannon." He looked over at me, his eyes dancing under the brim of his ball cap as he tried not to laugh. "She didn't tell me she knew you. I wonder why?"

"Because if I had a mortal enemy, it would be Shannon Green."

He burst out laughing. "What? Come on."

"We used to be friends. Really close friends, actually. We were on the cheerleading squad together and the soccer team. Then, one day after cheerleading practice I went to the field house to look for our coach, and I found her making out with my boyfriend, Jason Ward, in the locker room." I shook my head and watched the building pass outside of my window. "I've hated her ever since."

He chuckled and stared up ahead. "She's not too crazy about you either."

I leaned against the window. "I'll bet not. I convinced our whole school she had syphilis."

He cackled again. "Seriously?"

I nodded. "Yep."

He shook his head. "You're evil."

"She deserved it. You don't do that to a friend." I looked out the window. "I can't believe you're dating her."

He grinned over his shoulder. "Is that why you agreed to help me?"

I thought about it. "Not entirely, but that's definitely part of it."

"Why else then?" he asked.

I held out the card Kayleigh had made for me. I hadn't been able to leave it at home when he picked me up. "Kayleigh Neeland and her grandparents came by my house today, and she brought me this. She called me an angel. The thought crossed my mind, what if I hadn't agreed to help you and that little girl died alone in that attic? I wouldn't have been able to live with myself."

I took a deep breath. "Adrianne said to me recently, 'what's the point of being what you are if you can't use it to help people?' She was right. So I should, at least, try." My eyes glazed over, staring out the windshield. "All of those girls are dead, Nathan."

Nathan just nodded and kept driving.

Just outside of the city, in a smaller suburb called Arden, Nathan lived in a third floor apartment. I followed him inside and bit down on my lips to keep from laughing. The white walls of the room were bare, save for a large nail by the door. The few pieces of furniture—a futon couch and a recliner—were centered around the largest flat screen television I had ever seen. The only decor consisted of the black devices attached to the TV, a ridiculous collection of DVDs, and a family portrait that was leaning against the wall.

Nathan hung his keyring on the nail by the door and glanced around the room. "It's not much."

"That's the understatement of the year," I teased. "You don't even have a dining table. Where do you eat?"

He smiled. "Downtown."

I laughed and dropped my purse on the floor.

He turned toward the hallway. "Follow me."

At the end of the hall, a small bedroom had been converted into an office. It had more stuff crammed into it than the rest of the apartment combined. It was an impressive setup with a desk and a computer, a chair, a pin-board filled with paperwork and photographs, two filing cabinets, and a coffee pot.

On the desk lay the American flag patch I had seen on his ball cap. I looked up at his hat and noticed a different patch was on the front. It had a picture of an assault rifle and the caption 'I Plead the 2nd' below it. I laughed and picked the flag up off the desk. "It's velcro?" I asked.

He nodded and took the flag from my fingers. "The flag is my work patch."

I pointed at his hat. "And the assault rifle?"

He grinned. "I'm off work today."

I laughed and nodded my head. "That's cute."

His face scrunched in disgust. "It's not *cute.* It's rugged and funny, not cute."

I rolled my eyes. "Whatever you say, Nathan." I walked over and studied the timeline of the murders on the board. "Does Sheriff Davis know you're investigating this?"

He nodded and stepped over behind me. "Yeah. It's part of the reason he hired me," he said. "Raleigh didn't want me to leave because I've put so much time into the case."

I looked at his sister's picture on the board. "Isn't it sort of a conflict of interest, since you are so close to it personally?"

He shrugged his shoulders. "I suppose, but I don't think the reason really matters when you put in ten times the hours of any other investigator."

He sat down in the office chair and turned on the computer. I leaned over his shoulder and saw a photo of him and Shannon together on the desk. I reached over him and turned it face-down on the table. He laughed.

"Have a seat," he said.

I looked around the room. "On the floor?"

"Crap. I'm sorry." He stood up and offered me his chair. "I'll get some more furniture before you come over again."

"Already planning the second date, huh?" I joked as I sat down in his chair.

He smiled and knelt down beside me so he could open files on the computer.

The first two disappearances happened fairly close together in 2000. Melissa Jennings, like Nathan's sister, disappeared after a high school football game. Police and volunteers canvassed the area for weeks, but no sign of her was ever found. She was seventeen. Three weeks later, Nathan's sister Ashley vanished. At the time, police suspected the two cases may have been related, but no evidence to support the theory was ever found.

The next similar disappearance was almost a full year later in 2001. Angela Kearn, a nineteen year old student at Lenoir-Rhyne, went to her morning classes but returned to her dorm to change books for her afternoon classes and wasn't seen again.

Angela's disappearance seemed to be the beginning of a pattern. Each disappearance after Angela happened in an almost calculated timeframe. Every twelve to fifteen months, another girl would go missing from a very public place and never be seen or heard from again.

Many of the cases had gone cold over the years, but the most recent of the victims were still being actively investigated. The face of Joelle Lawson, a twenty-one year old nursing student from Winston-Salem, had been plastered on billboards all along I-40 since she disappeared in 2011. She had been at a fraternity party on October 2nd where she became sick from drinking too much alcohol and decided to call her roommate for a ride home. She was last seen waiting near the curb for her ride. When her roommate arrived, Joelle wasn't to be found. She assumed Joelle had changed her mind and returned to the party. The next day, when she didn't come home, her roommate called Joelle's family, who notified the police.

Colleen Webster, the most recent victim from Statesville, had been the subject of a couple of my press releases for a collaboration effort between our sheriff's office and that of Iredell County. Colleen was twenty-five and last seen on November 21st outside of a sports bar she frequented. She was laughing with the driver of a silver sedan, so no one suspected foul play. Two days later, her car was discovered in the driveway at the house where she lived alone. Her purse, phone, and keys were on the passenger's seat.

All of the victims were close in age, ranging from seventeen to twenty-five, and they were all attractive and from similar backgrounds. From looking at Nathan's map, I could see why he wondered if the next victim might be from Asheville. Like with the timeline, the murders seemed to be located in a pattern along the I-40 route through North Carolina.

I was chewing on a pen cap, staring at his elaborate pin-board. I put my feet up on the desk and reclined in the office chair. "What do we know about the killer?"

He looked around the room. "Hold up," he said. He went to the closet and pulled out a long piece of thick poster board. He rested it on the tray of the pin-board so I could see. It was covered in large, yellow sticky notes.

A few facts were written in thick black marker. He pointed to them. "Here's what the victims say about him: Number one. He blends in well with a crowd and seems to go unnoticed because no one reported seeing anyone remarkable at any of the locations. Number two. He's approachable and not threatening because there were no reports or signs of struggles at any of the crime scenes."

I raised my hand. "Out of all eleven cases, no one noticed anything out of the ordinary?"

He shook his head. "Not really."

I raised my hand again and held my pen over the pad I was using to take notes.

He leaned toward me. "This isn't a middle school history class. You don't have to raise your hand."

I stuck my tongue out at him. "Give me the ages of the victims in the order in which they were taken."

He straightened up and pointed to the board as he rattled off numbers and I wrote them down. "17, 16, 19, 18, 22, 19, 23, 24, 24, 21, 25."

I tapped my paper with the pen. "He's about their age. He's growing up with his victims."

He frowned at me. "If you would wait, that was point number three."

I put my hands up and bowed my head in apology. "Continue."

He turned toward the board. "I think the killer is likely from the Raleigh area and that he attended one of the metro schools. Both of the football games where my sister and Melissa disappeared were in the same district. The killer probably has some kind of ties to the different areas." He used his pen to point to the different cities on the maps.

I shrugged. "Or, he kidnaps them away from home and takes them to wherever he comes from."

He nodded. "That's a possibility too."

I squeezed my temples. "How is it even possible for someone to get away with this now with forensics, video surveillance, and crime scene investigation being as robust as they are? This person doesn't leave any evidence? No DNA? Fingerprints? Tire tread marks?" I found the whole thing incredibly implausible.

He almost laughed. "You watch too much television."

"I'm serious! And why hasn't anyone else picked up on these

possibly being related?" I asked. "It seems pretty obvious to me and I'm not a cop."

He sat down on the edge of the desk. "The first two happened so close in proximity and time that the police *did* think they were related, but all the rest have been spread out over the state and over so much time that it was hard to connect them together. There are over 10,000 missing person reports filed each year in the state of North Carolina alone. I've done a lot of eliminating to come up with this list. Imagine if you were looking at it among hundreds of thousands of reports."

I sighed. "I guess so. I just can't believe this is still even possible. You don't hear about serial killers anymore."

"That doesn't mean they don't exist. They just don't get the attention they did in the days of Bundy and Dahmer. Terrorists and school-shootings are the big media shockers now," he pointed out.

"Have there been any suspects?"

"There have been plenty of suspects." He pulled another file out of the cabinet and handed it to me before sitting down again. "But these are the only serious leads that have been pursued."

I opened it and found a few groupings of paperwork and photos. I pulled all of the stacks out and laid them in front of me. There were photos of four different men. I tapped my finger on the first mugshot of a middle-aged man with a thick brown mustache and a long scar over his right eye. "This guy is creepy, but he doesn't fit your profile at all."

He leaned over the paperwork. "That's Roger Watson," he said. "He was originally brought in for questioning because his prints were on my car when my sister disappeared. He was a teacher at our school and had been on security duty in the parking lot during the football game. He was never charged with anything."

"Then why does he have a mugshot?" I asked.

"Well, because it turns out you're right. He is a creep. He was arrested two years later for the sexual abuse of two boys on the basketball team. He's serving twenty-four years in federal prison," he explained.

"So he was in prison for most of the murders," I said.

Nathan nodded.

I looked at the other photos. I pointed to the one at the end—a twenty-something-year-old who looked like a Ken doll. "Well, if it's handsome here, then you have nothing to worry about. He's dead."

"I know," Nathan said. "He was killed in a car accident in 2010."

"And the other two?" I was carefully examining the remaining photos.

"These two have only been suspects in the individual disappearances of the respective victims in their areas, but I find them interesting enough that they are being watched." He pointed at the blonde on the left. "Logan Allen was the boyfriend of Christy Dumas who disappeared from her home in Hickory a couple of days after Christmas in 2005. He has two priors for domestic violence and a pretty nasty meth problem. He also has a grandmother in Winston-Salem and a sister who lives in Hendersonville."

I looked at the other guy who appeared to be the right age. He was attractive and obviously strong enough to easily subdue the small-framed victims, but I didn't get the sense that he was a horrible person. "This doesn't feel like a bad guy."

Nathan looked at me. "What do you mean?"

I remembered I hadn't told Nathan everything about my ability. "I have a really keen sense about people. Kind of like how I know if someone is alive or dead by looking at a picture, I sort of have an evil radar that goes off when someone is a rotten human being."

He looked up like he had just solved a great mystery. "That's why you don't like going to the jail."

I shuddered. "That's why I have to take sedatives before going to the jail. I can feel the evil radiating out of that place."

"Can you detect a person's tendencies?" he asked.

I leaned back in the chair. "Not exactly. There are a lot of good people who make really bad decisions. They don't seem evil to me at all, just lost."

"So you're saying that a person's decisions determine who they are?" he asked.

"I think what I'm saying is that you shouldn't put too much stock in feelings I get," I said. "You're not going to be able to convict people based on if they give the county publicist the heebie jeebies or not."

He nodded and stared at me for a moment. His gray eyes had flecks of blue in them that I hadn't noticed before. Finally, he put his finger on the picture. "Scott Bonham is the most likely suspect we have. He's thirty-two years old and was fired from the police force in Cary after being a cop for two years. He graduated from the same high school where Melissa attended and has family in Asheville. He hasn't held a stable job since he was fired in 2002 and has had residences in Raleigh, Asheville, and Winston-Salem."

"Is he in custody?" I asked.

"Nope. Again, not enough evidence," he said.

I thought for a moment. "Why was he fired?"

"For gross misconduct and sexual harassment. He was accused of groping two women during a routine traffic stop," he answered.

"But he wasn't arrested?" I asked.

He shook his head. "They decided not to press charges. He was let go among a flurry of embarrassing news reports."

"Where is he now?"

"Police in Winston-Salem try and keep tabs on him. That's his last known residence," he said.

Nathan's cell phone rang. He pulled it out of his pocket and answered it. "Hey," he said. "I'm working at home. What are you doing?" He listened for a moment. "No, I think I'm going to stay in today...No, don't come over. Maybe we will go to dinner tomorrow...Sure, church in the morning would be fine."

I laughed.

"Yep, OK. You too," he said and disconnected the call.

I folded my arms across my chest. "Are you going to church to repent for lying—again—to your girlfriend?"

"I didn't lie," he said with a pitch of offense in his voice.

"You didn't tell her I was here. That's lying by omission," I said.

He shook his head. "Nope. That was bypassing extra details for the benefit of everyone."

"What's with you saying 'you too'?" I asked.

"What?"

I cocked an eyebrow. "I'm pretty sure she says 'I love you' and you say 'you too'. What's up with that?"

He shifted uncomfortably on the desk. "I'm not sure that's any of your business."

I laughed. "Oh, it's not my business. I'm just curious. Are you in love with her?"

He stood up. "Sloan, that's a really inappropriate question."

"Why won't you answer it?" I asked, grinning up at him.

"Why are you so hung up on me and Shannon?" He folded his arms across his chest. "It didn't seem to bother you much when you and your friend left the bar last night with those two guys."

I laughed. "Now who's being inappropriate?"

Nathan walked out of the room. "Do you want something to drink?"

I got up and followed him to the kitchen. "You're completely blowing me off."

"Yep," he replied as he opened the refrigerator. "I've got beer and water."

I hoisted myself up onto his kitchen counter and tapped my fingers quizzically against my lips. "You say you're not using her, but you won't say you love her either."

He turned around and offered me a bottle of beer and a bottle of water. I took the water. He opened the beer and tipped it up to his lips. "Ready to get back to work?"

I kicked him lightly in the thigh. "Come on," I said. "You have forced me to get super personal with you in the past few weeks. I've told you stuff I haven't even told my mother."

"I didn't force you," he argued.

I cocked my head to the side. "Really?"

He shrugged. "I persuaded you."

"How did you meet her? How long have you been together?" I asked.

He groaned. "I met Shannon about six months ago when I was here researching the murder of Leslie Bryson," he said. "Some of the guys from the department here took me out for drinks, and I met her at the bar. We've been dating long distance ever since. Are you satisfied?" He turned and walked down the hall toward the office.

I jumped off the counter and followed him. "No. It's Shannon Green," I grumbled.

"She's not that bad," he said.

"She's high maintenance, spoiled, and has absolutely no loyalty."

He rounded on me and he wasn't laughing. "Let it go, Sloan."

I rolled my eyes and sat down in the chair. "Fine." I huffed and looked up at the board. "Tell me about Leslie Bryson."

Nathan cleared his throat. "Leslie worked at Chili's as a bartender. About twenty minutes after she clocked out at 10pm, she sent a text message to her roommate saying she was going to be late and to not wait up for her. She never came home."

"No other numbers on her phone?"

He shook his head. "None that were suspect."

"What about camera footage from the parking lot?" I asked. "Maybe she ran into the killer outside before she left."

He shrugged. "Maybe so, but there were no cameras."

"That's frustrating," I said. "What about GPS tracking on her phone?"

"Her purse and phone were found in her car which was abandoned at the Texaco gas station off of Tunnel Road," he answered.

I thought for a moment. "No one saw anything? That's a really crowded area."

He shook his head. "No witnesses."

I looked at the photos of the women and shook my head. "I still don't understand why there isn't some sort of public service announcement about this," I said. "It seems like the public should be made aware that there is a serial killer on the loose."

He sat down on the corner of the desk in front of me. "Well, I just found out a few days ago that all of these girls are dead. No bodies, remember? And there has been a lot of news coverage on all the kidnappings, just not all lumped together."

"I don't watch the news," I told him.

"You're a publicist," he said, surprised.

"The last thing I want to do at the end of my workday is come home and watch news stories about murders, missing people, and violence." I tapped my finger on the desk. "You know, all the stuff you've been throwing at me since we first met."

His smile was genuine and apologetic. "I really do appreciate your help."

"I know," I mumbled. I looked around the room at all of the work he had done, practically all on his own. "How are you going to convince the FBI that there is a serial killer involved? I don't think 'my publicist friend told me they're dead' is going to cut it with the Feds."

He chuckled. "They've been exploring it as a possibility for a while now. We've also considered it might be linked to human trafficking. Now I know which direction to focus on. It would really help if I could find the bodies."

I shook my head. "I'm not a cadaver dog."

He laughed. "I know."

"What do we do now? Just wait for someone else to go missing?" I asked.

He shrugged his shoulders. "Well, it helps now that I know that all of the victims are actually dead. Maybe you and I can find something that will help connect the dots." He kicked the side of the desk with his heel. "You know, even without your supernatural abilities, you're actually really good at this. Have you ever considered being a cop?"

I doubled over. "Me? Around criminals all the time? Seriously?"

He laughed and nodded his head. "Yeah, I didn't think about it that way."

"Supernatural, huh?" I asked.

"What do you call it?" he replied.

I rolled my eyes. "Lately, thanks to you, I call it a pain in my ass."

CHAPTER SEVEN

It was business as usual when I returned to work on Monday. The entire week was extraordinarily boring in comparison to the weekend as I hammered out the county newsletter; warned the citizens of West Asheville of a sewage backup off of Haywood Avenue; and reminded the city to not drink and drive during the upcoming Brewgrass Festival at Memorial Stadium. Most of the city would turn out for the festival, Adrianne and I included. It was my favorite event around the city all year.

I spent my downtime in the office and most of my evenings at home reading through some files Nathan had sent home with me. I found it difficult to believe that all of the women simply vanished without a trace of evidence and their bodies never surfaced, even by accident. I called Nathan at home on Thursday night to tell him as much, but he didn't answer. I hung up when the call went to his voicemail.

I got a text message from him a moment later. *On a call. What's up?*

I responded. *Nothing that can't wait, just brainstorming.*

I think I'm almost done here. Can I swing by on my way home?

The clock on the wall said it was almost 10 pm and I wasn't feeling sleepy yet. I tapped out a reply. *Yep.*

On my coffee table, I spread out each of the victims' summary sheets in the order in which they disappeared. Though I was sure that Nathan had already done the same thing, I searched for even the smallest similarities between the girls. After about a half hour of reading, the dates seemed to come together: all of the girls had been abducted during the fall and winter months. There weren't any that occurred in the spring or the summer. I jotted a list down in my notebook of the dates chronologically. They spanned from September 22nd to December 28th.

There was a knock at my door. When I opened it, Nathan was pulling off a pair of muddy boots. He was splattered in dried mud all the way up to his belly button. I looked at him sideways. "Have you been spelunking?"

He braced himself against my doorframe as he fought to free his foot from his left steel-toed boot. "Practically. I responded to a burglary call and ended up chasing a guy through a storm culvert."

I looked at the mud and then inside at my white furniture. "Why didn't you go home and take a shower?"

"Because I'm tired, and if I had gone home, I wouldn't have left again," he explained.

I thought about offering him a shower at my house, but I was pretty sure I wouldn't get any work done after knowing he had been naked in my bathroom. "Let's talk out here," I suggested.

He looked down at his ruined pants. "That's probably a good idea."

"One sec." I jogged to the living room to grab my notebook and tooth-mangled pen.

When I returned, he was sitting on the top of the steps, so I sat down beside him.

"What's up?" he asked.

I showed him my list. "Have you noticed the dates?"

"Yeah," he answered. "September through December."

"Don't you find that strange?" I asked. "Why just the cold months?"

"I've asked that question a lot. He could live seasonally in this area," he said.

I scowled and shook my head. "People live seasonally around here in the summer. They go to Florida for the winter."

"Older people go to Florida," he pointed out.

"Why would anyone live seasonally here when it's cold?" I asked.

"The leaves?" he suggested. "Tourist season starts here around what? September?"

I nodded. "Here, yes. But not in Raleigh, and it certainly doesn't last till December. Besides, do you really think anyone could be impressed by dying leaves so much that they would make a life change out of it? Particularly a guy in his twenties?"

"Good point," he said.

"Retail jobs are very seasonal," I said. "That's the same time that businesses start hiring for holiday help."

He thought about it. "Maybe. It could be how he finds his victims too."

I frowned and put a hand on my hip. "Are you suggesting that all women are shoppers?"

He laughed. "Yes."

I elbowed him in the side. "We're not all like Shannon."

He smiled. "It has to be more specific than retail though. You can do that anywhere in the country. Why here?"

"Because he's native to the area?" I offered.

"Perhaps, but a retail clerk moonlighting as a serial killer still seems pretty unlikely. It's too public. Someone would have suspected something," he said. "You got anything else?"

"Why were the bodies never found? It seems like it would be pretty hard to hide a body and get away with it," I said. "Where would you hide a body?"

He laughed. "I'm not sure I like where you're going with this."

"I'm serious. How do you make one disappear?" I asked.

He considered it. "I would incinerate it," he said. "Burn it to dust, then scatter and cover the evidence."

My nose wrinkled. "The smell would be suspicious."

He shrugged. "Not necessarily in this area. Moonshiners hide their smoke pretty well."

"How's a serial killer gonna tote an incinerator all over the state?" I shook my head. "You're not much help."

He laughed. "Probably because I'm tired. Let's continue this over the weekend."

"I'm going to the Brewgrass Festival this weekend at Memorial Stadium," I said.

"Oh, yeah. I've heard a lot about it. It's a good time, huh?" he asked.

I smiled. "If you like beer."

He stood up. "You know I do."

"So I'll see you there?" I asked.

"Maybe." He reached out his hand and pulled me to my feet. "I'm going to go home and pass out before I have to do this crap all over again tomorrow. I'm exhausted."

He picked up his boots and carried them down the stairs. As he stepped onto the sidewalk, the sound of rustling leaves between my house and the house next door caught both of our attention. Nathan grabbed a flashlight off his belt and I closed my eyes.

"There's no one there. Must be a cat or something." I leaned against the front handrail of my porch.

He panned the flashlight around the side of the house and then looked up at me. "How do you know?"

I smiled. "Maybe I'm a witch."

He shook his head and rolled his eyes. He yanked his driver's side door open and grumbled as he climbed inside. "I'm never going to get used to this. Goodnight, Sloan."

I waved to him. "Goodnight, Nathan."

When Saturday finally rolled around, I drove to Adrianne's townhouse to pick her up. She had on sunglasses that were bigger than her face. "You look ridiculous," I said as she got into my car.

She scowled over the top of her glasses at my black "This Girl Needs a Beer" tee and blue jeans. "Oh, you're the fashion expert now?" She noticed the angel pin on my shirt. "What's this?"

As I drove, I told her all about Kayleigh surprising me at home. When I finished, she slapped my leg. "See? Doesn't that feel good?" she asked.

I smiled. "Better than any feeling I've ever had before."

"And I've always thought you were a witch. Maybe you are an angel instead," she said.

I smirked. "You're so funny."

"How are things with the hot detective?" she asked.

I shrugged and turned toward the stadium. "Well, I agreed to help him with the serial killer case. We spent almost all day Saturday working on it." I looked over at her. "I want you to promise me you'll be careful, Adrianne."

She nodded. "No serial killers for me," she said. "I'm going to run every guy I talk to by you first."

"You have done that for the past several years and you *never* listen to me," I said.

"Well, you're a little overprotective. You need to tell me, 'that guy's a serial killer, Adrianne' and I won't go out with him," she assured me.

"They don't come with references and a background check," I said. "If I tell you I'm getting bad vibes, that should be enough."

She floated her hand through the air signaling she was bored with the conversation. "You've got our tickets?" she asked.

"They are in the bag next to the chairs," I said.

Memorial Stadium was already overflowing with people when we pulled into the grassy parking lot. "I hope you don't mind,"

Adrianne said as we got out and began unloading my trunk, "but I told Mark that we were going to be here today, and he said that he and Colin might come by."

"Who?" I pulled out a camping chair and slung it over my shoulder.

She retrieved the other chair. "Colin and Mark, the guys from the bar last weekend."

I groaned and leaned against my bumper. "Seriously, Adrianne? Case in point of you not listening to me. Please tell me that you're joking."

She shrugged. "They were cute and they paid our tabs."

"They were obnoxious. Especially Mark. And Colin was so full of himself I wanted to hit him over the head with my beer." I draped my backpack over my other shoulder.

We started toward the stadium. "You didn't like them because you're so hung up on that detective."

I adjusted my sunglasses against the mid-morning sun. "I didn't like them because they were jerks."

She looked over at me. "Is your boy coming today?"

"Nathan is not my boy, and I haven't talked to him in a few days. He said he would probably be here though," I said.

"With Shannon?" she asked.

My face twisted into a sour frown. "If I know my crappy luck, I'm sure she'll be with him."

She started laughing again. "She may have to cover a *serious* news situation."

I smiled. "Gridlock and drunk driving at the beer festival."

We found an open spot on the field, and I set up our chairs while Adrianne went to find our first beers of the day. A band was playing in what was normally the end zone of the football field, and a few people were dancing around the twenty yard line. Local breweries had tents set up all around the sidelines, offering samples and full-sized drafts of their craft brews.

The fragrant mix of sunshine, patchouli oil, booze, and

cannabis floated through the fall sky, reminding me I was at home in America's 'Freak Capital.' There were guys wearing broomstick skirts and girls with dreadlocks and facial piercings. In other groups, the boys wore tight pants and Buddy Holly glasses. Some people were dressed ready for Broadway, while others were dressed for a Renaissance festival. Scottish kilts seemed to be popular, and one man even carried a set of bagpipes. I looked down at my outfit and felt almost out of place. The Brewgrass Festival was people watching at its best.

My eyes scanned the crowd until they fell on someone, or some *thing*, that made my stomach leap into my throat. I coughed and blinked my eyes.

A man, tall with broad shoulders and shoulder-length black hair pulled back into ponytail, was watching me near a group of tents about fifty yards away. He had dark eyes set above high cheekbones and a square jaw. His gaze fixed on me when we locked eyes; it was like staring into the center of a black hole.

For the first time in my life, I sensed something I never had before. A stranger.

"Oktoberfest is out early this year!" Adrianne sang as she lowered a plastic cup over my head from behind. "Aren't you excited?"

I accepted the cup and she moved in front of me. When she had passed, the stranger was gone. Adrianne followed my gaze across the field. When she didn't see anything peculiar, she waved her hand in front of my face. "Yo, Sloan!"

I blinked again and focused on her face. She was still waving. "Huh?"

She leaned toward me. "What's up? You look like you've seen a ghost. You're all pale and stuff."

Sweat prickled on my forehead despite the autumn chill. "I think I have."

Seeing a ghost was *exactly* what it felt like. It was reminiscent of seeing Ray Whitmore lying in the doorway of the kitchen on

Clarksdale. The dark man could have been an animated corpse. There was nothing in him for me to read.

"Hey!" Adrianne shouted, snapping me back to reality again. "What the hell?" She kept looking around and then at me.

I pointed across the field. "There was a guy over there. A guy I didn't know." I strained again to see if I could find him.

She laughed. "There are thousands of people here you don't know."

I shook my head and stood up, craning my neck and searching through the crowds. "No. I mean I didn't *know* him."

"What?" She was looking at me like I had spoken in Mandarin.

I sat down. "Remember me telling you that I—"

"Hey, hey, hey!" someone cheered, stepping into our circle. It was Mark and Colin.

Adrianne stood up and hugged Mark, the guy with the ridiculously perfect teeth and the douchebag personality. She put her hand on his chest. "I thought you would be here later!"

Mark draped his arm across Adrianne's shoulders and held up the cup in his hand. "Oh no. We got here early and decided to try and make it through all forty brew stations before the day is over."

I rolled my eyes. "Of course you did."

"Hey, Sloan." Colin opened up an NC State folding chair and plopped it down on the grass next to me. "Whatcha drinkin'?"

I looked in my cup and realized I couldn't remember. I looked at Adrianne for help.

"Oktoberfest from Brevard Brewing," she answered. "Earth to Sloan."

I shook my head and stood up. "Excuse me for a second," I said. "I'll be right back."

Adrianne followed me and grabbed my arm. "What are you doing?"

I squeezed her hand in frustration. "I don't think you grasp exactly how big this is for me. I've never seen anyone I don't recognize. Ever. In all my life!"

Her face melted from irritation to worry. "What are you going to do?"

"I'm just going to walk around. I'll be back soon and I have my phone in my pocket."

"I'm coming with you," she said.

I shook my head. "No because Dumb and Dumber will follow. Just stay here and entertain. I'll be back in a second."

Her brow wrinkled with worry. "Please be careful."

"Of course," I assured her.

I took off in the direction of the tents before she could protest again. I sipped my beer as my eyes darted from face to face. Halfway around the field, I heard someone call my name. I turned to see Nathan walking hand in hand with Shannon toward me.

I had just passed a guy wearing a fur toga and a Viking helmet on his head, and then there was Shannon dressed in a silky sundress and high heels. Her heels kept sinking into the football field turf with each step that she took. *And I thought I wasn't dressed for the occasion,* I laughed to myself.

Nathan was in his standard tactical attire, except he was wearing a shirt that said "Conserve Water. Drink Beer" and the patch on the front of his hat said "Drinks Well With Others".

"I was wondering if we would bump into each other in this swarm of drunks," he said as they approached.

I held up my cup and forced a smile. "You found me."

"You need another beer," he said. "Let's go take care of that."

Shannon looked annoyed, so I agreed.

We walked toward the tents. "Let's see," he said. "Will it be Wicked Weed or Greenman?"

I looked at both tents. "I haven't tried Wicked Weed," I said.

He stepped toward the vendor leaving me alone with Shannon. "Nice dress," I said to break the uncomfortable silence.

She flipped her blond hair over her shoulder and angled her face toward the sky. "It's a LULUS exclusive."

I didn't know or care what that meant, so I went back to searching the crowd for the guy with the ponytail.

"Here you go." Nathan handed me a new full cup. "It's called the Freak of Nature Double IPA. It seemed appropriate for you."

I laughed and shoved him in the shoulder. "Hey!"

"Haha." He sipped on his beer. "This festival is pretty great. Do you come every year?"

I nodded. "Every year since they started it."

He laughed. "I had to drag Shannon here."

A smug "imagine that" slipped out before I could stop myself.

She huffed and crossed her arms across her chest.

"You looked like you were searching for someone," he said. "Are you lost?"

There was more than one reason I wished Shannon wasn't there. I really wanted to talk to him alone. "I saw this guy that was really strange to me," I said, trying to use words that Nathan would pick up on.

"Are you kidding?" Shannon asked. "Everyone here is strange."

Nathan nodded toward her. "She has a point."

"This guy was different." I cut my eyes at him, urging him to catch on to what I was trying to say.

We locked gazes for a moment. "What's he look like? I'll let you know if I see him."

"He's about your age and he's really tall. Maybe 6'2. He was wearing a dark blue shirt and blue jeans, and his hair was black, probably shoulder length or so in a ponytail."

Nathan was making mental notes. He took a quick look around. "I'll let you know if we see him."

I smiled. "Thanks. We are somewhere around the fifty yard line if you want to come by."

"Oh, we won't be here much longer," Shannon snapped.

I couldn't help myself. "Is there an important lane closure on I-40 that you need to go report?"

Her mouth fell open.

"I'll call you later," Nathan said, trying to sound defensive but not doing a convincing job of it.

I held up my beer as they walked away. "Y'all be careful, and stay away from 3rd South Street. I heard on the news that it's going to be blocked off all day for parking."

Nathan shot me a scowl over his shoulder and I laughed.

"Thanks for the beer!" I called after him.

"You're welcome," he replied. "Quit wandering around alone!"

I finished my lap around the field with no sign of the stranger. His face hung in my mind, like it was going to be permanently fixed there for a long time. Adrianne was at her intoxication stage of giggling by the time I returned. My cup was once again empty.

Colin stood up. "We were about to send a search party after you."

"Find anything?" Adrianne asked.

I shook my head.

"I'm about to get another beer. Want one?" Colin asked.

"Sure. Surprise me." I handed him my empty cup and plopped down into my seat.

He looked disappointed that I didn't offer to join him, but I didn't care.

I closed my eyes and pictured the stranger's dark eyes again. No matter how hard I searched the memory of his face with my gift, I couldn't register his soul. Thinking of the way he had watched me sent chills up my spine. There was some kind of connection there that my brain couldn't fit together.

Adrianne snapped her fingers in front of my nose. "Hey!"

My eyes popped open and settled on her. Mark had his arm across the back of her chair.

"Do you want to go to a dodgeball game tomorrow?" she asked.

"Um. What?" I asked.

"Adult dodgeball," she repeated.

I cocked an eyebrow. "Does that even exist?"

Mark nodded. "Yeah. Parks and Rec has a league. Colin and I play. We have a tournament tomorrow."

I looked at Adrianne. Her eyes were pleading. I didn't want to go but only slightly less than I wanted her to go anywhere alone with Mark. I didn't trust him. "Sure. What time?"

Adrianne smiled.

"It's at eleven in the morning," he said. "We'll come by and pick you up."

"No, we'll meet you there. Adrianne promised to go with me to the mall tomorrow, so we can swing by after," I said.

She tugged on his arm. "Oh yeah. Sorry, I forgot."

"That's cool, babe." He was a little closer to her face than I was comfortable with.

My cellphone buzzed in my pocket. I pulled it out to see a message from Nathan. It said, *Is this him?* A moment later a photo of the guy from behind appeared on my phone.

I dialed Nathan's number and he picked up on the first ring. "Yes! Where is he?"

"Gone," he replied. "I saw him ahead of us going toward the parking lot. He got into a black Dodge Challenger and took off. North Carolina tags and I got the plate number. Want me to run it?"

"Isn't that illegal?" I asked.

He chuckled. "I'll let you know what I find out," he said and disconnected.

Colin returned with my beer as I dropped the phone into the cup holder on my chair. Mark was whispering in Adrianne's ear.

"Hey Mark, what's your last name?" I asked.

"Higgins," he answered. "Why?"

I shrugged. "Just wondering." I was just wondering because I really didn't like Mark Higgins. Maybe I could convince Nathan to run him too.

When I roused myself from a restless sleep the next morning, my brain was still churning with thoughts of the soulless man from the day before. His face had haunted my dreams, taunting me with questions I couldn't answer. Who was he? *What* was he?

I might have spent all day lying there obsessing over him, had Adrianne not begun texting me to see if I was up and ready to go. I prayed that I could talk her out of going to the dodgeball game during shopping, but I failed. After a short trip to the mall, I drove to the downtown recreation gym, and for an hour, we watched grown men throw red rubber balls at each other.

I gestured toward the concession stand. "I'm going to go get a drink," I said. "You thirsty?"

"I'll take a diet soda," she replied.

I navigated the sideline to the concession window and got the attention of the girl behind the counter. "What can I get'cha?" she asked, chomping on a piece of bubblegum.

It was very unfortunate that the state restricted beer sales until after two o'clock on Sundays. Alcohol would be the only thing to make adult dodgeball more interesting. "Two diet sodas, please."

My phone rang. It was Nathan. "Where are you?" he asked.

"Dodgeball game," I answered over the sound of grown men screaming and the distinct squeak of tennis shoe soles on a gym floor.

There was silence on the other end of the line. "Did you say dodgeball?" he asked.

"Yep."

"Swing by my apartment when you're done," he said. "I went by your house and you weren't home."

"OK. Hopefully it won't be too long, but I have to take Adrianne home," I said.

"K," he said and disconnected.

I carried the drinks to the bleachers and realized the game must have ended since the two teams were shaking hands. I said a silent prayer of thanksgiving. I handed her the plastic cup. "Is it over?"

"Yep. They lost," she replied.

I smirked. "Shocker."

She threw a discarded piece of popcorn at me. "Be nice!"

Mark and Colin finally came out of the locker room carrying their gym bags. They had both showered and changed into fresh clothes. Mark had more product in his hair than Adrianne and I combined. He dropped his bag on the bleacher seat in front of us and smiled at me. "Who's hungry?" he asked.

"I'm hungry," Adrianne said.

"Me too," Colin added.

I bumped my friend with my shoulder. "I've got to go into work. No time for food."

"I'll take you home," Mark said to her.

I rolled my eyes and stared at Adrianne with blatant disapproval.

She raised an eyebrow at me. "You don't work on Sundays."

"I need to today. I promise. I've got to go and meet with Nathan," I told her.

"Well, then go. I'll ride with them," she said. "No worries."

But I was worried and she knew it.

She put her hand on my arm and stood up, slinging her purse strap over her shoulder. "I'll be fine. I'll call you tonight."

I knew there was no point in arguing with her. Adrianne always did what she wanted no matter my opinion or anyone else's. I sighed and followed them down the bleachers and out of the gym.

Before I stopped at my car, I grabbed her arm. "Seriously call me tonight," I said.

She smiled and hooked her arm through Mark's. "I promise," she said.

Obvious rejection was etched across Colin's face. "Are you sure you can't come, even if just for a little while?"

I opened my car door and sat down in the driver's seat. "Yeah, sorry. You guys have fun."

I watched them for a moment, unable to dismiss the nausea I felt over letting her go with them. All the way to Nathan's apartment, I reminded myself that I wasn't Adrianne's mother and that she was twenty-seven and fully capable of taking care of herself. I still felt sick though; staring at victims of a serial killer for hours on end had that effect.

There was no answer at Nathan's door when I knocked on it. I looked around the parking lot and his SUV was parked in his spot. I called his phone. He was out of breath when he answered. "Hello?"

"I'm at your door," I said.

"Oh. I thought you were going to be a while. I went for a run. Sit tight and I'll be right there," he said.

I ended the call and sank down on his welcome mat. His apartment building was built on a hill, so at least I had a decent view of the Blue Ridge mountains which were now thoroughly speckled with red, orange, and gold. The fall scenery was one of the things I loved most about the mountains of Western North Carolina. However, I couldn't help but be reminded that the killing season had just opened for our murderer.

As I sat there, I realized that the case was already tainting just about every area of my life, and I had only been involved for a handful of days. I wasn't sure how Nathan had lived with it for so many years.

After about five minutes, he appeared running up the hill in the parking lot. I stood up and brushed crumbled leaves off the seat of my yoga pants. A moment later, he was taking the steps two at a time up to the landing. He had on a white dry-fit shirt and a pair of black gym shorts. He had perfect calves.

He pulled his earbud speakers out of his ears and reached into his waistband for his keys. "I'm sorry. I thought I had plenty of time."

"Adrianne decided to go out and eat with the guys," I said.

He pushed the door open. "What guys?"

I followed him inside. "The ones we met at The Social Lounge."

He turned and looked at me. "You didn't go with them?"

I grimaced. "With Captain Douchebag Veneers and his side kick? No thank you."

He laughed as he wiped the beaded sweat off his forehead. "What was up with that guy's teeth?"

I threw my arms in the air. "I don't know. It looks like they were whitened with a nuclear agent."

He laughed and went to the kitchen. "Want some water?"

"Sure," I replied.

He came out and handed me a bottle of water. "I'm gonna take a quick shower. Make yourself at home."

"Ok."

He walked down the hallway and I sat down in the lone recliner in the living room. I studied the oversized remote before pressing the red ON button. Unfortunately, that was as far as I got. After pressing all of the other buttons, turning on a zombie video game, and possibly calling his mother on video chat, I gave up and turned the set off.

I walked to his office and found a new brown leather loveseat against the back wall. The couch was endearing, like it was a gift specifically put there for me. I stretched out across it and stared at the ceiling willing myself to think of anything except the sound of the shower running in the adjacent room.

After a few minutes, steam poured out of the bathroom door as it opened, and Nathan stepped into the hallway without a shirt on. I leaned a little too far over and fell off the couch with a loud thud.

"You all right?" he called from his bedroom.

"Fine!" I scrambled to my seat. I could feel my face pulsing with embarrassment, but he didn't seem to notice when he joined me a moment later. Thankfully, he was dressed in sweatpants and a t-shirt.

"You like the couch?" he asked.

"Very much."

"Did you fall off the couch?" he asked with a grin.

"Shut up."

While chuckling to himself, he looked under a pad on his desk and pulled out a sheet of paper. "I found your guy. He's clean." He handed me the paper and plopped down in the office chair.

I looked at the sheet. There was an identification photo in the top left corner. It was the guy I had seen at the festival. "Where'd you get this?"

He shrugged. "I have friends in important places."

I stared at the DMV photograph. "Nothing," I said out loud. "Absolutely nothing."

"Nothing?" he asked, confused.

I slapped the paper. "I don't get anything off this guy! If I didn't know any better, I would say he's dead." I raked my nails through my hair, tugging it in frustration. "This is so weird."

I scanned the paper. "Warren Michael Parish. Aliases: Shadow, Parish. Date of birth: August 27th, 1984. Lives in New Hope, NC. Honorable discharge from the Marines in 2010. No criminal records." I looked up at Nathan. "Who is this guy?"

"If he's in New Hope with a Marine background, I would assume he's with Claymore," he said.

"What's Claymore?" I asked.

"Hired mercenaries," he replied. "They go into high combat zones for the US and some of our allies, but they aren't governed by the Geneva Convention."

"That's scary. Why is a mercenary following me?" I asked.

He shrugged his shoulders. "That's a good question. How are you so sure he was concerned with you?"

"He was looking right at me," I said.

He laughed. "You're an attractive female. Of course he was looking at you."

I stood and began to slowly pace the room. "No. He was staring at me. He was staring at me like I was staring at him, but I couldn't tell anything about this guy. He was like...a void. I didn't know him at all."

"That's rare?" he asked.

I stopped and turned toward him. "That's non-existent."

He raised his eyebrows in doubt. "That never happens?"

"Never, Nathan. Unless someone is dead. That was the feeling I got from him. Like he was a corpse or a shell," I said.

He pondered my words for a while. I expected him to laugh or look at me like I was crazy. He never did. "*Was* the guy dead?" he finally asked.

"He was staring right at me," I said. "How could he be dead? It's impossible."

He leaned forward on the chair and rested his elbows on his knees. "Sloan, how can you tell if a person is alive or dead by looking at their photograph?" He leveled his gaze at me. "I'm beginning to think that less and less stuff is really impossible."

I sat down. "Good point."

"And you're sure he was staring at you? Could he have been just looking in your direction?" he asked.

"He was staring at me. No doubt about it," I said.

He was quiet again. "Do you have a carry permit?"

"Like a gun permit?" I asked.

"Yeah."

I laughed. "No. I've never shot a gun in my life."

He scowled and cocked his head to the side. "Seriously?"

"Never even touched one," I added.

He dropped his face into his hands. "But you're a mountain girl."

"What does that have to do with anything?" I asked.

"I thought it was like a rule or something, by nature, that you had to learn how to shoot if you live here," he said.

I was puzzled. "My dad's a doctor, not a hunter. Half the people of this city are granola vegetarians. Where would you get an idea like that?"

He groaned in exasperation and rubbed his palms over his eyes. "Well, I'm going to teach you," he said.

I looked around the room. "Right now?"

"No. Not right now. It will be dark soon," he said. "Maybe we can go—"

There was a noise in the front of the apartment. The door opened and we heard Shannon's voice. "Knock knock!"

"Uh oh," I said. I looked up to catch Nathan's surprised glance down the hallway in the direction of the front door. I tried to stifle a laugh as he darted from the room.

I didn't move.

"Hey," he said. "What are you doing here?"

"Since you blew me off all day, I decided to come by and bring you dinner," Shannon purred.

"You should've called," he said.

"I tried to call, but you haven't been answering your cell phone," she said. "What have you been doing all day?"

"Working," he answered. After a beat he added, "Sloan is here."

There was a distinct pause. "Sloan *Jordan* is here?" she asked like my name was some profane word that offended her to say. "Where? In your bedroom?"

I clapped my hand over my mouth to keep myself from bursting out in laughter.

"In my office," he clarified. "Sloan, can you come out here, please?"

Obediently, I got up and walked to the doorway of the office.

Shannon was poised with her hand on her hip by the kitchen. She was pissed. "What the hell are you doing here?" she shouted at me.

I couldn't contain my giggles any longer.

"We're working," he said again.

She forced a cough. "On what? Are you going to be on the six o'clock news, Nathan? She's a publicist, not a cop!"

She started to take a step in my direction, but he put his arm out to stop her. "Shannon, please go home. I'm sorry. I'll call you later."

She pointed an angry acrylic nail at me. "Tell *her* to go home!"

"She was invited," he snapped back.

That shut her up.

She stared at him with her mouth hanging open before slinging her purse over her shoulder and stalking to the front door. She looked to see if he would stop her. He didn't. She slammed the door on her way out.

He was frozen with his back to me. His hands were resting on his hipbones and he dropped his head and blew out a long huff of frustration. Finally, he turned around. I tried not to smile, but I couldn't help myself.

He walked to the office. "Oh, shut up."

"Trouble in paradise?" I asked as he brushed by me.

He plopped down in his chair. "Sometimes she makes me crazy."

"We have a club. Would you like a membership card?" I asked.

He scowled at me.

I hovered in the doorway. "Should I go so you can patch things up with her?" I asked, but I wasn't sure why.

He shook his head. "No. She needs to cool down anyway." Hesitantly, I walked to the loveseat and sat down. "Where were we?" he asked.

I folded my legs under me. "Gun range."

He nodded. "Tomorrow over lunch."

CHAPTER EIGHT

After finalizing our plans for bullets and targets over my lunch hour the next day, I said goodnight to Nathan and drove home. The sun had just finished sinking behind the horizon when I turned onto my street and found a black Dodge Challenger parked in front of my house. I slammed on my brakes.

Warren Parish heard the gravel shifting under my tires and looked up from where he was leaning against my front porch handrail.

"Dang it! I should have known!" I yelled at myself.

Quickly, I yanked out my cell phone and called Nathan.

The dark stranger was slowly walking toward me with his hands up in the surrender position. I knew I should put the car in reverse to get the hell out of there as fast as possible, but my insatiable curiosity got the best of me. I inched my car forward.

Nathan's voicemail picked up, so I left a message. "Hey. That guy, Warren Parish, is at my house. Thought you should know in case I turn up missing. I know it's probably not a smart idea, but I have to see why he's here."

I stopped behind his car in the middle of the street near the front of my house. I didn't put the car in park in case I needed to make a quick getaway. Warren stayed on the curb with his hands still raised. His black hair was pulled back and he was wearing a fitted white t-shirt and black jeans. I was terrified out of my wits, otherwise I probably would have been drooling. If Warren Parish was a corpse, death suited him.

I studied him for a moment before inching down my window enough to speak. "Who are you?" I snapped.

He slowly lowered his hands to his sides. "Warren." His voice was as deep as the void I felt when he spoke.

I was wringing the steering wheel with my sweaty hands. "I know you've been following me. What do you want?"

He gave an awkward laugh. "I'm not a hundred percent sure, other than I want to talk to you." After a pause, he lowered his face and cut his eyes up at me. "And I'm pretty sure you want to talk to me too."

I did want to talk to him. Desperately.

"How do I know you're not some lunatic who is trying to kill me?" I asked.

He cracked a smile. "I have an idea." He held his hands up again. "I'm going to give you my gun. It's loaded and ready to fire. All you have to do is pull the trigger and kill me if I even move too suddenly."

Oh geez. He's armed. My eyes narrowed. "You're crazy."

He nodded. "Probably so."

Slowly, he pulled his shirt up to display a black holster on his side. "I'm going to take it out and hand it to you. I won't move too fast."

My foot was poised and ready to slip from the brake to the gas pedal. My knuckles were white from my death grip on the steering wheel. He lifted the gun out of the holster and turned it around in his hand. He eased forward and passed it to me by the handle.

"Please don't shoot me," he said. "I promise I won't give you a reason to."

My hand was shaking as I took the gun through the open portion of the window. He stepped backward to the sidewalk again. I took a deep breath and slid the transmission into park without pulling the car over. I figured that I could only benefit from completely blocking the street with my car. I left the engine running and carefully got out.

His gun was shaking in my hand. "What are you doing here?" I asked.

He seemed to relax a little. "I saw you on the news. You helped save that little girl."

"And?" I asked.

He hesitated for a moment. "And I couldn't read you."

For a second, I thought my heart had stopped beating.

"I've never met anyone I couldn't read," he added. We stared at each other in loaded silence for what felt like an eternity. Finally, he spoke again. "What are you?"

"A publicist."

He laughed. "That's not what I meant."

I couldn't laugh if I had wanted to. "I know what you meant, but I don't have an answer for you. I don't know what I am. What are you?"

He shook his head. "I don't know either."

"I can't tell if you're good or evil," I admitted.

He laughed again. "Sometimes, I can't either."

I cut my eyes at him and studied his face in the light of the streetlamp. "Are you a serial killer?"

His eyes widened. "Are you?"

"No," I answered.

"Would you tell me if you were?" he asked.

"Probably not," I replied.

He shrugged again. "Then I guess it doesn't matter what I say, but I'm not a serial killer, and I promise I'm not here to hurt you. I just needed to meet you. Can we please talk?"

I thought about the stack of photographs of dead girls I had in my briefcase. "This isn't a really good time in my life to be talking to strangers."

He was quiet for a moment and then raised his hands again. "How about this? I'm going to empty my pockets and give you everything I have. I have a knife, and I'm going to open and close it, and then it's yours. Again, I promise I won't make any sudden moves."

Nervously, I nodded and raised the gun slightly.

He reached into his pockets and retrieved a large pocket knife from one and a set of keys from the other. He left his pockets turned out. He tossed the keys at my feet then pulled his wallet out of his back pocket and tossed it over. Next, he took the knife, opened it, and pricked his finger with the tip. He closed it again and slid it across the concrete toward me. "I'm going to walk to the front of your car," he said.

I was puzzled, but nodded again.

Slowly, with his hands still raised and blood trickling down his left index finger, he crossed in front of me to my front bumper. He wiped the blood on the hood of my car and then spat on it.

My mind raced trying to make sense of what was happening.

He raised his hands again and returned to the sidewalk. "Now you have my gun, my identification, my knife, my getaway keys, and enough of my DNA to clone me. Do you think we can relax and you can at least put my gun down on your car or something? You're shaking so bad that I'm afraid you might shoot yourself in the foot."

The tension began to leave my shoulders. Slowly, I placed the gun on the lid of my trunk.

He pointed to it. "Would you mind spinning the barrel away from us?"

I turned the gun so that it pointed down the street. He let out a deep sigh of relief.

I stretched my sweaty hands for a moment and took several deep breaths.

He sat down on the curb and looked up at me. "You OK?"

"Yeah." I sighed and looked down at him, but I was still unwilling to move from my spot. "Why did you come here?"

He shrugged his shoulders and draped his long arms over his knees. "Curiosity, I guess," he answered. "I've been all around the world a few times and have never encountered anything like you."

He was verbalizing my thoughts. "A stranger," I finally said.

"Yes!" He pointed at me. "That's exactly it!"

I nodded. "I feel the same way about you."

We studied each other. Finally, he spoke. "I know when people are alive or dead."

I narrowed my eyes. "Prove it."

He looked around the empty street. "How?"

My briefcase was in my house, but Nathan had given me the files of the suspects that evening. They were in the car. I pointed at him. "Don't move." He lifted his hands in the air again. I reached into my car and retrieved the folders from the passenger's seat. I pulled out the four photos of the suspects.

I looked at him from my car for a moment before taking a bold step forward. "Don't try anything," I warned him.

"You have my word," he said.

I sank down on the curb next to him and offered him the pictures. His hand brushed against mine and a jolt, like a warm, gentle buzz of electricity shot through me. Our eyes locked. He felt it too.

"That was weird," he said, wide-eyed with genuine surprise.

"Very weird," I agreed. "What was it?"

He shook his head and smiled a little. "I don't know, but it didn't hurt."

After a moment of letting the air settle down, I nodded to the pictures. "Tell me."

He flipped through them. "This guy is alive. This guy is alive. This guy is dead. And this guy is alive."

Slowly, my eyes met his. "You're like me."

The realization of what I had just said spread over his face. "Do you think that's why we can't sense each other?" he asked.

"Has to be," I said.

He raked the few strands of loose hair that had fallen around his face back toward his ponytail. "What the hell?" Suddenly, he began to laugh. "What are we?"

Within the span of seconds, I felt more understood by this random, seemingly menacing man than I had by anyone else in my entire life. I couldn't help but laugh with him. "I have no idea."

He looked at me with a handsome smile. "You're laughing," he said. "You're not afraid of me?"

I shook my head and looked up at the starry night sky. "Not anymore." I quickly pointed at him. "But don't prove me wrong!"

"I won't," he said as he nudged me with his shoulder.

I felt the buzz of energy again and it sent chills down my spine. "I don't think that's static electricity," I said.

He looked at me. "I don't think so either."

We both sat there in silence. There were frogs singing from the creek behind my house. After a while, he shifted his heels in the gravel. "People are always afraid of me," he said.

I chuckled. "You're kind of a big, scary dude with your black hair and your black car."

He shook his head. "No, I mean like *really* scared around me. I don't have a lot of friends."

"Hmm." I looked over at him. "That's different. People seem to like me for no reason at all. I'm way more popular than I should be."

He smirked. "You're hot and obviously pretty smart, and based on that little jitter dance you did holding my Glock, you're not intimidating *at all*."

I whined and buried my face in my knees. "That's the first time in my life I've ever touched a gun."

He burst out laughing. "Seriously?" He shook his head. "I'm glad you didn't kill us both, then."

"I'm supposed to learn to shoot tomorrow."

He chuckled a little. "Then I will certainly be on guard the next time we meet."

"Where are you from?" I asked.

"I live in New Hope, NC right now, working as a contractor for Claymore. Before that, I was all over the place with the Marines. Iraq, Kuwait, Afghanistan. I grew up in south Chicago," he said.

"Chicago," I repeated.

"Well, I don't know if I was born in Chicago. I really have no idea where I'm from originally," he added.

I sat up straight. "You're adopted?"

He shook his head. "Orphaned. Grew up in the system."

I blinked my eyes at him. "I'm adopted. I was a few days old when my mother found me. Maybe we're related!"

He looked at me out of the corner of his eye with a sly smile. "God, I hope not."

I blushed and laughed again. "You're going to feel really sleazy about that if it turns out that you're my brother."

We were quiet again. "What else can you do?" he finally asked.

I thought about where to begin, but before I could answer, an SUV—with blue lights ripping through the dark—screamed around the corner. "Oh no," I said. I jumped to my feet.

Warren didn't move. "You called the cops?"

I bit my lower lip. "Sort of. I'll handle it." I hesitated for a moment. "You don't need to, like, escape or anything do you?"

He laughed and shook his head. "No."

Nathan's SUV slid to a stop behind my car. I held my hands up as he ripped his driver's side door open. "It's OK!" I shouted. "It's OK. I'm fine!"

He stepped cautiously around his door with his hand on the gun at his side. "Sir, would you mind standing up, please? Keep your hands where I can see them."

Warren obediently stood with his hands raised over his head.

I stepped into his path and tried to block him with my body. "Nathan, you don't have to do this."

"Get out of my way, Sloan," he said.

I growled and moved out of his way.

"Please turn around," he said to Warren.

When Warren turned, Nathan carefully patted him down. While he searched, he carefully surveyed our surroundings. "Why is there a gun on your trunk, Sloan?" he asked without looking at me.

"I put it there," I said. "Seriously, it's OK."

"It's my gun, Officer—" Warren began, but he was cut off.

"I'm talking to her," Nathan barked.

I put my hands on his forearms. "Nathan, listen to me. I'm fine. I'm sorry I know I frightened you, but Warren and I have been talking and everything is—"

He cut me off. "Have you not been listening to a damn word I've been saying for the past couple of weeks? Do you want to get yourself killed?" There was genuine panic in his voice.

I looked around when a light flickered on outside of one of the neighboring houses. "Can we calm down and go inside, please?" I asked.

His eyes were still wide as he took a step away from Warren. "Do you mind if I see your information, buddy?" he asked.

Warren nodded to me. "She's got my wallet."

"Oh yeah." I dashed to the rear of my car to retrieve it. "He gave me everything in his pockets, including his gun." Nathan's eyes were dancing with confusion. I handed him the wallet. "Oh, and he wiped blood on my car so there would be DNA evidence if he hurt me."

Nathan blew out an angry huff and turned toward my car, but not before telling Warren not to move.

I looked at Warren. "I'm so sorry."

"Don't apologize. You can't be too careful," he said with a smile. "If you are my sister, I would expect no less from you."

Nathan perked up in the driver's seat and looked out at both of us. "Sister?"

"It's a long story," I said to him.

He finally stepped out of my car and handed Warren the wallet. "Here you go," he said. "Is that gun loaded?"

"Yes," Warren answered.

"Mind if I *unload* it?" Nathan asked.

Warren shook his head. "Go ahead."

Nathan picked up the gun, removed the magazine, and cleared the chamber. When he was done, he looked at Warren again. "Mind if I hold onto it while I'm here?" he asked.

Warren turned his hands out. "Be my guest."

"Sloan, you wanna move your car to the curb?" Nathan asked.

"Sure," I said. "I'm just gonna pull in my driveway, m'kay?"

"Fine," Nathan answered.

By the time we got our vehicles out of the road, two different neighbors were on their porches watching the ordeal. I waved to them as the three of us walked up the steps to my front door. "Sorry folks! Everything is OK. Nothing to see here!"

Mrs. Wilson, who lived across from me, was in her nightgown. She shook her head in disgust before disappearing inside. I groaned and unlocked the door. Warren and Nathan followed me.

When the door was closed, Nathan folded his arms over his chest. "Do you mind telling me what the hell is going on here?"

I urged him toward the living room. "Come on. We're not barbarians. Let's sit down and talk like civilized people," I said.

I sat on the couch, Warren took the loveseat, and Nathan scowled as he sat on the edge of the seat beside me.

Warren leaned forward, resting his elbows on his knees. "I'm really sorry I scared the shit out of everyone tonight. I couldn't bring myself to leave town without saying something."

"Saying what?" Nathan snapped.

I put my hand on his leg. "Simmer down. We're all friends here."

"No we're not," he said through a clenched jaw.

I realized I hadn't made introductions. "Warren, this is Detective Nathan McNamara. Nathan, you already know Mr. Parish," I said. "I'm sorry, Warren. Nathan and I have been through a lot here recently. We're both a little on edge."

"I told you, you don't have to apologize," Warren said.

"No! You *don't* have to apologize," Nathan barked at both of us. He cut his eyes at Warren. "Why were you here, waiting in the dark at her doorstep for her to come home alone?" he shouted across the room.

Warren shook his head. "I didn't know that she would be alone," he reasoned. "I tried to be as non-threatening as possible. I stayed outside of my car in the streetlight. I let all the neighbors get a good look at me—"

Nathan cut him off again. "It's bullshit! What are you doing here?"

"I wanted to talk to Sloan," he said.

"Why?"

Warren looked to me for help. I nodded my head. "It's OK. He knows," I assured him. I looked at Nathan and tried to get him to focus on my face. "He's like me."

That seemed to take Nathan back. He swallowed hard. "What do you mean? He's psychic?"

Warren cringed. "I hate that word."

"Me too!" I laughed, completely forgetting the seriousness of the moment.

Nathan wasn't laughing. "I don't like this, Sloan."

I patted his hand. "I know."

"Why are you stalking her?" Nathan asked.

Warren shook his head. "I wasn't trying to stalk her. I was actually trying to figure out how to approach her."

"And at night, at her house was your solution?" Nathan asked.

Warren shrugged. "It was a now or never moment. I've got to head home."

"To Claymore?" Nathan asked.

Warren nodded.

Nathan stood up and pointed at the front door. "Good. Go!"

"Whoa ho ho. Wait a minute." I reached out and grabbed Nathan by a belt loop. "You don't order people in and out of my house. This is *my* house and Warren can stay for as long as he likes."

Nathan was grinding his teeth, looking down at me. "Can I talk to you in private for a minute?"

I stood up.

Warren thrust his hand toward us. "By all means, say it to my face, bro," he said.

Nathan's face was burning with anger. "I'm not your 'bro' and I *will* say it to your face! I don't like you. I sure as hell don't trust you." He looked at me. "I can't even begin to explain how bad of an idea this is. You don't know this guy."

I smiled at the thought. "You're right. I don't know him. For the first time in my life I don't know someone!"

Nathan was looking at me like I was growing another nose on my face.

I put my hands on Nathan's arms which were flexed and not in a good way. "Do you have any idea how exhausting it is to see people everywhere you go and think, 'Hmm. Do I really know that person or do I just think I do because I'm a freak?' or 'I might know that woman, should I talk to her or will she think I'm a lunatic?' or even worse, 'That guy is terrifying! I wonder if he's planning to eat my face off!'"

I realized I was close to shouting, so I stopped and took a deep breath.

His hand shot out toward Warren. "But this—"

I cut him off. "*This* is not your business!" I forced him to look at me. "I know you think this is crazy, but crazy or not, he's here and he's not going anywhere until he wants to or I want him to."

Nathan's gray eyes were frantic.

Gently, I put my hands against his cheeks. "I've never in my life met anyone that understands as much about me as this guy. Not Adrianne, not my parents, and certainly not you. I sincerely appreciate you being so protective over me—I love it really, I do—but this isn't your call. This is something I can't ignore, even if it might get me killed."

That seemed to disarm Nathan ever so slightly. His jaw was working overtime, but his eyes relaxed a little. "All right," he forced out.

Nathan sucked in a deep breath and pulled the gun and clip out of his pocket. He handed it to Warren, but Warren shook his head. "Take the clip, man," he insisted.

After an awkward pause, Nathan placed the gun on the coffee table and then pointed a daring finger at Warren. "I swear to God, if you lay a finger on her, I will choke you to death on your own nutsack."

Warren pressed his lips together like I do when I'm trying not to laugh. "I promise she's safe."

I tugged on Nathan's sleeve and then wrapped my hand around his. "Come on. I'll walk you out."

We went to the front door and I opened it. He turned toward me, ran his hand up my jaw and pulled my ear to his lips. "Please don't do this," he begged.

I pulled back. "Nathan, trust me."

He shook his head. Then, out of nowhere, his lips crashed down on mine. As suddenly as he kissed me, he released me and walked out of the door. I was so stunned that I froze to the floor.

When he was halfway to his car, I shouted at him. "Wait! We're kissing now??"

He didn't respond, but he looked at me for a long second before getting in the SUV and starting the engine.

I groaned and closed the door.

When I returned to the living room, Warren was relaxed in the corner of the loveseat. "Well, that was very interesting," he said.

I sighed and fell onto the couch. "You have no idea." I sighed, staring at the ceiling. "I'm sorry, are you thirsty? Can I get you something to eat?"

He smiled and sat forward. "Some water would be great."

He followed me into the kitchen. I liked my kitchen, even if I rarely went into it. I had top of the line, shiny, stainless steel appliances, but the only one that ever got used was the coffee pot. I reached into the refrigerator and pulled out two bottles of water. I handed one to Warren and opened my own.

I tipped the bottle up to my lips and took a swig. "I hope Nathan doesn't call my parents."

He leaned against the white cabinets and motioned with his water bottle toward the door. "He loves you."

I choked on my water. "Ha. No, he doesn't. He just likes me because that's what people do—they like me." I shook my head. "And he was in RoboCop mode just now. We've been working on a really stressful case together and we're both really keyed up about it."

He raised an eyebrow. "A case? I thought I read that you were in public relations for the county."

I shrugged. "I'm pulling double duty these days ever since I slipped up and let the good detective know about my ability. Unpaid double duty," I added.

"Is that how you found that little girl? She was missing and you knew she was alive?" he asked.

I nodded. "You heard about that all the way out in New Hope?" I asked, astonished.

"Yep. Saw the video, on some news station website, of you carrying her out and everything. It went pretty viral," he said.

I rolled my eyes. "What did we ever do before the Internet? We all just stayed closed off in our neat little bubbles."

He shrugged his shoulders. "Relatively neat."

My phone rang. I pulled it out of my pocket, expecting it to be

Nathan. It was my mother, of course. I hit the answer button. "Hi Mom," I said, looking at Warren with I-told-you-so eyes.

He laughed.

"Hi honey," she said. "Just calling to check in. I haven't heard from you all weekend."

"I'm good, Mom. Did Detective McNamara call you?" I asked.

"Who?" she replied.

"Never mind," I said. "I actually have company over. Can I call you tomorrow?"

"Sure. Are you coming by for dinner tomorrow night?" she asked.

"Yep. I'll be there after work," I answered.

"OK, sweetie. I love you," she said.

"I love you, too," I replied and disconnected the call.

I held the phone out toward Warren. "Can you do that?"

He raised his eyebrows. "Talk to your mother?"

I walked toward the living room, sat down, and propped my feet up on the coffee table. "Summon people," I clarified.

Warren sat down next to me. "Summon people?" he asked.

I folded my legs under me and put my water bottle on the floor. "I seem to be able to call out for people and make them show up."

"Like, just now with your Mom calling?"

I nodded.

"You think you caused that?" he asked.

I shrugged. "It happens enough around me that I'm pretty convinced of it. Like, I had this long conversation with that detective about you this afternoon and then came home and you were at my house."

"I'm pretty sure I came all on my own," he said.

"You'll see for yourself if you hang around long enough," I told him.

He stretched his arm across the couch toward me and tapped the seat cushion between us with his fingers. "It's not that I don't believe you. Trust me. I believe you." He took a deep breath. "You make people show up; I make people disappear."

I turned my whole body toward him. "You what?"

He shrugged. "I don't know how."

"Like '*poof*' disappear?" Thoughts of a magician in a top hat with a bunny and a cloud of smoke came to mind.

He shook his head. "No. Like, if I had really wanted your buddy McNamara gone, I could have made it happen without having to say a word."

I didn't doubt him, but I was intrigued by what he meant. I rubbed my forehead. "This is all so crazy."

He nodded in agreement.

I looked over at him. "Does anyone else know about what you can do?" I asked.

He leaned against the armrest. "Not anymore. Well, not until tonight anyway. I told this girl one time, but she died a long time ago."

"I'm sorry," I said. "You know, I don't think I've ever known anyone who's died."

"Really?" he asked, surprised.

I thought about it and shook my head. "Not personally."

He was quiet for a while, seemingly lost in a memory that I wasn't privy to. "I think you and I have a lot more differences than we do similarities," he finally said.

"Do you get a sense if people are good or evil just by looking at them?" I asked.

"Yep," he said. "That was part of the reason I was so interested in you. I couldn't even tell if you were alive or dead. I kept waiting for the news to announce your death, but they never did, so I checked for myself. I've never seen anyone like you."

"Me too!" I said. "That's exactly what I told the detective about you. Of course, he sort of looked at me like I was crazy, and I'm pretty sure he wondered if you might be a zombie or something, but..."

He leaned toward me and lowered his voice. "Can I tell you something else?"

"Sure," I replied.

He thought for a moment. "Do you promise you won't get really freaked out about it?"

I smiled. "That's usually my line."

He smiled, but it quickly faded away. "When I say 'I make people disappear', what I mean is…I can kill people."

I blinked. "Kill people?" I tried to mute the panic in my voice as best I could.

He nodded.

I pulled my head back. "How?"

He turned his palms up and dropped them onto his lap. "Just by looking at them."

Suddenly, I realized that maybe Nathan had been right. Maybe this was a very bad idea. My eyes floated aimlessly around the room and settled on the unused, but beautifully decorated fireplace in the corner. My parents wedding picture was resting on the mantle. I briefly wondered if I would ever see them again. My mind was racing with a thousand different fears.

"I'm sorry. I've frightened you." Warren reached over and put his hand on my leg.

All at once, a calming warmth spread through me. My eyes closed, my pounding heart began to settle, and without thinking, I wrapped my fingers around his. I was quiet while my breathing returned to normal.

"You did," I admitted. "But I'm OK now." I squeezed his hand.

I wasn't sure what was happening whenever we touched, but it was magnetic. The man had just admitted he could end my life if he wanted to, and still, the sensation surging through me was so deliciously addicting that I never wanted to release him.

He looked down at our hands and then into my eyes. "I could stay here forever," he whispered.

"I don't know what this feeling is, but I don't want you to ever leave," I confessed. "A lot of really strange stuff has always happened around me, but this is by far the strangest."

For a long time we sat there, some unseen bond holding us together. I couldn't explain it, but I also didn't care. I felt like a lightning rod in the middle of a thunderstorm, completely content to soak up all the energy in the atmosphere.

He took in a slow deep breath and locked his eyes with mine. His eyes were so dark that I could hardly distinguish his pupils from the irises, save for a faint light halo of gold around the pupils. "I'm going to have to leave or I'm going to get really inappropriately close to you," he admitted. "This is like heroin."

He broke the connection of our hands and pushed himself up off the couch. It was like the room suddenly dropped ten degrees in temperature. I wanted to cry, but I didn't know why.

"I have a seven hour drive home." He sighed and stretched his arms over his head. "And I have to work tomorrow."

I stood up as he gathered his gun and keys from the table. I wanted to physically block his path to the door, but I didn't.

At the front door, he stopped and looked down at me for a several seconds before laughing. "I'm actually afraid to hug you goodbye. I might not leave."

I smiled and felt my face flush red. "Will I see you again?" I was almost afraid to hear his answer.

He sighed and twisted a strand of my hair around his finger. "Sooner than you think."

I pulled out my phone and brought up a new message. "What's your number? I'll text you mine."

He told me his phone number and I sent him a message.

"Let me know that you've made it home safely," I said as his phone beeped in his pocket.

He nodded. "I will." He drew in a deep breath. "Thanks for letting me in, Sloan."

Unable to stand our proximity without touching any longer, I stretched my arms up around his neck. I let out the breath I hadn't realized I was holding. "Thanks for finding me."

Enveloped in his dizzying embrace, I was sure that touching Warren was like connecting with destiny. In his arms was exactly where I was supposed to be.

CHAPTER NINE

I locked the door behind Warren and watched from the window till he got in his sports car and drove away. When he was gone, I turned around and leaned against the door. I closed my eyes and desperately tried to hold on to the feeling of his presence for as long as possible. The buzz faded with every second.

When I opened my eyes again, the room seemed brighter than usual. Even stranger, my dining room was missing. I blinked a few times and then looked straight at the dining room table. It was there, but to the right of it, the kitchen had disappeared. I pressed my palms to my eyes and walked forward, tripping over a fake flower arrangement that sat in the foyer. I turned toward the kitchen and saw it, but the wall to my right was gone. My heart was pounding so hard that I could feel my pulse throbbing in the side of my neck.

My phone was still in my hand, so I sent Nathan a message. *Warren is gone. I'm not feeling well, so I'm going to bed. I'll call you tomorrow.*

I turned toward the steps that led upstairs, but I was so dizzy I had to grasp the handrail for support. Each step of the staircase seemed to be broken. I couldn't see the right side of any of the steps before me.

By some miracle, I made it to my room but bumped into my bed before falling on top of it. Something was wrong. My phone buzzed in my hand. I looked down at the message on the screen, but most of the words and letters were missing. It was impossible to read. I tapped out a response the best I could and hit send just as it seemed that an invisible ice pick was jammed into the side of my skull. I crumpled onto the covers.

My phone rang. I knew I had to answer it. "Hello?" I drew my knees to my chest and rolled onto my side.

"Are you OK? Your messages aren't making any sense. Half of the words are missing or are misspelled," Nathan said.

I cringed. It was like he was screaming at me over the phone.

"I'm not OK," I said. "Something's wrong. I feel like my brain is bleeding."

"I'm on my way," he said. "Where are you in the house?"

"In my bed," I answered. "I can't see to make it back down the stairs and I locked the door."

There was a lot of noise on his end of the line. I held the phone away from my ear. "How can I get in? Do you have a key hidden?"

"Stop screaming," I begged.

"Sloan, I'm not screaming," he insisted.

I was rolling back and forth in pain. "No key," I choked out.

"Stay with me. I'm on my way."

I was in and out of consciousness, but sometime later I felt Nathan lift me off my bed. He was shouting at someone as he carried me down the stairs. There were bright lights flashing red and white, and each flash felt like a butcher knife to my brain. He laid me down and someone strapped a belt around my middle. Everyone was screaming.

"Shhh..." I cried. I covered my eyes with my arm to block out as much light as possible.

Someone was holding my hand. Whatever I was lying on felt like it was being knocked into walls and slammed against the ground. I tried to roll over onto my side, but the belt around my waist prevented it. "Sick," I mumbled.

"Are you going to be sick?" someone shouted as I began throwing up uncontrollably.

Everything went black.

When I opened my eyes again, I was in a dimly lit hospital room. My mother was seated next to me on the bed. Nathan was asleep in a chair in the corner. I heard my father's voice some distance away. I tried to raise my arm, but there was an IV in my hand that hurt like I had been shot. My head was throbbing with pain.

I tried to blink away the hazy film that covered my eyeballs. "What happened?"

My mother turned and leaned toward me. Nathan bolted out of his seat like he had been fired from a cannon.

Mom smoothed my hair gently with her hand. "How are you feeling?" she whispered.

Nathan came around to the other side of my bed and wrapped his hand around mine.

"Head hurts," I replied with a voice so raspy I hardly recognized it as my own. "What's wrong with me?" I asked as another figure appeared in the room.

It was my dad. Mom got up and moved out of the way so he could sit down beside me. "Hey, sweetheart," he said as he leaned down to kiss my forehead.

"Am I dying?"

He laughed softly. "No. You're not dying. You had a really severe migraine."

"A migraine? I'm in the hospital with a headache?" I groaned with embarrassment.

Dad rubbed my arm. "Sloan, you experienced a hemiplegic migraine. One of the most severe and serious forms of any migraine headache. You were paralyzed on your right side and couldn't speak," he said. "Nathan was right to call an ambulance and get you here."

Nathan squeezed my hand. "I thought you had been poisoned or that you were having a stroke or an aneurysm. You scared me to death."

I offered him a weak smile. "I'm sorry."

He kissed my fingers and held them against his lips. "I'm just glad you're OK."

"We already did a CT scan and it was clear. I'm thinking of ordering an MRI to be on the safe side," Dad explained.

"Did the hospital call you?" I asked.

He shook his head. "No. Nathan did."

"I took your phone and called them on our way to the hospital," he said.

"Thank you," I whispered. "Can you let Mary know I won't be at work tomorrow?"

"Today," he corrected me. "It's almost 11 am."

I looked around the room. "What? Seriously?"

"You've been asleep for a while," Mom said.

"Part of it is the drugs. Part of it is just the headache," Dad explained.

I groaned. "Nathan, shouldn't you be at work?"

He shook his head. "They can live without me for one day. You're much more important right now."

I squeezed his hand.

The hospital released me with a prescription for a migraine medication that I was instructed to keep with me at all times in case another headache began. They said that the ripples and holes in my vision that I experienced was usually the first sign of the onset of a migraine. Dad gave me strict orders to spend the day in bed. He and Mom drove Nathan and me to my house, since

Nathan had left his car there to ride with me in the ambulance. Dad went to his office, and Mom decided to spend the day as my personal nurse.

Nathan kept his arm tight around me the whole way up to my bed. I was feeling better, but my knees wobbled all the way up the stairs. Dad said it was the drugs still in my system.

I stretched out across the bed, and Nathan sat down next to me. My mom stood in the doorway. He gently brushed a loose strand of hair off my cheek and smiled at me. "Are you going to be OK?"

I nodded and reached for his arm. "Thank you for everything." I tugged on his sleeve. "I don't know what would have happened to me if you hadn't shown up."

He bent over me and kissed my forehead. "You may not be so thankful when you see what I did to your back door."

I laughed, but it hurt my head. "I don't even care."

"I'll come by and fix it later," he promised. "Or do you want me to stay? I can. We can curl up right here and watch movies or just sleep. I don't have anywhere else to be."

I shook my head. "I know you've got work to do, and you've been up all night, I'm sure." I glanced at my mother who was still waiting quietly by the door. "I'm in good hands."

He nodded, but he looked a little disappointed. If my mother hadn't been supervising, I might have changed my mind and invited him to crawl under my covers with me. He reached into the pocket of his fleece pullover and handed me my phone. "Will you call me if you need anything at all?"

I forced a smile as he laid the phone beside my pillow. "I will."

He leaned down and kissed my forehead again before getting up and walking across the room.

My mother hugged him at the door. "Thank you so much, Nathan," she said.

He shook his head. "No thanks needed, ma'am."

When he was gone, she looked at me. "If you don't marry that boy, I will disown you and cut you out of the will."

I had two missed calls and a text message from Warren. *Finally made it home. Had a pretty messed up night. Call me when you can.*

Later, while my mother was downstairs, I dialed his number.

He picked up on the first ring. "Hello?" He sounded a lot like I did.

"Hey, sorry I missed your calls," I said. "I've been in the hospital since last night."

"What? Are you OK?"

"I had this really debilitating migraine after you left. I was paralyzed and everything," I said.

"So did I," he said. "I actually blacked out when I stopped at a rest area."

"Oh my gosh, me too." I draped my arm across my forehead. "What is going on?"

"I have no idea," he said. "I've been sick all day. Feeling better now, but I never made it to work today. I guess I could've stayed another day with you."

"Do you think we would've gotten sick together?" I asked.

"I don't know," he said. "But it felt like I was detoxing off of you or something."

He was right. That's exactly what it felt like, though the only thing I had ever detoxed off of was caffeine. This was exponentially worse. "Warren, what do you think this means?"

He was quiet. "Either it means that we shouldn't be apart or that we never should have met in the first place. I don't know about you, but I'm pretty pissed that we haven't met until now."

"Me too," I agreed.

He sighed. "I think I need to pass out for a couple more hours. Can I call you later?" he asked.

"You don't have to ask," I said.

"OK," he said. "Take it easy and get some rest."

"You too," I said and hung up the phone.

The ceiling fan blades were spinning slowly overhead. I still felt like hell, but I knew I would rather feel that horrible for the rest of my life than to never feel the sensation of Warren's presence ever again. I had an even bigger problem than the migraine when I considered the events of the night before. What was going on with Nathan McNamara?

CHAPTER TEN

There was a smiley face balloon and a smiley face coffee mug full of chocolate candy on my desk when I returned to work the next day. Along with them was a note from my boss. *Hope you're feeling better. You gave us all quite the scare. - Mary.*

I smiled and sat down at my desk. A dull pain still throbbed in my skull, but my dad said it was normal and that it might take a couple of days to completely subside. My email inbox was full, and my voicemail light was showing nine new messages. I groaned and started sorting through the emails.

About halfway down the list was a bulletin from Catawba County. The subject line caught my attention. *Human Remains Discovered May Be That of Missing Hickory Woman.* I clicked the email open and read it aloud.

"Human remains were discovered on Monday underneath the home of Myrtle Allen, 82, of Hickory, N.C. Air conditioning contractors, working in a previously sealed off section of the home's crawl space, unearthed pieces of a human skeleton. Police believe that the remains may be that of Crystal Jennifer Dumas, a local woman who disappeared in 2005. Dumas was the girlfriend of Myrtle Allen's grandson, Logan Allen, 32, also of Hickory."

I picked up my phone and dialed Nathan's cell. A phone rang down the hallway, and a moment later he appeared in my office holding his phone. "You rang?" he asked.

I ended the call and pointed at the screen. "Come here. Have you seen this?"

He sat down in one of my chairs and put his feet up on the edge of my desk. "Christy Dumas?"

"Yes!"

He nodded. "Yep. I've seen it. They arrested Logan last night. I was coming by to see if you were up for a little road trip."

My eyes widened. "Nathan, I've got so much work to catch up on."

He pointed to the balloon. "I think Mary would understand if you said you still weren't feeling well." He plucked one of the chocolates out of the smiley face mug, unwrapped it, and popped it into his mouth.

I shook my head. "You're going to get me fired."

He leaned forward with his palms on my desk. He lowered his voice. "Do a little catch up work till lunch, and then tell her you're not feeling well and take the rest of the day off." He knocked his knuckles against my desk. "I'll pick you up at your house at"—he looked at his watch—"two o'clock."

He was gone before I could protest.

At five minutes till two I was sitting on my front porch steps feeling terribly guilty as I waited on Nathan. It was the first time I had ever lied to my boss to get out of work.

My phone rang. "Hello?" I answered.

"Hey, it's Warren."

"Hey there." I quickly forgot about my guilt and broke out into a smile. "What are you up to today?"

"I was wondering if you had plans this weekend," he said.

I thought for a moment. "I don't think so. What did you have in mind?"

"I was thinking about making another trip to Asheville," he said.

An uncontrollable giggle bubbled out before I could stop it. "I think that is a brilliant idea. You can stay with me as long as you promise to not tell my mother. I have a guest room."

He laughed. "OK. I promise not to tell your mother. I'm usually done with work by noon on Fridays, so I should be there around five or six."

"That's perfect," I said. "I get off at five."

"Are you working today?" he asked.

"Uhh, sort of," I said. "I went to work this morning, but now I'm on my way to Hickory to find a serial killer."

There was a pause. "You're doing what?"

I adjusted my sunglasses on my face. "Remember me telling you that I was working on a case with the detective? Well, they caught a guy in Hickory that we think is a suspect for a bunch of other murders."

"You didn't tell me it was a serial murder case." He started laughing. "No wonder that cop was so pissed off the other night."

"Yeah," I said.

"Do you want my help?" he asked.

I was surprised. "How can you help?"

Nathan's SUV turned onto my street.

"The stack of photos you quizzed me on the other night. Was that your group of suspects?" he asked.

"Yeah, why?" I asked.

"None of the guys you showed me in that stack are serial killers," he said. "One of them has murdered someone, but only that one person."

"Which guy?" I asked.

"Blonde hair with a goatee," he said.

"Logan Allen. That's who we are going to see today," I told him. "How do you know he's only killed one person?"

"I just know. It's kind of like people who have killed have death attached to them. Like they carry it with them," he said. "I can tell exactly how many there are and that Logan guy only has one."

Nathan rolled to a stop in front of the curb, and I got up and walked around the front of the vehicle.

"I never get anything that specific," I said to Warren. "I only get an impression if someone is good or not."

"Hmm. I find evil and death really well. Goodness, not so much," he said. "I wonder if it's because I've been around it more and have paid more attention to it."

"I don't know. Maybe. I've been pretty sheltered," I admitted. I got in the passenger's seat of the SUV and fastened my seatbelt. "What do you mean by you can find death?" I asked. "Like, can you find corpses?"

Nathan looked over at me, catching the tail end of my question.

"Sure. If I know where to look," Warren said.

I turned the thought over in my mind. "When I was in the house where we found that little girl, there was a dead body in there and I didn't feel anything. I knew Kayleigh—or someone else who was alive—was there, but I didn't get anything off the corpse."

"Sloan, I do the opposite," he said.

I swallowed hard. "Huh."

"We'll talk more about it later," he said. "I've got to get back to work."

"Ok," I said.

When I disconnected the call, I sat there in stunned silence till Nathan punched me in the shoulder. "What was all that about?" he asked.

I turned in my seat to look at him. "Warren can find dead bodies."

"Really?" He pulled away from the curb. "Tell him I'm looking for ten more."

I stared out of the window. "He said he would have to know where to look, like a general area I guess."

"That dude is weird," he said.

I looked at him. "I'm weird."

He nodded. "Yes you are."

I sat back against my seat. "You know, a month ago my life was pretty dang normal. Then you showed up and turned everything —absolutely everything—upside down."

His ball cap, with the American flag in place, was pulled down close over his eyes. One arm was draped over the steering wheel. "No offense, but I don't think anything about your life has ever been exactly normal."

I pointed at him. "No, but it was peaceful. I went to work. I hung out with my friends. I had dinner with my parents on Mondays. Now look at me. I'm lying to my boss, skipping work, and I'm on my way to Hickory to meet a guy that murdered his girlfriend and shoved her under his granny's house."

"And maybe a lot of other girls," he added.

I shook my head. "Warren doesn't think so. He said Logan Allen has only killed one person. He's not a serial killer."

He looked at me with a raised eyebrow. "I think I would rather investigate it for myself than just take Warren's word for it."

I folded my arms across my chest. "How come you're so certain about things that I tell you, but you have no faith in what he says?"

"Because I think Warren is a con. I think that he's dangerous, and I don't think you should be involved with him at all," he said.

I frowned. "A con? How could he possibly be conning me? No one knows about what I can do except for you and Adrianne. Now, unless one of you has posted some tell-all about me that I'm unaware of, I don't see how he could know as much as he does unless he was telling the truth."

"I don't like him," he said.

I nodded. "Obviously, but you'd better start getting used to him being in the picture if we're going to keep working together."

He glanced over. "Why?"

"Because he's coming again on Friday," I said.

"Why? Are you dating him now?" he asked, his voice jumping up a few decibels.

"If I was, it wouldn't be any of your business," I reminded him.

"None of my business? This guy stalks you, shows up at your house, and I wind up carrying you to an ambulance when he leaves, and you don't think this is any of my business?" He was close to shouting.

I leaned toward him and narrowed my eyes. "Let's call Shannon and see if she agrees that this is your business."

He was gripping the steering wheel so tight I was afraid he might break it off the column and send us careening off the highway. I sat back in my seat again and stared at the road ahead. He was leaning against his door with his hand over his mouth. We rode in complete silence until we crossed out of Buncombe County.

Finally, he spoke. "I'm sorry. I don't want to fight with you this whole trip."

"I'm sorry too," I said, still staring straight ahead.

After another moment, I looked over at him. "Why did you kiss me the other night?"

He dragged his knuckles over his bottom lip, then turned his hand up and shrugged. "I thought there might be a good chance I wouldn't see you again. Warren gives off really bad vibes."

"He's supposed to," I said.

His eyebrows scrunched together. "What?"

I shrugged. "He gives off bad vibes like I give off good vibes," I said. "People like me and people hate him."

Nathan cracked a smile for the first time in thirty miles. "Shannon doesn't like you."

I laughed. "Touché."

"If he gives off bad vibes, why doesn't he bother you?" he asked.

"I don't feel him giving off anything. I told you, I don't read anything on him at all," I said.

"Can he read you?" he asked.

I shook my head. "No, and I think it's one of the reasons why I like him so much," I admitted. "I always wonder if people really want to be around me or if they are just attracted to whatever power it is that I give off. Like, I wonder if it forces people to like me. I don't worry about that with Warren."

Nathan looked over his shoulder at me. "Do you worry about that with me? Do you think I only want to be around you because of the vibes you give off?"

I laughed and shook my head. "Nathan McNamara, I can't figure out a damn thing about you."

When we passed into Hickory, I looked over at him. "How close are we?"

"About five minutes," he answered.

I nodded and pulled out my purse. I retrieved my bottle of Xanax and put a half of a tablet under my tongue.

He watched me tuck the pill bottle back into my purse. "Do you do that every time?"

"Every time I visit a jail? Yes," I said.

"When you go in there, what's it like exactly?" he asked.

I shook my head. "You wouldn't understand."

"Help me understand," he said.

I thought for a moment. "Were you ever afraid of the dark when you were a kid?" I asked.

"No," he answered quickly.

I looked at him with a raised eyebrow.

"Maybe. Shut up," he whined.

"It's like that. It's like walking into the blackest, most all-consuming darkness you can imagine. It's that feeling that you're trapped in the dark, unable to find the light switch, and that at any second, whatever is hiding in the darkness is going to rip you apart." I shuddered. "And it's frustrating because I know I'm safe, like I know nothing can really hurt me, but I just can't feel safe. It gets so bad sometimes that I can't even breathe."

"Damn. That sucks," he said.

I nodded. "Sucks doesn't cover it. My dad put me on anti-anxiety meds when I was in the seventh grade because I started having panic attacks at school. It turned out that my math teacher was a pedophile, and once he was removed from the school, I was fine again."

He shook his head. "That's nuts."

"Yep," I agreed. "I'm a walking, talking evil barometer."

He reached over and put his hand on my knee. "Well, we will make this as quick as we can. If, at any point, you need to leave, you just say so and we're out. No questions asked."

I smiled at him and squeezed his hand. "Thanks, Nathan."

It turned out that our trip to the Catawba County Jail wasn't as bad as I had feared that it would be. Without a doubt, Logan Allen had a dark soul, but Warren had been right—he wasn't a serial killer.

Nathan and I walked out into the setting sun. "Well, that was a complete waste of a sick day," I said.

"You never know," Nathan said. "He might still be our guy."

I stopped and turned to look at him. "He was in there bawling like a toddler. You saw the look on his face when you started asking about the other girls. He's *not* our guy."

Nathan slapped the file folder he was carrying against his thigh and groaned. "Oh well," he said. "I'm hungry. Let's go eat."

We went to the Bleachers Sports Bar & Restaurant that we had passed on our way into town and ordered burgers. Nathan ordered a Snickers pie as an appetizer.

When the waitress walked away from the table, I looked at him sideways. "How in the hell do you stay in such good shape eating like that all the time?" I asked. "I honestly don't think I've ever seen you eat anything that's remotely healthy."

He laughed and shrugged his shoulders. "I have good genes, I guess."

I shook my head. "I'm so jealous. In fact, I hate you a little bit."

He winked at me from across the table. "You can't hate me. I'm the 'cute little blond boy', remember?"

I laughed and rolled my eyes.

The waitress returned with Nathan's slice of pie and he picked up his fork. "How are you feeling after yesterday?"

"Pretty good now. I still have a little dull pain, but nothing like it was," I said. "I really can't thank you enough for what you did."

He put his hand to his forehead. "You scared me to death. I literally thought I was watching you die. I was sure he had poisoned you."

"He didn't poison me," I said.

"Well, I know that now," he said. "I made them run a blood test to check for toxins."

"Really?"

He nodded. "Oh yeah."

I was eyeballing Nathan's pie and wishing I had ordered a slice for myself. "I want a bite." I opened my mouth wide.

He cut off a forkful and held it to my lips. "One bite," he said with a hint of warning in his tone.

The sweet cold chocolate and cream almost made my eyes roll back in my head. I licked my lips. When I looked at Nathan again, he was staring at me with the fork still frozen in the air. I covered my mouth and laughed.

He cast his eyes down at his plate and cleared his throat. "What were we talking about?"

"Migraines and poisoning," I reminded him. "Warren actually got really sick too. Same thing happened to him on the way home."

"Good," Nathan mumbled. He picked a piece of candy bar off of the top of his pie and dropped it into his mouth.

I wadded up my napkin and threw it at him.

My phone rang. "Lo and behold." I turned my phone around so he could see that it was Warren.

He shook his head and shoveled another forkful of pie into his mouth. "You're a creepy chick," he said with his mouth full.

I answered the call. "Hey. I was just talking about you."

"And here I am," he said, laughing. "What are you doing?"

"I am sitting at a sports bar in Hickory with Nathan. What are you doing?" I asked.

"I am watching football at home. How'd it go at the jail?" he asked.

"Not our guy," I said.

"I told you," he said.

I nodded. "I know you did."

Nathan nudged me with his foot under the table. "Ask him what he needs to find someone."

"What you were saying earlier about finding bodies, how do you do that?" I asked.

"I guess the same way you found that kid. You knew where to look and when you got there, you knew she was there," he said.

"Well, I knew someone was there. I didn't necessarily know it was Kayleigh," I clarified.

"Same thing with me," he said.

I made a sour face. "You can sense dead bodies anywhere? That seems like it would get exhausting."

"Ehh, no more so than you being around people and sensing life all the time," he said. "You get kind of used to it."

"I guess that makes sense. What kind of radius are we talking about here as far as a search area goes?" I asked.

"It depends. Where do you think they are?" he asked.

I bit the tip of my index finger. "Between Asheville and Raleigh."

He laughed. "Yeah, I need it to be a little more specific than that. Like maybe the size of a football field," he said.

I nodded. "OK. I don't know that much."

"We'll talk more about it this weekend," he said. "You sure you don't mind if I come?"

"Are you kidding?" I laughed. "I can't wait."

"Me either. Well, I'll let you get back to whatever you're doing. Give my regards to the detective," he said.

I laughed. "I will. I'll text you later." I hung up and looked at Nathan. "He said to tell you hello."

"Yay," he said, feigning interest.

"When we get home, we need to go over the map again," I said.

"How come?" he asked.

"Warren said if we could narrow down the area, he can tell us if anything is there," I told him.

"How does he do it?"

I wiggled my fingers in front of his face. "Magic."

He smiled and wiped his mouth.

On our ride home, I looked over at him. "You never told me what happened with Shannon after I left your house the other night."

"Well, she was pissed," he said. "I actually didn't call her back until last night. That didn't help things much."

"Seriously?" I asked.

He shrugged. "Well, I was going to call her, but then I got your message saying that some stalker was at your house, so I took off. Then, I was so mad when I left your place that I didn't want to talk to anyone. After that I was at the hospital with you all night. I didn't really have the time."

"I so would have dumped you," I said, shaking my head.

He nodded. "I know you would have."

"Did you fix things with her?" I asked.

"I guess. I don't really know if I even want to fix things with her. Dating her long distance is quite different than it being a full-time gig," he said.

"Ladies and Gentlemen, he's finally making some sense," I teased.

"Shut up," he said.

"You know, without Christy Dumas being a part of the group anymore, your theory about the next victim being from Asheville is completely shot to hell," I pointed out.

He nodded. "I know. I already thought of that."

I rolled my head against the headrest to face him. "And if you dump your girlfriend, you really have no reason to be here anymore."

He looked over at me. "You don't think so?" It was a loaded question. He was curious about a lot more than my opinion.

I felt my cheeks flush, and I looked out the window without giving him an answer.

"Hey," he said.

I looked toward him again.

He was still staring at me over the arm that was resting on the steering wheel. "I can promise you, it's more than your vibes, Sloan."

I swallowed hard. "You don't know that."

He raised his eyebrows. "Don't I?"

I looked away, signaling the end of the conversation. With Warren suddenly in the picture, the timing couldn't be any worse for a heart-to-heart conversation about romance with Nathan.

He was quiet for a moment. "I can always go back to Raleigh."

I wasn't sure where my heart landed on that idea. I was just starting to get used to having him around. I certainly wouldn't tell him that, so I decided to change the subject.

"We should've gone by Lenoir-Rhyne University before we left Hickory," I said. "I would've liked to look around where the other girl was taken."

"Angela Kearn," he said.

I kicked off my shoes and put my feet up on his dashboard. "You really have lived, slept, and breathed this stuff, haven't you?"

"Wouldn't you?" he asked.

"Probably." I looked out of my window up at the night sky. "But I've never had any siblings."

"I didn't know that," he said.

"My parents couldn't have any children of their own," I said.

He looked over at me surprised. "You're adopted?"

I nodded. "I was abandoned at the hospital. You know what's weird?"

He raised his eyebrows in question.

"Warren's adopted. Well, orphaned. He was given away by his birth parents too," I said.

He looked ahead. "That is weird. You both have these crazy abilities and neither of you know your birth parents."

"I keep wondering if we might be related," I said. "Maybe we are brother and sister."

"That would explain a lot." He was silent for a moment, and then he laughed. "I'll keep my fingers crossed."

I pointed at him and smiled. "Don't get your hopes up."

He reached out and playfully grabbed my finger. He held onto it for a little longer than was appropriate, but I didn't stop him.

When we got to my house, he walked me inside and took a look around. The back door was boarded up and held closed with nails. "I haven't forgotten that I promised to fix that," he said.

I laughed as we walked to the front door. "Maybe I'll hold your shirt for ransom till it gets fixed."

He reached up and ran his thumb over the angel pin on my collar. "Keep the shirt. It looks better on you anyway."

He studied my face in the moonlight for a long moment. I might have had the ability to read Nathan's soul, but I had no idea what was on his mind. Gently, he pulled on my collar and touched his lips to mine. Without another word, he was gone.

CHAPTER ELEVEN

By Friday, I was caught up on the work that had piled up at the beginning of the week. I wasn't exactly sure how I got it done because my mind seemed to be everywhere else except in the county building. Between Nathan and Warren, I had so much confusion and excitement rolling around in my head that I could hardly think straight.

Just before five o'clock, Nathan walked into my office dressed in black from head to toe. I was a little surprised to see him. "Hey, Nathan."

"Hey," he said. "I know you've got a full weekend, but I was wondering if you wanted to grab a beer before you went home."

I looked up at the clock. "I'm sorry. I don't have time. Do you need something?"

"I was hoping to talk some sense into you, I guess." He was looking at the ground and lightly kicking the toe of his boot against the leg of my desk.

I walked around my desk and pinched his nose. "You're so cute when you're worried," I said in a munchkin voice. "Stop being so paranoid. I will be fine."

He caught me by the arm and looked at me seriously. "The last time you said that, I had to sleep in a chair listening to your IV machine beep all night."

I squeezed his hand. "I'm going to be fine."

As I turned to pick up my purse, he grabbed me by the arm and pulled me back. "We need to talk."

"Then you should've come by earlier. I'm going to be late," I told him.

"Don't go with him, Sloan."

I laughed. "That's not an option, Nathan."

He slid his hand down my arm and tangled his fingers with mine. "Yes, it is an option. Have I been misreading everything with you for the past few weeks?" He took another half-step closer to me and lowered his voice. "I want to be with you."

The space between us was dangerously close, and his eyes were fixed on my mouth. I took a deep breath and backed away from him. "Damn it, Nathan. I can't do this right now! A week ago, yes. A week from now, maybe, but I can't do this today!"

He stepped back and leaned against the wall. "So it's him."

I pulled on his arm. "I don't know if it's him, but I do know that you're with Shannon and I just met Warren. The Shannon thing I could probably overlook—actually, I know I could forget about Shannon—but I *can't* forget about Warren. He is, literally, a once in a lifetime thing for me. It's not fair to anyone if you and I try to do this now and you know it."

He nodded his head, but his jaw was set.

I picked up my purse and stopped in front of him. "Please don't be mad at me."

"I'm not mad at you," he said.

I touched his forearm. "I'm really sorry." And I meant it.

He nodded, but he wasn't happy about it. I locked my office and we walked down the hallway together in silence. He held open the back door and when we walked outside, Warren was leaning against the hood of his muscle car.

Nathan shook his head and slipped on his sunglasses. "Have a good weekend, Sloan," he said and took off in the opposite direction. My shoulders slumped as I watched him jog down the steps and cross the parking lot.

I shook my head and made my way down the steps.

Warren stood and smiled as I approached. His missing soul was still as shocking to me as if he wasn't wearing pants. He was wearing pants, however, blue jeans and a black button-up shirt. His hair was parted just off center and hanging loose to his shoulders.

"I thought you were going to meet me at home," I said when I reached him.

He shrugged. "I got here a little early and I didn't want to wait."

I stepped into his open arms and into the magnetic surge. Every nerve ending inside me began to tingle. Never in my life had I experimented with drugs, but if being with Warren was anything like being high, I had a newfound sympathy for addicts and junkies. I took a deep whiff of his faint cologne. "I'm so glad you're here."

He rested his chin on the top of my head as he held me. "I'm glad you let me come back."

It was hard to pull away from him, but I had to or we would never make it out of the parking lot. I stepped away, but he still gently held onto my wrist. I looked up at him against the setting sun. "Well, what do you want to do this weekend?"

He shrugged and laughed. "I don't know. Know anywhere open on the weekends that does DNA testing?"

I laughed, but it quickly faded. I looked at my watch. "Actually, I do," I said with wide eyes. "Get in the car. We have to go now."

"I was joking," he said.

I shook my head. "I'm not. Come on. My dad's office is open until six, but we've got to hurry."

He opened the passenger side door, and I slid into the warm, black leather seat. The car was immaculate. I thought of the Diet Coke cans and junk mail that littered my car and felt ashamed. He got in and cranked up the engine. The machine roared to life under me. "Where to?" he asked.

"Turn left out of the lot," I said.

He rolled out of the spot and toward the exit.

I trailed my fingers along the soft leather. "This car is awesome."

He smiled. "Yes." He turned left onto the street. "I traded my truck in for it a few months ago."

I scrunched up my nose. "I'm kinda jealous."

He grinned at me. "Where are we going?"

"My father's a doctor. His office is part of a larger medical facility that's associated with the hospital. I know they have a lab somewhere in the building," I said. "Turn right at the light."

Warren looked over at me. "I'm meeting your dad?"

My eyes doubled in size. "Is that OK?"

He laughed. "It's fine with me," he said. "Just be warned, he's not going to approve."

Nervously, I squished my mouth to one side. "My mom will probably be there too."

"OK." He started laughing. "This is an interesting way to start the weekend."

Realizing that I may have just gone way too far way too fast, I reached over and touched his forearm that was stretched toward the gear stick. "We don't have to do this," I said. "Not if you don't want to."

He looked down at my hand and then covered it with his own. "No, I want to know. The sooner the better." He winked an eye at me.

My father's office was located on the third floor of a five story building adjacent to the hospital. When we went inside and walked onto the elevator, Warren leaned against the wall and stared at the floor.

I leaned next to him. "You look nervous."

"I don't like hospitals. I don't like being around dying people," he said. "It feels like it sucks the life out of me."

I looked at my watch again. "They shouldn't be taking any more patients, so it's probably close to empty in there."

With a mechanical ding, the doors opened to the bright and airy hallway. I reached for Warren's hand and exchanged a smile with him at the tingle. I tugged him down the hall. "Come on. It's this way."

I pushed the door open and the petite, brunette receptionist smiled. "Hi, can I help you?" she asked.

"I'm here to see Dr. Jordan," I said.

She looked puzzled and glanced up at the clock on the wall. "Do you have an appointment?"

"I'm his daughter."

She covered her eyes, embarrassed. "Of course you are. I know you from the pictures that your dad has all over his office. I'll let him know you're here."

"Is my mom in today?" I asked.

"She is." She disappeared through the door behind her.

I turned around and Warren raised an eyebrow. "Your dad's secretary doesn't know who you are?" he asked.

"I try to avoid coming here. I had to come a lot when I was a kid, but these old people flock to me and it always makes me uncomfortable," I explained.

"That's interesting," he said.

A moment later, the receptionist reappeared. "Come on back, Sloan," she said.

I nodded and pulled the door in front of us open. My mom was walking toward us wearing white scrubs covered in pink breast cancer ribbons. "Hey, Mom."

Her eyes were puzzled. "Hi, honey. Is everything OK?"

I nodded. "Yeah. I just need a little help with something. Can I talk to Dad?"

"In a minute. He's finishing up with his last patient." She looked at Warren then at me. "Who's your friend?"

"Mom, this is Warren Parish," I said. "Warren, this is my mom, Audrey."

He smiled and offered his hand. "Hi, Mrs. Jordan," he said.

She looked confused, but her smile was genuine. "Nice to meet you, Warren." She looked at me again. "Can I talk to you a second?" she asked, her voice a little higher than usual.

Warren nudged me. "Go ahead. I'm fine."

I stepped across the room and behind a partition near my father's office door. "Who is that?" she asked with wide eyes.

"A new friend of mine. Isn't he cute?" I whispered.

She cocked her head to the side. "Yes, he's handsome, but who is he? And what about Detective McNamara?"

I sighed. "Mom, I'm not dating Nathan."

She put her hands on her hips. "Well, you could have fooled me by the way that boy hovered over you all night at the hospital."

Just then, my dad's office door swung open. A small white-haired woman, with thick pink-framed glasses and blue polyester pants pulled up almost to her chin, stepped out into the hall. A younger woman held her carefully by the arm as she shuffled forward. The old woman saw me and her face lit up.

She stepped toward me with her hands stretched out. She was smiling from ear to ear. "Sloan Jordan!"

My mouth smiled, but my eyes danced with bewilderment and worry. "Hi there."

She took my hands and squeezed them. "You are just as beautiful as you are on the television screen. We saw you carrying that little girl out of that house on the news last week. Your parents must be so proud of you!"

My mother leaned close to the woman's ear. "We are very proud of her!" My mother was over enunciating and almost shouting.

The woman looked at her, obviously annoyed. "Goodness gracious, you don't have to yell, Audrey."

My mother exchanged a puzzled glance with the woman's daughter.

"It's very nice to meet you," I said, stumbling over the end of my sentence because I had no idea how this woman knew me.

She tapped her chest. "I'm Geraldine Flynn. This is my daughter, Ann. It's been wonderful to meet you as well."

My dad's head was peeking around his door. His eyes were wide and glancing between the old woman and my mother. He looked as confused as I felt.

I patted her shoulder politely. "You have a good day now, Mrs. Flynn."

She nodded and Ann took her by the arm and led her across the room.

When she was a few feet away, my mom looked at my dad. "Did you hear that, Robert?"

The old woman stopped short of the door when she neared Warren. She looked back at us. "My ride's here, doctor!" she shouted. "I'm going home with handsome here!"

My father was scratching his head. "Well, that was unusual."

Mom touched the sleeve of his white lab coat. "Did you hear her talking to Sloan?"

"I caught bits and pieces of it," he said.

I looked back and forth at them. "What's going on?"

"I can't tell you because of confidentiality reasons, but she's practically deaf and I haven't heard her that lucid in a very long time," he said.

"Years," my mother added.

Dad shrugged his shoulders, then stepped out of his office and hugged me. "This is a surprise. How are you feeling?"

"I'm fine now. I actually have a reason for being here and it's sort of time-sensitive," I said.

"I assumed you wouldn't show up without needing something," he said with a teasing wink. "What do you need?"

"Can the lab here do DNA testing?" I asked.

He looked puzzled again. "They would have to send it to the hospital, but yes. Why? And who is that man?"

I wished I had prepared more for this conversation. "It's kind of hard to explain, but his name is Warren and we just met recently. Because of some really big similarities, I'm curious to see if he and I might be related to each other."

"Biologically?" he asked surprised.

My mother's mouth fell open. "You want to do a DNA test?"

I nodded. "Yeah. Is that possible? I'll pay whatever it costs."

Dad's brow furrowed. "Why do you think you might be related?"

I shrugged. "We have a lot in common. We both have dark hair and similar skin tone, and he was abandoned when he was a baby a couple of years before I was."

They exchanged awkward looks.

I grabbed my dad's arm. "I know this seems really crazy, but it's really important to me. I need to know, and we've got to do it today because he's only in town for the weekend."

Dad patted my hand. "The results aren't immediate. They will take a few days, but I'll order the test."

I stretched up on my tiptoes and kissed his cheek. "Thank you, Daddy."

He nodded toward Warren. "Well, introduce me at least."

I tugged on his sleeve and Warren met us halfway across the office. My dad extended his hand and Warren shook it. "Warren, is it?" he asked.

Warren nodded. "Yes, you must be Dr. Jordan. Sloan's father."

My dad shook his head. "Call me Robert."

Warren smiled.

Dad looked at the clock. "If you want to make it to the lab, you had better hurry. Your mom will call them on your way."

Mom smiled in agreement.

I kissed his cheek again.

Warren nodded. "Thank you, sir."

Dad looked at me. "Well, my daughter doesn't ask for much, and this must be pretty important to her, so no thanks needed. The lab is on the second floor, on your left when you get off the elevator. Warren, perhaps we will see you again soon."

Warren smiled down at me. "I certainly hope so," he said.

I hooked my arm through Warren's. "Thanks," I said to my parents. "I'll call you later!"

They both nodded and stared curiously as we left the office.

When we were in the hallway, Warren looked down at me. "Well, that was easy."

I smiled up at him. "I'm a bit of a daddy's girl."

The elevator doors opened and we stepped inside. "He seems like a really good man," he said.

I nodded and punched the button for floor two. "He's the best."

We walked into the lab and a nurse was waiting for us. She was a heavyset black woman who reminded me a bit of Ms. Claybrooks at the jail. "Sloan?" she asked.

"Yes," I said.

She held the door open for us. "Come on back. My name is Joyce. Your mother called to let me know you were on your way up here."

We followed her down the hallway to a sterile white room with a padded blue chair and a large collection of syringes and specimen bottles. Joyce rubbed her hands together. "Who am I sticking first?" she asked.

I looked at Warren. "I'll go first," he said with a touch of reluctance. He unbuttoned his black shirt revealing a white ribbed tank top underneath.

He handed me the shirt and sat down in the chair. She sat down on the office chair in front of him and pulled on some purple rubber gloves. He extended his toned arm out on the armrest and she grabbed it with both hands.

She pulled his arm forwards and gasped with glee. "Look at those beautiful veins!"

He cut his eyes up at her. "So it will be easy?"

She smiled and shook her head in amazement. "Honey, this is like nurse porn right here."

I laughed. "Nurse porn?"

"Heck yeah, girl. I could do this with my eyes closed." She prepared the needle and rubbed alcohol across the bend in his arm.

"Please keep your eyes open," he begged, his voice cracking a little bit.

I stuck out my lower lip. "Oh, are you scared of needles?"

"Shut up," he said, not looking up at me.

The nurse slid the needle into his vein. He cringed and she shook her head. "It's always the big tough ones who freak out on me the most." As the vial was filling, she tapped her finger on the black tribal tattoo that was wound around his bicep and shoulder before it disappeared under his tank top. "Men, all day long, sit through huge tattoos like this but one tiny little stick for blood and they become the biggest babies."

"I'm not a baby," he protested.

I laughed.

She removed the needle and capped the lid on the vial. "All done," she said. "Was that so terrible?" She covered the spot with a cotton ball and a Band-Aid.

"No," he said, but didn't mean it.

Warren got up and I handed him his shirt. He shrugged into it and started securing the buttons as I pushed up the sleeve of my sweater and sat down.

"You're Dr. Jordan's daughter?" Joyce asked.

I nodded. "Yes. My name is Sloan. Can I ask you a question?"

"Sure, honey," she said as she tied a tourniquet above my elbow.

"How accurate is DNA testing?" I asked.

"Depends on what kind. Paternity?" she asked.

I shook my head. "Sibling."

She shrugged. "Pretty accurate. Science is so advanced these days, they can even tell if you're half-siblings or full ones," she said. "Why? Are you two related?"

"We don't know," I answered.

She stuck the needle in my arm and then looked from Warren's face to mine while my blood drained out into her vial. "Nah," she said. "I'd place money on it."

He leaned his shoulder against the wall and crossed one black boot over the other. "You don't think so?" he asked.

She shook her head. "I mean, I don't know for sure, but everything's different. Bone structure, eyes, nose, mouth. Nah. I don't think so."

He stuffed his hands into the pockets on his blue jeans and smiled over at me. "I'm really hoping not."

She smiled. "Oh, I see. Y'all have some Days of our Lives stuff going on."

He laughed. "More like Stephen King stuff."

She removed the needle from my arm and patched me up. "All done. I'll send it over before I leave for the day. I got your information from your mother. I just need his. What's your name, sir?"

"Warren Parish," he said.

"Date of birth?" she asked.

"August 27th, 1984," he answered.

She nodded. "I'm gonna put the same address and phone number." She filled in the blanks on the paperwork in front of her. "I think that's all I need."

I tugged my sleeve down and stood up. "Thank you so much."

She smiled. "Y'all have a good weekend."

We walked out of the office. Warren glanced down at this watch. "Well, I've been here for an hour, and I've met your parents and had my blood taken. This is shaping up to be a very interesting weekend."

I laughed as we got on the elevator. "You hungry?" I asked.

"Starving actually," he answered.

"I say we grab some food to go and find a spot by the river somewhere that we can talk in private," I suggested.

He nodded. "That's a perfect idea."

We picked up fast food sandwiches and drinks and drove out to a picnic area by the French Broad River. There was a father and son fishing from the bank, but other than that we were alone. I sat down on the picnic table and he straddled the bench.

He looked out over the wide river. "This looks like something off of a postcard."

I laughed. "I'm sure this very scene is on many postcards, actually."

Towering red oaks and orange and yellow maple trees dotted the mountains that confined the rushing waters of the river. The water was deep, but just up ahead, huge rocks formed a series of churning rapids. The sun was setting over the jagged Carolina horizon, casting pink and purple streaks across the blue sky.

"What river is this?" he asked.

"The French Broad," I answered. "They say it's the third oldest river in the world."

He looked up at me and cocked an eyebrow. "How do they know that?"

I shrugged my shoulders. "Not a clue."

He laughed and looked out over the water. "Well, it's really pretty."

I nodded and sucked on my straw. "It looks pretty, but don't get in it." I pointed just offshore. "Adrianne and I once saw a cow's head floating right by here."

"Nice." He laughed and took a bite of his sandwich. "Who's Adrianne?"

"She's been my best friend for forever. I'm sure you'll meet her soon." My phone began to ring in my pocket. "Wanna take bets?" I asked with a smile.

"No," he said.

I pulled out the phone and showed him Adrianne's face that was lit up on the screen.

He shook his head and picked up his drink. "That's crazy."

I ignored her call and tucked my phone back into my pocket. "I know."

"How does it work?" he asked.

I shrugged. "I'm not really sure. I figured out a few years ago that it happens more often when I mention someone while picturing them in my mind. It doesn't always happen, but it's becoming more and more frequent that they show up in some way."

"So it's not always in person?" he asked.

"No. Sometimes it's just a phone call or email or on Facebook. Other times, I don't get anything," I said. "I'm not sure why it seems that sometimes I make it happen and other times I can't do it at all."

He thought for a second. "I think whatever we can do is like working out. The more we use our muscles, the stronger they get."

I nodded. "That makes sense. It began getting a whole lot stronger after I finally opened up about it."

He pointed the straw from his drink at me. "You accepted it."

"Yeah."

"Do your parents know?" he asked.

I leaned forward against my knees and told him about what had happened when I was eight. "It was pretty traumatic," I explained. "I learned not to bring it up after all that happened."

He reached up and lightly ran his thumb over the scar on my eyebrow. "I don't blame you." He shifted on the bench. "Only your friend and the detective know?"

"And now you," I added.

He nodded. "I have to ask. What's going on with you and the detective?"

I laughed. "I really don't want to talk about him. We don't need him showing up here right now."

He didn't laugh. "You know we have to talk about him. The two of you seem to have a lot of history."

"Oh no." I feverishly shook my head. "We don't have any history at all. I just met him like a month ago."

His head snapped back with surprise. "Really?"

"Really," I said. "He sort of walked into my life and turned it all upside down."

"He's into you," he said.

"I know. Well, he's been interested in me since you showed up anyway. I think it's a territorial thing," I said. "He has a girlfriend."

"Do you like him?" he asked.

I took a deep breath. "I'm not going to lie to you about it. I've liked him since I met him, but then you showed up."

He nodded. "And complicated things."

I squeezed my eyes closed and smiled. "Definitely complicated things."

He looked up at me and shrugged. "But it might turn out that I'm your brother and that would make things easier for you."

I laughed and threw a pickle at him. "You're not my brother."

He smiled and put his straw to his lips. "I know I'm not."

I finished off the last of my sandwich just as he did, and I got up and carried our trash to the garbage can. As I walked back to the table, he turned around backward on his seat and reached his arms out toward me. I took his hands, and he pulled me close and rested his head against my stomach. I couldn't help but run my fingers through his silky smooth hair as I stood in front of him. His touch was absolutely intoxicating.

"What do you think this is?" He looked up at me, resting his chin on my belly button. "It's like I can't get close enough to you."

I pushed his hair behind his ears. "It's like we're magnets," I said. "I'm the positive. You're the negative. We're drawn together."

He nodded. "That makes a lot of sense actually. We're the same, but we have different purposes."

"And it's really hard to separate us," I added.

He pulled away. "Isn't it? What was up with the headaches?"

I sat down next to him. "I have no idea, but I thought I was dying. My dad said it's called a hemiplegic migraine. The most severe kind there is. I couldn't move or talk for hours."

He shook his head. "Me either, and I was on the interstate. I ended up sleeping in my car for a while."

I shuddered. "I can't even imagine. Nathan called an ambulance to come and get me."

"I hope it's not like that every time I leave," he said. "That will be very problematic till my contract with Claymore ends."

"What do you do exactly?" I asked.

"I'm transitioning out of being a High Threat Personal Security Contractor for Claymore Worldwide Security," he said.

My eyes glazed over. "A what?"

He smiled. "It's a private military company. We're contracted by the US Government and other governments for doing things the regular military can't do," he explained.

"Mercenaries?"

He cringed. "That makes us sound like traitors."

"And you do what exactly?" I asked.

He took a deep breath. "Well, I was just a hired gun when I was recruited in 2010, but two years ago I became a team leader. I just got back from Afghanistan, and I'm filling in as an instructor until my contract ends." He sighed and shook his head. "I'm done with being deployed."

"What did you do in the Marines?" I asked.

"I was a sniper," he answered.

I raised an eyebrow. "Seems a little ironic being what you are, doesn't it?"

He laughed. "I guess it does."

"I want to hear about *that,* too," I said.

"You will. That's more of a 'behind closed doors' conversation, you know?" he said.

I nodded. "Oh, I know."

He looked at me sideways. "That doesn't scare you?"

"It did at first," I admitted. "But people who live in glass houses shouldn't throw stones."

He pointed at me. "You save people. That's quite a bit different."

I smiled and showed him the angel pin on my lapel. "The little girl I pulled out of that attic told me I was her angel."

"Huh." He stood and tugged up his shirt and tank top, displaying the gun on his hip. He pushed his waistband down, and under the holster, tattooed on his side, was the word *Azrael.*

Without thinking, my fingers traced the letters. I looked up at him. "The Angel of Death."

CHAPTER TWELVE

We left my car at the office for the evening and went straight to my house. I unlocked the front door and we walked inside. "Home sweet home," I announced.

He stopped at the end of the foyer and looked across the room. "What happened to your back door?"

"That night when I had the migraine, the detective broke it down to get to me," I said. "He patched it up for now."

"I'll fix it before I leave," he said.

I tugged on his arm. "Come on, I'll show you to your room." He followed me toward the stairs.

At the top of the steps was a small hallway. I pointed to the right. "This is my room." I turned to the left. "And this is the guest room and bathroom." I flipped on the light to the small guest bedroom that I had decorated in pastel blues and greens. It reminded me of the beach.

He walked to the queen sized bed and put his tactical black bag on top of the seashell comforter. "It's a nice house," he said.

I leaned against the doorframe. "I like it. I've lived here for a couple of years now. It was the first thing I ever bought that made me feel like a grownup." I motioned toward my room. "I'm going to go change out of my work clothes. Do you think you might want to go out again tonight, or am I safe changing into my comfy clothes?"

He smiled at me. "I didn't come here to see the city, so I would be perfectly happy staying in tonight if that's what you want to do."

"Great." I backed out of the room and into the hallway. "Make yourself at home."

He nodded and I went to my room.

I kicked off my heels, stripped out of my slacks and sweater, and pulled on a pair of blue Victoria's Secret sweatpants, a sports bra, and a black tank top. I stopped in the bathroom to fix my ponytail and brush my teeth before rejoining him downstairs.

Warren was standing in front of my refrigerator laughing when I walked in. He looked at me. "Your fridge looks like mine. Water, cheese, and beer."

"Don't tell my mom." I reached around him and retrieved a beer.

He grabbed one too and followed me to the living room. He nodded to the fireplace. "Want me to build a fire?"

I hesitated. "Ehhh...I haven't used that thing since I moved in. It might burn the house down."

He laughed and picked up the couple of pieces of wood that I brought inside just for looks. "We'll call the fire department if we need to."

I sat down on the sofa and watched him as I drank my beer. He had pulled his hair back and taken off the black shirt, but he was still in the same tank top and blue jeans. His shoulder tattoo apparently went down his arm and completely down his side. I could see a hint of black on his skin through his shirt.

After a few minutes, a flicker of fire began to dance between the logs. He got up and dusted his hands off on his jeans. "See, that wasn't hard." He picked up his beer and joined me on the couch.

"Have you always had long hair?" I asked.

"Oh no. I had to keep it within military regulations for eight years." He gripped his ponytail. "I think this is still out of rebellion."

I laughed. "Makes sense. I like it. It looks really good on you."

"Thanks." He tipped the beer bottle up to his lips then looked over at me. His face was serious. "Are you ready for the conversation to get heavy?"

I tucked my feet under me. "Yes."

"You're sure? He raised an eyebrow. "I've never told anyone what I'm about to tell you."

I swallowed hard but nodded with confidence. "I'm sure." A strange mix of fear and excitement seemed to bubble inside of me.

"And you promise what I say here doesn't leave this room?" he asked. "This is some really bad stuff that I'm getting ready to admit to."

I held out my little finger. "Pinky swear."

He hooked his little finger with mine, spurring another small electric shock. It made him jump a little and he laughed. "I'm not sure I'll ever get used to that."

I rubbed my finger. "Me either."

He blew out a deep breath. "OK. Here goes," he said. "When I was eight, I was in the foster system. Me and this other girl who was seven were living with a couple in the suburbs of Chicago. The woman was all right, but the man gave me nightmares. Just evil at the core. You know what I'm talking about."

I nodded and shivered with familiarity. "Yes."

"The little girl's name was Alice. She and I were in the system together for a while. She was a little slow and had a speech impediment, but she was really nice to me when a lot of the other kids weren't. After we had been there for about a month, the man started picking us up from school. We would go to the house and he would take her into his room," he said.

I put my hand over my mouth and closed my eyes.

"Well, you can guess," he said. "I didn't know what was happening, but I knew this guy was a monster. Alice began to shut down. She cried a lot and wouldn't talk to me or play with me anymore."

My heart was pounding, and my stomach churned with nausea.

"One day, we came home from school, and he started to take her to his room. She started crying. I yelled and told him to stop. He said that he might have to make me come too. I started crying. Alice was sobbing. I just knew, even at eight, that he shouldn't be allowed to be alive. I screamed, and there was a crack that reverberated around the room. It sounded like lightning striking a tree. The guy fell to his knees and face-planted on the carpet. I took Alice by the hand and we ran to the neighbor's house." He paused and took a deep breath.

"He was dead?" I asked.

He nodded. "His heart stopped."

I sat back and rolled my head against the cushion. "That's horrific."

"I knew, even then, I had done it," he said. "I tried to tell my caseworker I had caused it, but of course he didn't believe me."

"Of course," I said.

"After that, Alice and I were split up and sent to different foster homes. Then when I was fourteen, I was sent to a group home in the city," he said. "No families ever kept me for longer than six months because everyone seemed to be afraid of me."

I rested my head on my hand. "That must have been traumatic."

He nodded. "In a way, but there was this huge part of me that was so fiercely protective of other people. I knew I wasn't a bad person. I never felt like a bad kid." He took another long sip from the bottle. "Then, when I was sixteen, me and a couple of the other boys from the group home went to the movies. They embodied all the horror stories you hear about system kids. Smoking, drinking, drugs, gangs...you name it. But they were the only people that didn't seem to mind being around me.

"After the movie was over, we were supposed to walk home, but they decided to follow this girl who had left alone. I think she must have lived close by. They cornered her in this alley. I grabbed one of them, this kid named Rex, by his hair and threw him backward. The other guy, Travis, lunged at the girl and shoved her into the corner of this dumpster. It split her head open pretty bad. Travis jumped on top of her and pounded her in the face. Rex had me by the back of the shirt, but I was focused on Travis. He was going to kill that girl if I didn't stop him. Then there was another crack like lightning."

"And it stopped his heart," I said.

He nodded. "Rex was so shocked that he backed off. When I turned toward him, he took off running."

"What happened to the girl?" I asked.

"I picked her up and carried her to the gas station around the corner. They called 911, and I took off into the streets before the police arrived. I'm pretty sure she lived though," he said.

I rubbed my hands over my face. "Wow."

He finished his beer and placed the empty bottle on the floor beside him. "I made it on the streets till I turned eighteen and could join the military. That was my only way out."

"And you became a sniper," I said.

He shrugged his shoulders. "I was already a killer."

I shook my head. "No you weren't. You were a savior."

He turned his palms up. "It doesn't feel that way when you know you've stopped a beating heart."

I let out a long puff of air. "How many times have you done it?"

"Nine times," he said. "Three of them at once in Iraq in 2006."

"I guess that ability comes in handy during wartime," I said.

He nodded. "Yes, it does."

"How does it work? Can you do it at will now?" I asked.

"I wouldn't say 'at will' exactly, but I can do it when I have no other choice," he said.

"Whatever happened to Alice?" I asked.

He took a deep breath and leaned his head back on the couch. After a moment of awkward silence it became clear that he didn't want to talk about her.

I put my hand on his. "It's OK. You don't have to tell me."

He sighed and shook his head. "No, I need to tell you," he said. "Alice is dead."

My head snapped back with surprise. "How?"

He was silent again. He looked down at his hands and then back up at me. There were tears brimming along the edges of his dark eyes. "I killed her."

I swallowed hard but didn't release his hand. "How did it happen?"

"I didn't see her again until after I ran away from the group home. When I found her, she was holed up in a crack house on the wrong side of the city. I stayed with her for a while and tried to help get her cleaned up, but one night I came back from buying us food and she was overdosing on something. I still don't know what she took." He dropped his head.

His hand was sweaty in mine.

"She was choking to death on her own vomit and convulsing. I tried to clear her airway, but there was too much," he said. "I could feel her slipping away, and I knew she was in pain. I didn't have a phone to call for help. No one else was there. So I stopped it."

I put my arms around his neck and pulled him close to me. I didn't know if he was crying, but his breaths were rapid and shallow. Uncontrollable tears were dripping off my cheeks. "You didn't kill her." I shook my head. "You helped her find peace. No one should die in that much pain."

He didn't move for the longest time. Neither did I. I just raked my nails through his hair, till his breathing returned to normal. He was just a kid when Alice died. She had been his only semblance of family. Suddenly, I felt guilty for having such a charmed life growing up. Warren and I may have had our similarities, but he had lived through things worse than anything I could even imagine.

Finally, he straightened and wiped at his eyes. "She was the one I told about what I could do. She was the only person until now who ever knew."

I tucked his hair behind his ear. "Warren, I'm so sorry."

He nodded. "I am too. I've always felt so responsible for her. I should've protected her when we were in that awful house together. I should've been able to save her when she died." He sniffed.

I shook my head. "It wasn't your responsibility."

"Wasn't it?" he asked, his voice full of sincere doubt.

"No," I said. "You were a kid. No kid should carry that much."

He nodded, but he wasn't convinced. Perhaps he never would be.

After a while, his shoulders seemed to relax. "Wow, I've never told that stuff to anyone."

"It will never leave this room," I promised.

He smiled. "I know." He stared at me for a minute. "All this time, I thought I was all alone. I thought I would always be alone, carrying this shit around with me."

I tangled my fingers with his and remembered the sting of my face being split open on the third grade play ground. I kissed his knuckles and whispered, "Never again."

Our conversation took a lighter turn after that and I told him about growing up in Asheville and about college at UNC. I told him about Ms. Claybrooks at the jail and about wishing syphilis on Nathan's girlfriend. We laughed and talked until almost two in the morning.

Finally, he yawned and he shook his head. "I don't want to, but I have to go to bed. I've been up since four this morning." He looked down at the large black watch encircling his wrist. "That's almost twenty-four hours ago."

"You're right. I don't want to sleep the day away tomorrow," I said.

He stood up and offered me his hand. "What's on the agenda for tomorrow?"

I shrugged. "I don't know. Maybe matching tattoos or running away to Mexico."

He laughed and pulled me to my feet. "I would go with you to Mexico."

I smiled and he followed me upstairs. When we reached the top, I turned toward him. "Well, goodnight, Warren."

He leaned down and pressed a kiss to my forehead. "Goodnight, Sloan."

I went to my room and left the door cracked open. I brushed my teeth and climbed under the sheets and the down blanket. My brain was spinning, sleep nowhere to be found. My body twisted under the covers. I hugged my pillow and pushed it aside. I rolled to the other side of the mattress. I kicked my blanket off only to wrap it around my legs again.

My Xanax was in my purse downstairs. A full tablet would lull me into a coma. As I contemplated the hangover it would cause the next morning, my bedroom door creaked open, and Warren crept inside.

"You OK?" I asked across the moonlit room.

"Yeah." He was slowly walking toward me. "I'm coming to ask your forgiveness."

I watched over my shoulder as he stopped at the edge of my bed. "Ask my forgiveness for what?"

He lifted the covers and lay down behind me. His arm slipped around my waist, and he rested his head on my pillow. "You're going to have to forgive me for climbing into your bed," he whispered. He pulled me tight against his body, making the bed hum with electricity.

I hadn't slept that well in years.

The sound of a hammer downstairs jarred me from a deep sleep the next morning. I was alone in my bed. While our 'sleeping together' was confined to the very literal sense of the phrase, my body was so exhaustively satisfied that my brain couldn't help but wander to all sorts of 'what if' fantasies. My toes curled at the thought.

The scent of fresh coffee urged my unwilling body parts out of the bed, and my legs wobbled as I took the first step toward the bathroom. My muscles felt like Jell-O.

Downstairs, Warren was pounding nails into a new door frame around my back door. "Where did you get the tools?" I asked at the bottom of the steps.

He looked up and smiled. "I had to go buy them, but I rented the saw. Good morning," he said.

"Good morning. How long have you been up?" I crossed the room toward the kitchen.

"I slept in and got up around seven," he said.

I laughed. "Seven is sleeping in?"

"I'm always up by four," he replied.

I shook my head and pulled a coffee mug out of the cabinet. "And you made coffee? I could get used to this."

I carried the coffee to the living room and stretched out on the couch. He was in his white tank top, and I admired watching his biceps flex as he used the hammer.

He caught me grinning. "What are you doing?" he asked.

I blushed over the rim of my mug. "Enjoying the view."

He laughed. "I had to get you a new door. The other one was broken beyond repair. McNamara must have kicked it in."

"Probably. He's like a bull in a china shop sometimes," I said. "Let me know how much I owe you, and I'll pay you back."

"Shut up." He swung the door back and forth. "How did you sleep?"

I moaned and stretched my head back. "Better than I ever have in my life."

He smiled. "Me too."

The doorbell rang. I sat up to answer it, but he held out his hand to stop me. "I can get it."

He opened the door, and Adrianne froze when she saw Warren. "Uh, who are you?" she asked with wide eyes.

"It's OK!" I called out to her. "I'm in here."

She looked Warren up and down as she crept past him.

"Warren, that's my best friend Adrianne," I said. "Adrianne, that's Warren."

He shook her hand. "I've heard a lot about you," he said.

Her mouth was hanging open. "I haven't heard a word about you." She looked at me for an answer.

"Sure you have!" She slowly sank down on the couch beside my feet and I leaned toward her. "He's the guy I was looking for at the festival last weekend."

"The one that you said reminded you of a corpse? Now he's here installing a door." She dropped her head to one side, her eyes bewildered. "I'm so freaking confused right now."

"I tried to call you Wednesday night to explain, but you didn't answer or call me back," I said. "A lot has happened since Sunday."

Warren laughed and returned to fixing the door. "That's an understatement."

She put her purse on the coffee table and crossed her legs. "Please catch me up," she begged.

"I met Warren last Sunday. Remember me trying to explain to you at the festival that I couldn't read him?" I asked.

"Yeah," she said.

I nudged her in the thigh with my toe. "He's like me. That's why I couldn't tell anything about him."

"He can do your weird voodoo stuff?" she asked.

"Yeah. More or less," I said.

She rubbed her forehead. "I'm so lost."

I took a deep breath. "Let me see if I can sum this all up. Warren lives near the beach. He saw me on the news. He couldn't read me, like I couldn't read him, so he came here to find me. On Sunday night, I came home and he was here."

She looked at Warren. "Did you break in her house?" She pointed to the door.

I shook my head. "No, Nathan did."

"The detective? Why did he break in your house?" she asked, her voice jumping up an octave.

"To take me to the hospital," I said.

"Hospital?!" she shrieked.

I looked at Warren who was leaning against the door laughing.

"This really isn't making any sense is it?" I asked him.

He shook his head. "The more you talk, the crazier you sound."

Adrianne picked up her keys and shook her head. "Maybe I should leave and come again later. I was just stopping by to see if you wanted to grab breakfast. My brain is not nearly awake enough to handle this kind of information."

I laughed. "No. Stay," I said trying to hold her with my feet.

"I'm assuming he stayed here last night?" she asked, pointing to my pajamas.

"Yes."

"Are you like *together* now?" she asked.

Warren lost his composure and burst out laughing again. "Not until we find out if I'm her brother!"

I doubled over and buried my face in my knees. "Ha!"

She stood up. "I've got to be in the wrong house."

I reached out and grabbed her by the arm. "I'm sorry. This sounds a whole lot worse than it really is."

"I hope so," she said as I pulled her back to the couch.

I rested my head on her shoulder. "He's really great and you're going to love him."

She looked down at me and then over at Warren. "You're talking about him like he's a puppy."

He shook his head. "I am certainly not a puppy." He knocked his knuckles against the door. "I'm going to clean this mess up and jump in the shower. Maybe that will give you enough time to fill Adrianne in."

"OK," I said. He winked at me before he walked outside.

In a slower version, I recapped the events of the week for my friend until she finally understood some of what I was saying. When I was done, she shook her head. "You're such a freak. Only this kind of crap happens to you."

I nodded. "I know."

"When do you find out the DNA test results?" She pointed up the stairs. "Because if he is your brother, I'm totally going to ask him out."

"He's hot, isn't he?" I asked.

"Smoking hot," she said. "What does he do?"

"He's a sniper," I said with a wild, excited smile.

She sighed and rolled her eyes. "Of course he is."

"Oh, guess what else?" I asked.

She held up her palms and shook her head. "There is absolutely no telling."

I punched her in the shoulder. "In the past week, the hot detective kissed me *twice*." I waved two fingers in front of her face. "Twice, Adrianne!"

She laughed. "No way."

"Yep. He is crazy jealous," I said.

"So you already have a backup plan."

"Nathan isn't a backup plan," I said. "I really don't think Warren and I are related."

She smiled. "For your sake, I hope not. For my sake, I'm going to pray that you are."

I laughed and kicked her in the thigh.

Warren came down a few minutes later with wet hair, wearing a fitted gray thermal shirt and jeans. He sat down on the love seat and placed his black boots on the floor beside him. "Did you ladies get everything figured out?"

"I think so." Adrianne sighed. "That's a pretty unbelievable story."

He laughed. "Which part?"

"All of it." She stood up and slung her purse over her shoulder. "Well, I'm going to take off. Warren, it was really great to meet you."

Warren and I stood up. He wrapped his arms around me from behind. "You too, Adrianne. I'm sure I'll be seeing you again soon," he said.

She smiled. "I'm sure you will." She pointed at me. "You and I are having lunch on Monday, and I want every detail of how the rest of this weekend plays out."

Warren looked from her down at me. "What's happening the rest of the weekend?"

Adrianne shook her head. "With this girl, you never know. She's a complete freak of nature."

"Bye," I said with a little wave. "I'll call you later."

When she was gone, I sat down and Warren stretched out on the sofa, resting his head in my lap.

"You're all wet," I said, running my nails through his hair.

He smiled up at me. "You don't care."

He was right.

I looked down at him. "You know, I think you're wrong."

He angled his neck to look at me. "Wrong about what?"

"About nobody liking you. Neither Mom, Dad, or Adrianne seemed freaked out by you at all. Adrianne even says she's going to ask you out if it turns out we're related."

He laughed. "Really?"

"Yup," I said.

"I think it's really strange. Everyone I've met with you has made me feel...normal. They don't automatically dislike me," he said. "Except Detective McNamara. He clearly doesn't like me."

I laughed. "That's a testosterone issue."

"That's probably part of it," he agreed.

"You know, I wonder if we sort of neutralize each other. Like, maybe you're more likable around me," I said.

"People don't seem to like you any less with me around," he said.

"That's because I'm adorable." I said as I batted my eyelashes down at him.

He chuckled. "That you are." He closed his eyes. "Tell me about this serial killer case. We haven't discussed that subject much."

It took a while, but I relayed all of the information that Nathan had given me.

"I've heard about some of those missing girls," he said. "I wasn't aware they were related to anything else."

"Well, that's just all coming together now," I said.

"So they are all about the same age, race, and similar appearance. Anything else?" he asked.

"Yes. They were all kidnapped—and I assume killed—during the fall and winter months. September through December," I said.

"Huh. That's interesting," he said.

"It's very interesting," I agreed. "Have you ever met a serial killer in person?"

He shrugged. "That's a pretty vague definition. I've met many people who have murdered more than one person."

"No, I mean like the sick and twisted Ted Bundy type," I said.

He thought for a moment. "There was one guy over in Afghanistan. He went nuts and killed a bunch of civilians while I was doing private security work. He was pretty twisted," he said.

"Do you think that killing someone always reads the same when we look at them?" I asked.

He shrugged. "Considering how many people I've taken out, I certainly hope not. I do know there's a big difference between me looking at my comrades who have fought and killed in war and a guy that shot a bunch of kids in their sleep."

I thought about it. "I've always assumed that it is something to do with the soul that I can detect. The actual essence of a person that thinks, makes decisions, and experiences emotions."

"I can get on board with that theory, but I don't think that people are born good or evil. I think their choices determine which side of the moral divide they fall on," he said. "I've never met a little kid who felt dark."

"Me either," I agreed.

"So the choices people make taint their souls," I said.

He nodded. "I think so because some people are definitely more evil than others."

Warren continued. "And some people that I've known for several years have become more evil over time."

"Yeah, I'm beginning to notice that more and more," I said.

He looked up at me. "Because you're paying more attention and trying to figure it out now. I told you, it's like exercise."

"That's why you're so much better at everything than I am?" I asked. "You've been practicing it longer?"

"Having the power to end someone's life kinda makes you want to work at mastering it," he said. "You don't want that kind of loose cannon flailing around."

"Makes sense," I said.

He pointed at me. "Here's a bigger question. If it is their souls that we can see, does that mean you and I don't have souls since we can't read each other?"

I raised my eyebrows. "That's scary."

He smiled. "I wouldn't be surprised if I didn't have a soul."

I shook my head. "Shut up." I drummed my nails on his chest, and my thoughts returned to the girls who were missing. "Do you really think that if we found a suspected area that you could tell if there was a dead body there?"

He closed his eyes as I played with his hair. "Absolutely."

I shuddered at the thought of feeling death everywhere I went. "I know you said it isn't a big deal, but that has to be creepy."

"I'm pretty used to it," he said.

I scrunched up my nose. "I'll bet you freak out around cemeteries."

He laughed. "Not exactly."

I shook my head. "I don't want to talk about murders and death anymore. What do you want to do today?"

He didn't open his eyes. "I'm doing it right now."

I rubbed my hands down his chest. "I say, we go get some food, maybe pick up some movies from Redbox, and then spend the rest of the day doing exactly this."

He smiled and pushed himself up. "I can get on board with that plan."

We drove to the Sunnyside Cafe for breakfast, and on the way home, we stopped at the gas station near my house to pick up some movies from Redbox. "I think I'm going to get some more beer. What do you want?" I asked.

He was pulling the movies out of the kiosk. "Hold on, I'll come with you."

The door chimed as we walked into the store. I retrieved a six pack of Highland Brewing's Pale Ale, grabbed a bag of Doritos, and followed Warren to the counter. A burly man wearing camouflage pants with suspenders was ahead of us in line.

Warren leaned down close to my ear. "Do you think if I moved up here, I could pull off wearing those pants?" he whispered.

I honestly thought Warren could pull off a burlap sack if he really wanted to. I motioned toward the window, drawing his attention to the camouflage truck parked at the gas pump. "Only if you get the truck to go with them," I said.

He laughed.

I cut my eyes at him. "More important than the pants, what is this you say about moving here?"

He shrugged his broad shoulders. "It's just a thought. I don't wanna keep driving back and forth forever."

I smiled but didn't say anything.

"What's there to do around here?" he asked. "Sell me on Asheville, and don't talk about the leaves changing colors. I don't give a shit about leaves."

I laughed. "Well, the only things to do around here in the fall, besides looking at leaves, are hunting and watching football. If you're not into either of those, you're screwed in the fall and the winter."

A bell *dinged* in my mind.

"I thought you guys have some ski slopes around here—" he began.

I held up my hand to silence him. "Hold on. When is hunting season?"

His face twisted with confusion. "What?"

I tugged on his sleeve. "Seriously! When is hunting season?"

"Well, it depends on what you're hunting. Deer season is the biggest sport, and it usually runs from September to January depending on what weapon you're using and where you are in the state. Why?"

My eyes widened. I put the beer on the counter and gripped his forearms. "September to December!" I almost shouted at him. "The murders happen during deer season! The killer is a hunter!"

CHAPTER THIRTEEN

"Nathan, are you at home?" I shouted into the phone as I buckled my seatbelt.

"I just got back. Why?" he asked. "Are you all right?"

"Warren and I are on our way to your house." I looked at Warren and moved the phone away from my mouth. "Turn right."

"Umm...excuse me?" Nathan asked.

"Nathan, I know what the connection is with the dates," I said. "The killer is a hunter! These girls are buried in the woods. I need a topographical map and a list of hunting areas. We'll be there in ten minutes." I disconnected the call before he had the chance to object.

I looked over at Warren. "Are you sure you don't mind?" I asked. "I wouldn't do this if it weren't a big deal."

He shook his head. "No, I get it. I'm not sure if McNamara is going to let me in the house though."

"He will if he wants my help," I said. "Take the next left."

Nathan was brooding when he answered the door, but he nodded hello to Warren and let us inside. He motioned toward the office. "Come on back."

He had a topographical map up on the board with pins stuck

in the areas where the girls disappeared. "Did you get the list?" I asked.

He nodded. "It's on the computer," he said. "What is all this about?"

"Remember how we said all this time that this killer is seasonal?" I reminded him. He nodded and I gripped his forearm. "Hunting season is during the same time frame. That's the only thing that has made any sense to me so far about this whole case!"

He laughed and crossed his arms over his chest. "That's a long shot, Sloan."

"Maybe," I agreed, looking down at the computer screen. "But it's better than any other lead we've had."

Nathan stepped over behind me. "But deer season is the busiest time of the year in those woods. Why would the killer hide bodies during such a high time of traffic? And how would he do it without being seen?" Nathan shook his head. "That doesn't make sense."

"I think the idea has some merit," Warren said. "If I were going to bury bodies in the woods, I would do it when I knew a lot of different tracks were going to be covering up mine. Also, the wildlife service makes sure the woods are cleared of poachers every day at sundown, so witnesses wouldn't be likely."

Nathan turned and shot him a hateful glare "Given this a lot of thought, have you?"

I punched him in the arm. "Shut up. He's just trying to help."

"He shouldn't be here," Nathan mumbled.

That was it. I whirled around at him. "OK. I'm putting an end to this crap right now!" I pointed at Warren who was sitting on the couch eating my bag of Doritos. "Let me remind you, Detective, that this man wouldn't be here if it weren't for *you.* You put me in the middle of the media spotlight and he saw me. That's not his fault. And neither of us are here because this is what we want to be doing right now. As much as I like you, Nathan, I would really rather be working on my own mystery that I've been trying to solve all my life—figuring out what I am! We are here because you begged for my help on this case. So you can either stop being a jackass right now, or I'm walking and you're on your own."

By the end of my rant, both of their mouths were hanging open.

I leaned toward him. "Do we understand each other?"

He nodded, snapping his mouth shut.

I put my hands on my hips and looked back at the map. "Now, where was I?"

"Poachers," Warren answered with a mouthful of chips.

"Right." I tapped my fingernail on the computer screen. "If we try and narrow these down to a small search field, we can check it out and see what we find."

"You don't want to start here in Asheville," Nathan said. "There's way too much hunting ground here to cover."

I looked at the map. "Which of these areas where girls went missing has the least amount of hunting land?"

"Raleigh," they said at the same time.

I looked at Nathan. "Where can you hunt around Raleigh?"

"Private or public?" he asked.

"Public," Warren answered. "If it's the same guy, nobody has access to private hunting land all over the state."

Nathan squeezed his eyes shut. "OK, public game lands would be Jordan Lake or Butner-Falls around Raleigh." He grabbed a marker and circled the areas on the map. "Butner-Falls would be closest to the murders, but we're talking about an area of about ten square miles."

"Minus the water," I said. "Wait. Could the bodies have been dumped in the water?" I looked between the two of them as I waited for an answer.

Warren shook his head. "Very doubtful. I imagine that river system has a really fluctuating current. Even if someone weighed down the body, chances are still high that it would eventually surface when it was swept to the smaller waterways."

"So, ten square miles minus the water," I said.

Warren crossed the ankle of his boot over his knee. "We could cover that in a day. We won't need to hike all of it."

"We?" Nathan asked, surprised.

Warren shrugged. "You can't exactly call in a search team with our unreasonable suspicion. So yeah, I'll do it if you want my help."

I leaned against the desk. "Warren, is there any kind of time limit on these bodies? The ones in Raleigh disappeared about thirteen years ago."

He shook his head. "There's no expiration date on death."

Nathan and I both halted at his statement. "Good point," Nathan finally said.

"I'm heading that way tomorrow. If you guys want to come, you can ride back together, and I can go on home," Warren offered.

I held my hands up in the air. "We're doing this?"

Nathan put his hands on his hips and shook his head. "This is such a long shot."

"I think she's on to something," Warren said.

I wrung my hands. "I'm right. I know I am."

Nathan sighed. "Yeah. Let's do it. One big happy family going on a hike in the woods."

I clapped my hands together and squealed.

"We're going to need some supplies if we're going to be trekking through the woods all day," Warren said. "I didn't bring any gear with me."

"I've got a couple of packs we can take," Nathan said. "Sloan, do you have any hiking boots?"

I laughed. "Nope."

"Where is a sporting store around here?" Warren asked.

"River Hills," I answered.

"Good. We'll need some hunter safety orange this time of year too," Warren said.

"We can go do some shopping on the way home," I told him.

Nathan leaned against his desk. "What time do you want to head out tomorrow?"

Warren shrugged. "I'm up at four."

"Five, then?" Nathan asked. "That would put us there by nine."

I frowned. "Five in the morning?"

"I promise you'll live, babe," Warren said. He stood up and offered his hand to Nathan. "See you in the morning, then?"

Nathan hesitated for a moment looking down at Warren's outstretched hand. I elbowed him in the ribs, and he finally shook it. "Yeah. See you in the morning. Thanks," he said.

Warren and I left Nathan's house and went shopping for hiking supplies before picking up dinner and returning to my house. "I'm sorry our day on the couch got pretty screwed up," I said as we lugged bags up my front steps.

"I'm here. That's all that matters," he said.

I unlocked the front door and smiled at him. "You're pretty remarkable."

He smirked. "No, I'm not."

"Yes, you are. You hardly know me, and yet you're willing to go to all this trouble for me and another guy that you don't even like. That's really impressive." We walked inside and I flipped on the light.

He placed the bags in his hands behind the sofa and carried the beer to the refrigerator. "I think even though it's only technically been a week, I know you pretty well." He smiled over at me. "And this is important to you and you're important to me."

"Just know I really appreciate it," I said. "Nathan does too, even if he's kind of an ass about it."

He started laughing as we went to the living room. "Holy crap, you went off on him back there. That was one of the sexiest things I've ever seen in my life."

I put the movies we had picked out on top of the DVD player.

"He deserved it. Everything that has happened here recently really is all of his doing."

He groaned and hooked a finger in my belt loop, turning me around to face him. "Oh, don't say that. I don't want to have to be grateful to him at all for bringing us together when I know he's trying to work his way in here when I'm not around."

I put my hands on his strong chest. "Nobody is going to be doing anything when you're not around." I looked up at him and motioned between us. "This is different."

He nodded and rested his forehead against mine. "*Different* doesn't even begin to cover what this is."

I closed my eyes and mindlessly traced my fingernails up his forearms. "We've still got to take this really slow until we know for sure."

"Sloan." His voice was commanding.

I looked at him.

He cupped my face in his strong hands.

When his lips touched mine, the rest of the world was obliterated. Every nerve in my body pulsed with energy as I melted into him. His fingers tangled in my hair and pulled my head back, forcing my mouth to open for him. I could no longer tell where his lips ended and mine began.

After what felt like an eternity that could never last long enough, he broke the kiss. The break in energy was like a shower of ice water. We were both breathless.

His deep voice was rough and desperate. "If we don't stop now, I'm not going to be able to."

"That was..."

"I know," he whispered.

Warren didn't sleep in my bed that night. We possessed superpowers, but defying temptation after that kiss wasn't one of them.

There was a fine line between 'playing it safe' and 'who cares if it might be incest', and that line was sandwiched between Warren Parish's perfect lips. That mind-blowing kiss was the first thought in my head when I woke up to the sound of a knock at my door the next morning.

"You awake?" Warren asked.

He was already showered and dressed in the tactical pants and black and bright orange pullover he had purchased the night before. I groaned and rolled over away from him. His boots clunked against the hardwood as he crossed my bedroom.

"What time is it?" I asked into the dark.

"4:15," he answered. "I let you sleep in a little longer."

"Fifteen minutes. You're not very generous," I whined.

The bed sank under his weight, and he ran his hand along my back. "How did you sleep?" he asked.

"Terribly." I thought of how well I had slept in his arms before. "You ruined me."

"I slept like crap too." He began massaging the muscles around my spine. "Come on. I made coffee."

I felt him move to get up, so I twisted my arm around and grabbed a handful of the front of his shirt. I pulled him toward me and he leaned down over my back.

His hand slid along the length of my arm till his fingers tangled with mine underneath my cushy pillow. "This is a bad idea," he moaned.

His warm breath dampened my skin as he dragged his lips across my neck.

"I don't care," I said.

For a second, I felt his weight press into me, but he quickly pushed himself off the bed. I rolled onto my back and looked up at him. He put his hands on his hips and shook his head. "You've got to get out of that bed, *right now.*"

I smiled.

He pointed at me. "Get up. I'm going downstairs." He turned

on his heel and left my room before I could tempt him any further.

When I came downstairs, ten minutes later, he was leaning against the kitchen counter drinking a cup of coffee. He smiled over the top of the mug. "Good morning, you evil woman."

I yawned and reached for an empty mug. "There is no such thing as a good morning."

He wrapped his arms around my waist from behind. "That's not entirely true. For a moment there, I was very tempted to make this a really good morning," he said, his lips against my ear.

I poured my coffee and smiled over my shoulder. "You know, it's not too late to say screw it all and go back to bed."

He pulled away and pointed at me again. "Don't even start."

I laughed and looked at the clock on the oven. "I'm surprised Nathan isn't here yet."

The doorbell rang. Warren shook his head and pushed passed me, smacking me on the backside as he went. "Adrianne's right. You are a freak."

"Those are big words coming from the guy who can sniff out dead bodies," I teased.

Warren chuckled as he pulled the front door open. "Morning," he said, stepping aside.

Nathan walked in. "Morning." He wiped the bottom of his boots on the welcome mat. "It's pouring out there."

Warren followed him to the kitchen. "I checked the weather in Raleigh. This storm will be there by the time we get there," he said.

I frowned. "Ugh."

"It will be better for us. There won't be as many hunters in the woods," Warren said. "I'd rather get wet than get shot."

Nathan laughed. "For real." Nathan's eyes fell on my new back door. He put his hand on his hip and glared in my direction. Under the brim of his ball cap his eyes echoed the patch on his hat that read, 'Whiskey. Tango. Foxtrot.'

"Want some coffee?" I asked, smiling like I was oblivious to the insult that had just occurred.

He shook his head. "Thanks. I've got some in my truck." He produced a large paper book from his jacket. "I talked to some buddies of mine last night and asked them where the most heavily tracked parts of the game land are. I figured those should be the last places we should check. I also picked up this book of hunting maps last night."

Warren nodded. "That's good." He pointed to the book. "May I?"

Nathan handed it to him. "Have you been there before?"

Warren shook his head. "No, but I'm no stranger to the woods."

I raised my hand. "I have a question. What are we going to do if we actually find something today? We can't exactly say we were out hiking in the rain and happened upon it." I looked at Nathan. "Not with you being so close to the case."

Warren flipped through the book. "I figured that out last night," he said. "I can call it in after you guys leave. I will say I was on my way home from visiting my girlfriend and was scouting the woods for escape and evasion drills in the spring."

Nathan crossed his arms over his chest. "Your girlfriend or your sister?"

I pointed at Nathan. "Don't start."

Warren was smiling down at the book.

I pushed away from the counter and stretched my arms up over my head. "Come on boys. I didn't get up before the sun to stand around chatting in my kitchen. If we hang out here much longer, I'm going back to bed."

It was a four hour drive to Raleigh. It rained the entire way. Thankfully, when we pulled into a parking area at Butner-Falls, the storm had minimized to a drizzle. The parking lot was almost empty. Nathan pulled his blue four-door truck up beside us, and we got out of the car. When we stopped in Winston-Salem,

Warren let me drive the Challenger the rest of the distance. I didn't think I would ever be satisfied with my car again.

Warren spread out the map on the hood of Nathan's truck. "I went over this on the way here. I think we should hit these areas first." He was pointing to three red circles he had drawn on the map. "Coupled with the list you provided, these areas are the most secluded. There are few trails for hikers to come stumbling through, and they are heavily wooded with lots of ground covering."

I adjusted the ball cap I had stolen out of the back seat of Nathan's truck. "If there aren't any trails, how are we going to find our way through the woods and back again?"

Warren and Nathan looked at each other and smiled for the first time ever at each other. "I think we'll be OK," Nathan said.

Warren made some notes on the map, and we started off into the woods.

I shook my head. "This feels like the set up to a really bad, B-rated horror movie. 'A sniper, a detective, and a publicist go into the woods...'"

Nathan laughed behind me. "Or a really bad joke."

I peeked over my shoulder at him. "Speaking of really bad jokes, how's your girlfriend?"

He stuck his middle finger up in the air and I laughed.

"Who do we think is buried out here anyway?" Warren asked over his shoulder.

"My sister," Nathan answered.

Warren turned around so suddenly that I slammed into his chest. "Oh shit. Seriously?" he asked.

Nathan nodded. "She's been missing for almost thirteen years."

"Man, I'm sorry. I had no idea." Warren shook his head and turned away again. "I was wondering why you are working on a case in Raleigh when you live in Asheville."

"He's been working on it his whole career," I said.

"Haven't had any good information until I met Sloan," Nathan said. "We didn't even know they were all dead."

"But you still don't know that they are all connected, right?" Warren asked.

"No, but it seems that they are," Nathan said.

"Follow your gut, man. If I've learned anything being whatever it is that I am, it's to follow your gut," Warren said.

After a half an hour of walking seemingly nowhere, I asked, "How big is that circle?" All I could see were trees in every direction.

"About a hundred and fifty acres," Warren answered over his shoulder.

"Um, I'm no expert, but I'm pretty sure that's a little bigger than a football field," I said.

"It's about a hundred football fields," Nathan said.

My mind flashed back to grueling laps around the football field during high school cheerleading practice. Back then, the terrain was flat and there were cute football players to discuss with Adrianne. Butner-Falls was cold and wet and without a level concrete path. The eye candy was definitely sufficient, but even the view of Warren from behind wasn't able to distract me from the dread of trekking through a hundred mountainous football fields in the rain. I wondered how much sweet-talking it would take to get one of my companions to give me a piggy-back ride.

I was really beginning to doubt myself and my theory about the murders when Warren finally stopped in a clearing with a view of the lake and shook his head. "There's nothing here," he said. "It's not this section."

I almost burst into tears.

"How do you know?" Nathan asked.

Warren turned and took my hand as he led me past Nathan. "The same way Sloan knew those girls were dead."

"You just know?" Nathan asked with an arrogant tone.

"I just know," Warren repeated.

"Sloan, why can't you do this?" Nathan asked.

I shrugged my shoulders. "I don't know. Why can't you do it?"

He smirked. "Funny," he said. "You know, not too long ago I was a real detective who did real police work. Now I'm wandering around the woods in the rain looking for dead bodies with two psychics."

"Ick," I said. "Don't use that word."

"I hate it." Warren laughed and looked down at me. "It always makes me want to break out singing, 'That's What Friends are For' by Dionne Warwick."

"That singer with the Psychic Friends Network?" Nathan asked.

"Ha! Yes," I answered. I smiled up at Warren. "And I think you should sing."

"I second that," Nathan agreed.

Warren was shaking his head. "Singing it in my head is bad enough."

We stopped for a sandwich when we got to the parking lot, and then we drove to the second spot Warren had circled. I didn't like the sight of it from the road. The incline was steep, and it went on for farther than my legs were willing to go. We parked in a grassy spot near a guardrail, and I got out and looked up. Straight up.

"I think I'm going to sit this one out, boys. I'll wait in the car with the heater and the radio on," I said.

Warren slung his backpack over his shoulders. He raised an eyebrow. "We're out here looking for the body of two dead girls who we believe were murdered by a serial killer in this vicinity, and you want to stay in the car alone?"

"I could wait with her," Nathan suggested with a sneaky grin.

Warren smiled and cut his eyes over at Nathan. "Then they might have to look for three bodies."

I groaned and re-tied my shoelaces. "Who would bury bodies on this cliff? That's stupid."

Warren looked at the map. "If the bodies are here, they will be on the other side of this hill. We could hike in from the access road on the other side, it's not as steep, but it is about eight times as far, and we would have to cross a river. The hill is our fastest route."

I looked down at my drenched clothes. "I don't think the river is a deterrent at this point. And stop calling that thing a hill." I pointed at the incline. "That's a mountain."

Warren shoved the map into his back pocket and offered me his hand. "Come on. It's not as bad as it looks," he said. "We'll be there before you know it."

I put my hand in his, and the three of us walked down into a creek before starting up the mountain on the other side. Some parts were so steep that we had to pull ourselves upward using tree roots that poked out of the ground. Halfway to the top, the sky opened up and the rain poured down once again.

"This is every single bit as bad as it looks, Warren," I whined as he helped me up onto a boulder near the top.

Nathan hoisted himself up after me. "I would like to take this opportunity to remind you, Sloan: this was *your* brilliant idea."

Warren put his backpack down and pulled out the map. I plopped down next to the pack and pulled out a water bottle. I offered it to Nathan. He took it and then stepped closer to look over Warren's shoulder. My wet hair was matted to my face, and my teeth were chattering. Cold rain drizzled down the bridge of my nose like a freshwater spring.

The other side of the mountain leveled off after a small decline from where we were. I could see the lake in the distance.

"It was a brilliant idea," Warren finally said. He was straining his eyes out over the view. "This is it."

I jumped up, causing water to squish out of my new boots in every direction. "What did you just say?"

Nathan stepped forward. "Where?"

Warren held his hand out. "That direction," he said, reaching for his pack. "Come on."

I had initially hoped that knowing we were on the right track would renew my strength, but the screaming pain in my legs proved otherwise. The only thing that improved was the rain finally let up again. Still, I didn't want to take another step. "OK, I'm done." I was dragging my heavy feet through the fallen leaves and the mud. "Who wants to carry me?"

"We're almost there," Warren insisted.

I tossed my head back over my shoulder. "Nathan, you wanna carry me?"

"No he doesn't," Warren said.

"This time, he's right," Nathan agreed.

We walked for another half a mile to an area thick with twisted mountain laurel and kudzu. Warren stopped so suddenly that I slammed into his backpack once again.

I rubbed my head where it smacked into a piece of the pack's hard plastic. "You've got to start warning me before you do that," I griped. "Maybe get a set of brake lights."

"There's a body buried under there." He was pointing to a spot on the ground, just beyond a fallen tree covered with moss and mushrooms.

My head snapped up. I looked around him for confirmation but didn't see anything suspicious in the mess of woodland brush. All I saw was a patch of decaying flowers and a mulberry bush.

Warren spun around to his left and started walking again.

"How can you tell?" I asked. "Can you describe it?"

He thought for a moment. "It kind of feels like the sucking force of a vacuum. Like the spot is swallowing up the life around it."

"That actually makes a lot of sense. I always know when a person is nearby because it seems like they are pulsing with energy and I can sense the vibrations," I said.

Nathan looked puzzled.

I put my hand on his arm. "It's OK. You wouldn't get it."

Warren began walking a wide circle, leaving Nathan and me watching him like he might sprout a long nose and a tail at any moment. He was like a six-foot-two bloodhound scouring the ground with his eyes.

About forty feet away from us, he finally looked in our direction. "There's another one this way." He took a few more steps to his left. "This one is easier to get to." He started toward a wild rhododendron.

"Should we disturb it?" I asked when we got closer.

Warren looked up at me. "How am I going to convince anyone there is a body up here if I don't have something to show them?" he reminded me. "I'll say I was scoping out areas for foxholes. I'll dig up some other places too."

He put his pack down and pulled out a large knife. I started to go with him, but Nathan blocked me with his arm. "Stay back. You and I should keep our distance. We aren't supposed to be here."

Warren ducked under the rhododendron and fought his way through more kudzu before he knelt down and began scraping at the ground with his blade. A few minutes passed and he finally stopped. "Bingo," he said.

I dug my nails into Nathan's arm.

Warren's hand came up, and resting on his fingers was a piece of bone that was hooked like the letter *J*. It was four or five inches long. He raised his eyebrows.

"Oh god," Nathan moaned. He folded his arms over top of his head and began to pace around.

"What is it?" I asked as Warren stood up still examining it.

Nathan paced the other direction and groaned. "It's a jawbone."

CHAPTER FOURTEEN

Even though we had been talking about it for two days, Nathan obviously wasn't prepared to actually find his sister's remains. If he hadn't been so worried about tainting the crime scene, I was sure he would've been vomiting. It wasn't the first time he had seen human bones, but it was the first bones that carried the probability of being his baby sister.

Warren carefully walked over and put the bone into a zip lock bag he had brought along. He turned it over in his hand so I could see the teeth that were still attached. I felt my stomach do a back-flip. I turned and covered my mouth with the back of my hand.

He nodded toward Nathan who had wandered farther away. "Go check on him," he mouthed.

Cautiously, I crossed the grass. "Nathan? You OK?"

He nodded, but didn't answer. His eyes were closed as he paced.

"Why don't you sit down?" I suggested. "Have a drink of water."

He shook his head furiously and walked away rubbing his hands over his face.

Warren caught up with us. The bone was tucked securely somewhere in his pack. "Let's get him out of here," he said quietly.

He walked over and clapped Nathan on his back. "Hey man, we've got to get out of here before you and Sloan leave too much of your presence behind."

Nathan blew out a hard puff of air and nodded. His hands were visibly shaking. He shoved his arms through the arm holes of his pack and turned in the direction of the cliff we had just scaled.

Warren let him lead the way back to the car. I was pretty sure it was to keep Nathan completely focused on where he was putting his feet instead of on what Warren was toting down with us. If that was his reason, it worked. Nathan was more himself when we reached the bottom, but he still went directly to his truck and climbed in the cab without saying a word. He sat there with his head on the steering wheel while I walked with Warren to the Challenger.

"What do we do now?" I asked him.

Warren carefully put the pack in the back seat. "You and Nathan need to get on the road. The sooner he gets home the better because I'm sure the cops around here are going to be blowing up his phone when they find out about it. I'm going to give you a few minutes head start so he's not recognized by some of the local law enforcement. I just can't wait too long because they won't be able to do anything if it gets dark."

I nodded. "OK."

He pointed over at Nathan. "Make sure he goes straight to Asheville. He's probably going to want to be with his family, but he needs to get home," he said.

I frowned. "I just realized this is going to be a really abrupt goodbye."

He draped his forearms over my shoulders. "I know. It sucks, but at least it's for a good reason," he said. "I'm glad we were able to find them."

I nodded. "Me too." I put my arms around his waist and my head on his chest. "Thank you so much, Warren."

He kissed the top of my head. "I'm glad I could help."

I looked up at him. "When will I see you again?"

"Next weekend. I'll come to you or I can fly you to New Hope," he suggested.

"Let's see how this week goes and we will figure it out," I said. "I'm sorry it's been such a crazy weekend."

He smiled. "Something tells me we're going to be having a lot of those."

I stretched up on my toes and kissed him quickly, knowing that I couldn't linger too long without us both of us being catapulted into the stratosphere and losing all track of time. "I'm going to miss you," I said.

"I miss you already," he said. "Come on. I'll put your things in Nate's truck."

Nathan was still face down on the steering wheel when we approached the truck. Warren opened the back door and put my bag inside. When he closed it, Nathan sat up. He looked a little better than he had at the top of the mountain, but his face was pale and his eyes were bloodshot. He stepped out of the truck and offered his hand to Warren.

"I can't thank you enough, Warren," he said.

Warren shook his hand and squeezed his arm. "I'm really sorry about all this, but I hope it helps."

Nathan nodded. "It does."

Warren put his hand on my shoulder. "You guys need to get out of here. I've got to call this in before it gets too late in the day, but I want you long gone before they start coming this direction."

"Why don't you let me drive?" I asked Nathan.

He shook his head. "Nah, I'm good. I can drive. Are you ready to go?"

I nodded. "Yeah."

Warren walked me around to the passenger's side and opened the door. "Keep me updated on where you guys are. Please be careful," he said.

I smiled. "I promise. Call me in a little while."

He pressed a kiss to my forehead and lingered for a moment. "I will."

Nathan and I drove for miles in complete silence. I couldn't imagine what was going on inside his head, and I certainly didn't know what to say, so I just rested my hand on the back of his neck. I watched the road ahead, lost in my thoughts, until the right side of my vision became a little blurred. Soon, the entire right side of the road was missing from my field of vision.

I groaned. "Oh no."

Nathan looked over at me. "What's the matter?"

I bent forward and opened my backpack. Thankfully, I had remembered to pack the medicine they gave me at the hospital. "Another migraine is starting." I fumbled through the pack. "Nathan, I need your help."

"Hold on." He flipped on his emergency lights and jerked the truck over into the emergency lane on the side of the interstate.

My hands were beginning to tremble. "I can't find my medicine. It's a white box with a prescription label. I can't see to find it!"

He slammed the truck into park and yanked my bag up onto the seat. He dumped its entire contents before finding the small white box. "Here, here!" He ripped the packaging open and popped the seal around the capsules inside their plastic. "It says you're supposed to take two at the onset." He thrust two pills into my hand.

I took some deep breaths and dropped the pills into my mouth without waiting for water to swallow them. He put a bottle of water up to my lips and instructed me to drink.

I laid my head against my seat. "Oh god, this is going to be bad."

"Should I find a hospital?" he asked.

I covered my face with my hands. "No. No. Just drive home.

We need to get out of here." I felt dizzy, and the pain was beginning like a pinprick in my skull just above the top of my ear.

"Where's your phone?" he asked.

I handed it to him.

A moment later, I heard his voice. "Warren, it's Nate. Sloan is getting another migraine. Really?" I felt his hand on my shoulder. "He's getting one too. He wants to know if he should meet us somewhere."

I reached toward him, grasping for the phone with my eyes clamped shut. "Let me talk." I pressed the phone to my ear. "Hey."

"Where are you guys? I'll come to you."

"No. We need to get home. Are you OK?" I asked.

"I'm getting worse by the second," he admitted. "I'm hoping they will be done with questioning me soon. I'm at the police station now."

"Nathan, drive," I said.

"It might stop if I come to you," Warren argued.

"You said it yourself. No stopping. We've got to get back to Asheville. I took the meds they gave me at the hospital. I'm hoping that will lessen the blow," I said.

"Ok," he said. "I'll call in and check on you."

"Please be careful, Warren." I was unable to imagine how he could begin to cope with dealing with the police in this state.

"Let me talk to Nate," he said.

I handed Nathan the phone as the car rolled onto smooth pavement. "Yeah?" Nathan asked. "OK. Of course. I've got her phone."

The medicine certainly helped. At the very least, I wasn't paralyzed or vomiting all over the truck. I was, however, slumped over the seat with my head in Nathan's lap for the rest of the drive. I also had his jacket shrouding my head to prevent the pangs from the headlights of oncoming cars. I cried the entire last fifty miles of the trip.

It didn't help that Nathan's phone started ringing non-stop by the time we crossed into Buncombe County. Though Nathan switched his phone to vibrate and tried to talk as quietly as possible, every word I heard was like an axe being driven into my skull. Even the silent buzz from his phone felt like a jackhammer. Finally, he turned his phone off when he realized my writhing intensified whenever he was on a call.

When we got to my house, I sat up and fumbled for the passenger side door.

"Wait, I've got it," he said.

He came around to my side of the truck and opened the door. "I'm going to get your keys and open up the house. Sit tight and I'll come back for you."

Sitting up was apparently a bad idea, and before he had gotten farther than a few steps away I started hurling, thankfully, onto the street. He held my ponytail out of the way and kept a firm hand on my shoulder to ensure that I didn't flop forward and crash into the asphalt.

When the puking subsided, he rubbed my back. "Can I take you to the hospital now?"

"No. Take me to bed, please," I begged.

He unlocked the door and carried me into the house. I held onto his neck until we got to my room and he carefully placed me on my bed. "I'll be right back," he whispered.

I reached for him. "No, Nathan. Go home. I'm fine."

"You're a terrible liar. I'm not leaving," he said.

I closed my eyes and tried to ignore the pounding of his footsteps against the hardwood floor. He turned on the water in the bathroom, and a moment later, my side of the bed dipped down under his weight. A cool washcloth touched my cheek. It felt like a kiss from heaven.

"I'm going to put this over your eyes to block out the light. They did it at the hospital and it seemed to help," he said. A moment later, the cool cloth was resting over my eyes.

His hands went to work on my boots and he carefully placed

each of them on the floor. Next, he stripped off my socks and then tugged my blanket up around my waist. I felt his hand on my thigh.

"I've got to make some phone calls, but I'll be back. I put a trashcan by the bed in case you've got anything left in your stomach."

I fumbled around until I found his fingers. "Thank you," I whispered.

He squeezed my hand, and then he was gone.

The next morning I woke up to the sound of an alarm I didn't recognize. My headache had calmed to a dull throb. I looked over to see Nathan reaching for his cell phone on my nightstand. The early morning sun filled the room.

I rubbed my hand over my face. "What happened?"

He silenced the alarm and rolled onto his side to face me. He was in a white t-shirt and what I assumed were a pair of blue, plaid boxer shorts.

"Are you in your underwear?" I asked.

He grimaced. "Well, you puked all over my pants."

I groaned and draped my arms over my face.

"And my boots," he added.

"Oh, this is so embarrassing."

He laughed softly. "How are you feeling?"

"My head hurts, but better." I looked over at him. "You stayed with me all night?"

He winked an eye at me. "And slept in your bed."

"Warren's going to be so pissed," I told him.

"Warren threatened my life if I left you alone," he said.

"Really?" I asked surprised.

He laughed and nodded his head. "Yeah. First, I threatened to kill him. Now he's threatened to kill me. I think we've reached the first level of friendship."

I raised an eyebrow. "Friendship?"

He laughed. "OK, maybe not exactly."

"What time is it?" I asked.

"Six," he said. "Do you think you'll go into work today?"

I groaned. "I have to. I have a feeling this is going to be a crazy week for all of us."

He nodded and sat up. "I'm sure it is. I'm probably going to head to Raleigh today."

"What happened last night? I could hear you talking on the phone, but I couldn't make sense of anything because of the pain," I said.

He swung his legs off the bed and wrapped the bed sheet around his waist for the sake of decency. He walked to my bathroom and rinsed out his mouth with my mouthwash.

"Well, some of my buddies in Raleigh called to tell me that some guy found a skeleton at Buckner-Falls. They said they thought it might be a young female, but they wouldn't know for certain until they heard from the medical examiner. I told them I had a theory about the suspect being an avid hunter and that they should canvass the area with cadaver dogs. They said they were going to today. My story sounded plausible enough, I guess."

I pushed myself up in the bed. "How are you doing with it all?" Nathan had removed my hiking boots and socks, but I was still dressed in my jeans and even my rain-resistant, bright orange pullover.

He splashed water on his face. "I'm all right. It was a pretty big shock yesterday, but I feel better knowing we found her, if in fact it is her," he said.

"Have you talked to Warren? Did he make it home?" I asked.

"He was in pretty bad shape when he was threatening my life. They questioned him for a few hours but released him without any suspicion. I think he was going to stop and rest for a while before trying to drive," he said.

I walked into the bathroom behind him and grabbed my toothbrush. "Where are your clothes?"

"In the dryer. I washed them last night while you were passed out," he said. "I hope that's OK."

I laughed and squeezed toothpaste onto the brush. "I puked all over you. The least I can do is let you wash your clothes." I looked up at our reflections in the bathroom mirror. My hair was halfway in and out of my ponytail, my face was black with mascara and dirt, and my eyes were swollen and puffy. "Well, I look awesome."

He laughed. "Like a princess."

I spat toothpaste into the sink and stuck my tongue out at him.

He smiled and left the bathroom. A few minutes later, I turned on the shower and he walked into my bedroom fully dressed as I was picking out an outfit for work. He strapped on his tactical belt and checked his gun before tucking into his side holster.

"I've got to run home and change and head to the department. Call me later and let me know how you're doing," he said.

I walked across the room and put my arms around his neck. "Thank you so much, Nathan."

He was smiling when he pulled back, and he wiped a smudge of black out from under my eye. "Anytime, Sloan."

A couple of pain pills knocked out what was left of my headache on my drive into work. Still, the world seemed a little too bright, and my brain seemed to be half a step behind in processing thoughts and paperwork. It was like having a hangover without having the good time the night before.

The morning was exceptionally mundane except for the news articles that kept coming through my email from the state capital. By that afternoon police had located the other body in the woods, and the medical examiner confirmed that the first skeleton was that of a teenage female. The police and the media were all speculating that the remains were of Ashley McNamara and Melissa

Jennings, and some reporters were already saying the murders may be the work of a serial killer.

I didn't hear from Nathan again that day other than a text message to check on how I was feeling.

I had called Warren that morning before leaving the house. He was awake but still in a great deal of pain. He promised to call me later, after he figured out if he was going to make it to work. When his name popped up on my caller ID again, I was sitting in my office with my feet propped up on my desk, eating a bag of pretzels and drinking a Diet Coke out of the vending machine.

I pressed the answer button and held the phone to my ear. "Hello."

"Hey," Warren said.

I popped another pretzel into my mouth. "Hey. How are you feeling?"

He groaned. "Like someone took a battle axe to my skull last night. I came into work, but I'm counting the seconds till I can leave and go home."

"You should stop leaving me," I said.

"I agree," he said. "Did the meds help you last night? Was it any better this time?"

"It was definitely better, but I still ended up puking all over Nathan," I said.

He chuckled softly. "So I heard."

"Did you also hear that he slept in my bed last night?" I asked.

His end of the line was quiet for a beat. "No," he finally said. "I asked him to stay with you, but that's not exactly what I meant."

I smiled. "Not to worry. I woke up in my blue jeans and rain coat."

"Still," he grumbled and blew out a sigh. "What are you going to do tonight?"

"It's Monday," I said. "I have dinner with my parents on Monday nights."

"Do you think your dad has had a chance to get the results of our blood test?" he asked.

"That's what I'm hoping to find out," I said.

"Well, call me as soon as you can if you find anything out. I've got to get back to work," he said.

"I promise."

I was lost in my office. Putting together announcements about road closures and the submissions deadline for the county online cook-book almost seemed insulting after discovering a human jawbone the day before. I was thankful when five o'clock came and I could head to my parents' house for dinner. I didn't feel like going. I really wanted to go home and climb back into my bed. That desire, however, was trumped by my curiosity to know if Dad had heard anything from the lab about the DNA test.

I was surprised to find Dad's car in the driveway when I got to their house. Dinner was already on the table, and Mom was filling three glasses with sweet tea when I walked in and put my purse down on the counter. "Hey," I said. "Where's Dad?"

"Upstairs," she answered as I leaned over to give her a welcoming kiss on the cheek. "He will be down in a minute."

Looking at my mother, something snagged my attention once again. I couldn't put my finger on what it was, but something felt strange about her. I studied her face until she sheepishly blushed.

She touched her cheek. "What?"

I smiled. "Nothing. Can I help with dinner?"

She shook her head and smiled. "I've got it," she replied. "How was your day?"

"Better than my night," I groaned.

"What happened last night?" she asked.

I leaned against the counter. "Another migraine."

She put the tea pitcher down and walked over to me. "You should've called me," she said. "Or you should've gone to the emergency room."

"Mom, I can't go to the ER every time I have a headache," I said.

She pointed at me. "You shouldn't be alone when those things hit you. That's pretty dangerous."

I shook my head. "I wasn't alone. Detective McNamara stayed with me."

She raised her eyebrows and smiled. "Oh really?"

"Yes, but stop looking at me like that. There is nothing going on with me and Nathan," I said.

Her smile grew and she shook her head. "I'm not so sure about that."

I rolled my eyes and laughed. To be honest, I wasn't so sure either.

Dad appeared in the kitchen. He came over and gave me a hug. "Hi, sweetheart."

"Hi, Daddy," I answered. "How was work?"

He smiled. "Not too bad. I left a little early today at your mother's insistence, so I'm not complaining. How are you?"

Mom squeezed my shoulder. "Your daughter had another migraine last night."

His brow wrinkled. "Really?"

I nodded. "Yes. I took the medicine though, so it wasn't as severe."

He shook his head. "I don't like this, Sloan. I think we should schedule some more tests. Maybe it's time to meet with a neurologist."

"No, Dad," I objected. My eyes brightened. "But…speaking of tests?"

A thin smile spread across his lips and he lifted an envelope in his right hand.

I beamed at him, but he shook his head and motioned to the table. "Let's sit so the food doesn't get cold."

The tone of his voice sounded ominous. The DNA test results were in that envelope. I knew it.

We all sat down to three steaming plates of meatloaf, mashed potatoes, green beans, and bread. Monday night dinner was usually the only homemade meal of the week that I ever had. When I put a forkful of buttery mashed potatoes in my mouth, I regretted not paying attention more when my mother cooked.

The table was silent for a few minutes. My father looked lost in thought as he chewed his food and my mother looked nervous. I wiped my mouth and put my napkin on the table. "OK, what is going on? You guys are killing me."

My dad reached for my mother's hand and gave it a reassuring squeeze. "The lab rushed your test results for me and I have them."

I sat forward on the edge of my seat. "Well, what does it say?"

Dad shook his head. "I don't know. It would be illegal for me, as your father, to look at them without your permission."

I shot my hand out. "Well, *gimme*!"

He slid the envelope toward me, but pressed his fingers down to prevent me from picking it up. "Sloan, your mother and I want you to know that no matter what, you will always be our little girl, even if you do want to know who your birth family is."

I focused on their faces. My mother looked like she might melt into a puddle of tears at any second. I had been insensitive with my vague explanations of how this had all transpired. I took my hand off the envelope and pushed my plate back. "Mom, Dad, of course I've always been curious as to where I came from, but I'm not on a quest to replace you. I met Warren by accident and we had a lot of similarities and I got curious. That's all this is. I promise."

"Well," my mother began, "if he is your brother, we want you to know we are truly happy for you, and we will always do whatever we can to support you. Even in finding your birth family."

I smiled. "Thank you."

She seemed to relax a little.

Dad released the envelope and I snatched it up. I tore it open and pulled out the letter inside which contained a spreadsheet full of letters and numbers that I didn't understand. The results might as well have been written in hieroglyphics. "Uh, what is this?"

"If you're looking for a green check mark or a red letter 'x' you're not going to find it." My dad was grinning. "Want me to have a look?"

I handed it to him and sat on my hands to keep them from shaking completely off of the ends of my arms. "Please."

He examined the paper for a moment. My mother was leaning toward him. He adjusted his glasses. "Well, sibling tests done without a sample from at least the mother are very difficult to determine. This is actually two different tests. One of them assumes you have the same mother and the other assumes you do not. You and Warren do share some of the same alleles, but both tests fall on the probable side that you are not siblings. The percentages and odds are extremely low."

"He's not my brother?"

Dad handed me the piece of paper. "No one can say with absolute certainty, but the DNA test says most likely not."

I sat back in my seat. My mother reached across the table and squeezed my hand. Her smile was sympathetic. "I'm sorry, honey."

I laughed. "I'm not."

She looked surprised, and she glanced from me to my father.

"You weren't hoping you had found your brother?" Dad asked with a raised eyebrow.

"No." I laughed and shook my head. "I mean, it would have been nice to know I had a brother out there and maybe finally get some answers to questions I've had all my life, but no. I was really, *really* hoping Warren wasn't related to me."

Dad's shoulders relaxed like he had been preparing for me to have a meltdown. "Well, congratulations are in order, then!"

I laughed with relief. "Do you mind if I excuse myself for a moment? I need to call Warren."

"Go ahead, honey," Mom answered.

I grabbed my phone from my purse and carried it out onto the back porch. I looked out over the light-speckled mountains which suddenly seemed full of hope and possibilities. I dialed Warren's number.

"Hey." His voice was groggy.

"Were you sleeping?" I asked.

"A little. I came in and fell asleep on my couch right after work. It's been a rough day," he said.

"Are you ready for it to get a whole lot better?" I asked.

After a beat of silence his voice came over the line much more coherent than it had been before. "I told you I wasn't your brother."

A blue truck was parked at my curb when I got home. Nathan looked up from his cell phone as I slowly drove by. I waved and pulled into my driveway. He was standing under the streetlight on the sidewalk when I made it around to the front.

"Hey." I fumbled through my keyring. "What are you doing here? Returning for another slumber party?"

He laughed and followed me up the front porch steps. "I don't know. Is that an invitation?"

I grinned at him over my shoulder as I used my key to tumble the deadbolt. "Come on in," I said as I pushed the door open. "Have you been here long?"

He shook his head as we stepped inside. "I had just pulled up when you came home."

I turned on the light switch. "You should have called me."

He stripped off his ball cap and placed it with his keys on the table in my foyer. "I was on my way home and decided to drop by."

"You don't live anywhere near here." I smiled at him as I shrugged out of my jacket and hung it on the hook near the door.

He winked a steel gray eye at me. "I decided to take the long way home."

I smiled and flipped on the light in the living room. "Fair

enough."

He followed me to the living room. "I was surprised you weren't home when I got here. I came by assuming you would be in your pajamas by now."

I looked over my shoulder at him. "Well, I thought I would be too, but it's Monday and that means it's dinner night with my parents. I didn't want to cancel it because my dad had some really big news to tell me."

"News?" he asked.

"Yeah. Warren and I had a DNA test done last week, and Dad got the results in today," I answered.

Nathan faltered a step as we walked into the living room. "Really? Can I ask what it said?"

I sat down in the corner of the sofa and tucked my legs underneath me. "We're not related."

He sank down on the edge of the seat next to me. He nodded and forced a smile. "Well, I guess I should congratulate you."

I lowered my gaze at him. "I know you wouldn't mean it."

He shrugged his shoulders. "I want you to be happy, Sloan, and I get why you're with him. He's got an edge nobody can compete with."

It was really hard for me to know that my happiness was unintentionally painful for Nathan. I cared about him so much, but he was right; there wasn't anyone who could compete with the connection I had with Warren. Still, I felt Nathan deserved my apology. "Can you keep a secret?" I asked.

He raised his eyebrows in question.

I leaned toward him. "From the moment I saw you at the sheriff's office during your oath ceremony, I had the biggest crush on you. I was so devastated when you told me you had a girlfriend that I almost cried in your car."

He laughed. "Really?"

"True story," I answered.

He looked down at his hands. "I'm really sorry about that."

I reached over and squeezed his forearm. "I'm sorry about this now."

"I know," he replied.

I nudged him. "Different subject. Why did you come by here on your 'long way home'?" I asked. "I wasn't expecting to see you again tonight."

He leaned forward, resting his elbows on his knees. "I wanted to stop by to see how you were feeling and to tell you goodbye. I'm leaving in the morning and don't know how long I'll be gone."

"Raleigh?"

He nodded. "Yeah. My mom is pretty hysterical, understandably so. And if it is Ashley, then we will have to make a lot of arrangements for her body."

My stomach felt queasy thinking about the jawbone Warren had found. "How long will it take them to know for sure if it's her or not?"

He shrugged his shoulders. "I'm sure it will at least be a few weeks," he said. "The investigation will go on for a while, but we will eventually have a burial service for her, I guess. We already had a memorial service a couple of years after she disappeared."

I groaned. "That sucks. Will you keep me updated on what's going on out there? And, certainly, let me know if there's anything I can do to help."

"Of course." He raked his fingers through his hair. "You know, we've been through a hell of a lot together in a really short time."

I laughed. "You can say that again."

He pushed himself up off the couch and offered his hand to help me up. When he pulled me to my feet, he looked down to where his hand was wrapped around mine. "Can you keep a secret?" he asked quietly.

I smiled. "Yeah."

He tugged on my hand and stepped toward me. His free hand slipped behind my head as he brought his lips down onto mine. Nathan tasted like Skittles.

CHAPTER FIFTEEN

Warren said he would be late on Friday, but that he was coming for the weekend. He had a meeting on Friday afternoon, and he said he would leave as soon as he was able. I was at home waiting for him that night when there was a knock at my door around nine o'clock.

It was Adrianne, wearing a party dress and enough makeup to be in a televised beauty pageant. "You haven't been answering your phone," she said.

I stepped aside to let her in. "I've been busy and didn't have time to talk."

She looked around my living room. "Where's your boy toy?"

"He's on his way. What are you doing here?"

"I had to run over to the salon because I ran out of bobby pins." She framed her hands around her formal updo. "Like my hair?"

It was spectacular, as usual. "It's gorgeous."

She pointed at me. "Since you've forgotten how to use a phone, I came by to kidnap you for this party." She looked up and down at my blue jeans and black V-neck sweater. "But you need to change."

I looked down at my outfit. "What's wrong with my clothes? I thought I looked pretty good." I had actually spent over an hour getting redressed after work.

She tugged on the hem of my sweater. "You can't go to a party like that."

I pushed her hand away. "I'm not going to a party at all." I sat down on the couch. "Warren will be here soon, and we are spending the night at home."

She smiled and leaned against the armrest with a mischievous grin. "Like, spending the night at home or *spending the night at home?*"

My face flushed. "He and I have a lot to talk about."

She laughed. "Yes. I'm sure there will be plenty of talking."

"Either way, we're not going out," I said. "What party is it?"

"Mark and I are going to the opening of a new club on Merrimon Avenue. It's called Crush. Everybody's been talking about it," she said.

With all that had happened in the past week, I had almost forgotten that Mark Higgins even existed. I choked back the bit of nausea that seemed to accompany thoughts of him and put my feet up on the coffee table. "I guess I've been too wrapped up in skeletons and boy problems to hear about the latest buzz in the Asheville nightlife."

"How's the detective doing since they identified his sister?" she asked.

The thought of Nathan's kiss resurfaced in my memory, triggering a mix of butterflies and guilt in the pit of my stomach. I hadn't told anyone about that night.

I pushed the thought away and shrugged my shoulders. "I don't really know. He's been in Raleigh all week with his family."

Adrianne sighed. "That's so sad."

"Yep, but at least I think they have some closure now," I said. "I think not knowing is worse."

Her phone beeped. She looked down at the screen and then up

at me. "I've got to run. Mark's going to pick me up at my house in five minutes."

I stood up and walked with her to the door. "Are you dating Mark now?"

She laughed and waved her hand toward me. "Just having fun," she said. "It's nothing serious. Maybe we can double date sometime soon."

"Sure. I would *love* to hear Warren's opinion about him," I said with a smirk.

I opened the front door just as Warren had raised his hand to knock.

Adrianne shook her head and looked at me. "I don't think I'm ever going to get used to you being such a freak." She kissed me on the cheek. "Call me if you change your mind. Hey, Warren!"

"Hi, Adrianne," he replied.

"I'm not going to change my mind!" I called after her as she walked out.

She giggled as she carefully maneuvered her way down the stairs in her heels. "Have fun you crazy kids."

"You have fun, and be careful!" I shouted.

I looked up at Warren, and my breath caught in my throat. "You're finally here!"

He stepped inside. "I'm sorry I'm so late." He put his bag down by the door and reached for my hand. "I had a really important meeting at work."

"About what?" I asked.

He pulled me to him. "I'll tell you in a minute." He bent and covered my mouth with his. He pushed the front door closed and moved me back against it. When he finally released me, I would have fallen to the floor had he not had his arms around me.

I laughed as he rested his forehead against mine and the world seemed to swirl back into place. "I'm almost afraid for us to go any further than that," I admitted. "I worry my heart might stop or my brain might explode."

He smiled against my cheek. "That would be a hell of a way to go out." He pulled away and looked at me as he bit his lower lip. "I plan on testing it out very soon, but I want to talk to you first."

I exhaled slowly, still trying to catch my breath. "Talk to me about what?"

He tugged on my hand, and I followed him to the living room. "What did Adrianne want?"

"She wanted us to go to a party with her and this creep, Mark, tonight. I told her no."

He sat down on the sofa and pulled me down next to him. "Do you want to go?"

I laughed and leaned into him. "Hell no."

He draped his arm over my shoulders, and I reached up to hold onto his hand.

"Have you heard from Nathan?" he asked.

The guilt returned. "I got a text from him this morning saying he convinced the FBI and the state to send search teams into the game lands around the areas where the girls disappeared."

He nodded. "That's good. Did he say if they positively identified the bodies?"

I shook my head. "He's pretty sure it's his sister and the other girl, but he said it could take a while to get anything from the medical examiner. Before he left, he told me they are planning to do a burial service for his sister sometime, but they can't till the state has finished with her remains."

He wove his fingers in and out of mine. "Are you going to the service?"

"Probably so," I said. "I can't imagine how hard this has to be for him."

Warren kissed my temple. "I can't either. I may hate him, but Nate's not a bad guy."

I smiled over my shoulder at him. "You don't hate Nathan."

"If I hadn't been as sick as I was on Monday, I would've driven back over here and kicked his ass for sleeping in your bed," he said.

I laughed. "You told him to stay."

He nodded. "He could've slept on the floor."

It felt like an angel and a demon were arguing on my shoulders about whether or not I should tell Warren about Nathan kissing me. Nathan had asked me to keep it a secret, but it felt wrong. "He stopped by before he went to Raleigh, and I told him the DNA results said we aren't related." Silently, I gave one point to the good angel on my left shoulder who was urging me to be honest.

"How did that go?"

I sighed. "He was pretty obviously disappointed, but he said he understood why you and I are together. He even said, 'congratulations'."

Warren chuckled. "That's bullshit."

"Maybe," I agreed.

"Not 'maybe'. Nathan is in love with you," he said.

I kissed his fingertips. "But I'm with you now," I said, and I knew I meant it.

I sighed and decided to give a point to the demon on my right shoulder by changing the subject before the conversation about Nathan went any further. "What did you want to talk to me about? I know it's not about Nathan McNamara."

He nodded and turned in his seat. I turned around sideways so I could look at him, folding my legs under me. He tucked his hair behind his ears. "You know how I'm a contractor for Claymore, right?"

I nodded.

He took my hands and rested them on my lap. "So you understand that it's only for a contracted period of time with no guarantees for a continuation after the contract is over, correct?"

I nodded. "Yes."

He sucked in a deep breath. "Well, they offered me a permanent position with them today. That's what the meeting was about."

"Really?" I asked surprised. "That's a good thing, right?"

He moved his head from side to side. "Well, the money is great. So are the benefits."

I raised an eyebrow. "But?"

He looked down at my hands. "The job is in Oregon."

My mouth dropped open. "Wow."

He nodded. "Yeah. It's a pretty big deal."

"What did you tell them?" I asked.

He sighed. "I told them I would have to think about it. I said I had some reservations about moving that far."

"What are your reservations?" I asked.

He squeezed my hands. "You. You are my only reservation."

I took in a slow, deep breath and then blew it out even slower. "Wow. OK," I said. "So if I weren't in the picture, you would take this job."

He nodded. "In a heartbeat."

It was like the weight of the world fell onto my chest. My shoulders sank down, and I balanced my elbows on my knees for support. It was a lot of pressure, especially considering I had cheese in my refrigerator that had been around longer than Warren.

He put his finger under my chin to lift my eyes to meet his. "I know this is a lot to put on you. We've technically only known each other for what? Twelve, thirteen days maybe?"

I laughed. "Yeah."

He pulled my fingers up to his lips and kissed them. "Sloan, I don't know about you, but I feel like I am finally where I'm supposed to be for the first time in my life. When I'm with you, it's just...right. It's like gravity has aligned when we are together."

I knew what he was talking about. There was something there. Something between us that couldn't be seen or explained or probably understood by anyone else in the world. It wasn't necessarily love; in many ways, it felt much bigger than that. Whatever it was seemed to be a cosmic or even supernatural desperation to be connected. I had never been one to believe in fate or predestination... not until I first brushed the hand of Warren Parish.

He shook his head. "I don't know what to tell them."

"When do you have to give them an answer?" I asked.

He gave a reluctant smile. "That's kind of good news. They gave me the next week off to really think about it and come to a decision."

"What happens if you accept?"

"Then I would be on the West Coast by mid-October," he said.

"That's just a few weeks away," I said.

He nodded. "I know."

"And if you turn it down?" I asked.

He shrugged. "Then they probably won't offer me another contract when mine runs out at the end of the month. Or, maybe they will. I don't know for sure."

I rubbed my face over my hands. "Wow. That's big."

He dropped his head. "I know. I'm sorry. This is way too much, way too fast, but I couldn't make this decision without talking to you first."

My mind was racing. "What are you asking me, Warren?"

He brushed a loose strand of hair out of my face. "I realize this is absolutely crazy, but would you ever consider going with me to Oregon?"

My mouth dropped open again. I laughed. "Really? Seriously? Are you asking me to move to the other side of the country?"

He turned his hands over. "I need to know if it's a possibility."

I thought of Adrianne and our lunches with martinis and goat cheese grits. I thought about Monday night dinners with my parents and the fact that I still didn't know how to make her mashed potatoes. I even thought of Nathan McNamara leaning against the wall in my office. "Warren, I've got my Mom and Dad here and Adrianne. I've got my career and my house—"

He nodded. "I know. That's why I'm asking."

My phone rang. Adrianne's face was on the screen. I hit ignore and put the phone on silent before placing it on the coffee table.

I turned my palms up. "I can't make this decision for you, Warren. If you want to go, we will just have to figure it out."

"Sloan, you don't understand." He pressed his eyes closed and then opened them. "If you won't even consider it, then I'm turning the job down. End of story. I can't stand being on the opposite side of the state from you, I can't imagine how much harder it would be if I were on the other side of the country."

"You're going to turn it down?" I asked.

He wrapped his fingers around mine. "I'm not asking you for some big commitment or anything, but I do know that no matter whether or not you and I end up together, I can't be that far away from you."

"But what will you do?" I asked. "Where will you work?"

He laughed. "I'm a marksman. This is probably the easiest place in the US for me to get a job. It may not pay six figures a year, but it would be near you."

"Six figures?" I asked.

He nodded. "Yeah. Does that change your mind?"

I laughed and shook my head. "No. I can't leave my family. At least not in a few weeks. But I don't want to be without you either." I clasped my hands over my heart. "Is that really selfish of me? That I want to stand in the way of a really great opportunity for you?"

He ran his fingers through my hair. "Do you realize that no one ever in my life has been selfish for me? I would give up all the money in the world to be wanted that badly."

He hooked his finger inside the collar of my sweater and pulled me close. His lips touched mine, sending sparks through my body. He pulled back and smiled. "Did we just decide I'm moving here?"

I giggled. "I think we did."

He grinned and stood up, offering me his hand. When I was on my feet, he tucked my hair behind my ear and trailed his knuckles down the side of my neck. His eyes, dancing with mischief, glanced to the stairs behind me. "Can I take you upstairs and try to kill us both now?"

I laughed. "Please!"

Without another word, he bent down and grabbed me around my thighs. He slung me over his shoulder, and I laughed all the way up the stairs. When he returned me to my feet at the foot of my bed, I nearly fell over from all the blood rushing from my head. He smiled and smoothed my hair into place. His dark eyes searched mine and my giggles quickly faded.

I bit my lip as he slowly reached for the top button on his white shirt. When all of the buttons were undone, I pushed his shirt off of his shoulders. Underneath was a black, fitted t-shirt with a distressed picture of the Grim Reaper on the front. I looked up at him in silence as I untucked the shirt and pulled it up. When I couldn't reach any higher, he tugged the shirt off over his head.

For the first time, I could see the full length of his tribal tattoo. I traced the lines with my fingertips. There was a claw that came down the center of his chest and curved to a point toward his ribcage. The lines came up along his left collarbone and spread wide over his shoulder and down to his elbow. He slowly turned to show me the back. There were three more large claws that stretched from his shoulder to halfway down his spine. It was a talon, like that of a massive eagle, gripping his body from above.

"Wow," I whispered.

He turned back around and slid his hands up the curve of my jaw. He tipped my face up and slowly brought his lips down to meet mine. His touch was gentle at first, but as his fingers twisted into my hair, the kiss deepened until he released every reservation he had held each time before. With one smooth motion, my sweater was on the floor and his hands were working at the clasp of my bra. He pulled my body against his as he slipped the straps off my shoulders. I pressed my teeth into his salty skin at the bend of his neck and heard my name.

But…my name wasn't coming from Warren.

"Sloan?" I heard again, closer this time. I broke free from him.

"That's my mother!" I said in a panicked whisper.

"Sloa...oh oh!" Mom nearly choked on my name as she staggered backward as soon as she walked into my room.

"Mom!" I snatched up the closest discarded shred of clothing my fingers found and wrapped it around my chest.

She had stumbled out of my room to the hallway. Warren sat down on the edge of the bed, laughing.

I looked around the corner to see my mom panting and gripping her chest. She was leaning against the wall. "Mom, what are you doing in my house?"

"I used my key. You didn't answer when I rang!"

"I didn't hear the doorbell!"

She threw her hands in the air. "Obviously." She was still panting. "I'm sorry. I didn't know you had company."

"What do you want?"

Her face sobered. "You need to get dressed. Your father just called me from the hospital. It's Adrianne. There's been an accident!"

Warren stood and I darted out into the hall and grabbed my mother by the arm. "What?"

"Your dad called and said they brought her in by ambulance. It's bad. You need to go," she said.

I pressed my eyes closed and reached out into the world with my gift to find my best friend. She was alive, but that was all I knew.

Warren came out in his black t-shirt and handed me my sweater. "Let's go," he said.

CHAPTER SIXTEEN

Mark Higgins had been drunk when he came by to pick up Adrianne. They never made it to the party because he had driven his Jeep off an extra high road shoulder, flipping it. As is the case with most drunk drivers, Mark was practically unscathed; Adrianne, however, had been ejected.

My father had been on call and was at the hospital with a patient when they brought her in. He had tried to call me several times, but my phone had been on silent. When the three of us got to the hospital, I ran to the emergency room's waiting area.

Her mother, Gloria, who was like a second mom to me, crossed the room when we walked in. She started crying, and she gripped me so tight I feared my head might pop off.

"How is she?" I asked as I pushed her back enough to search her bloodshot eyes.

She sniffed and wiped her runny nose on the cuff of her sleeve. "I don't know," she cried. "They had to take her into emergency surgery because of swelling on her brain."

My father came in right behind us and slipped his arm around my shoulders giving me a gentle squeeze. "Hey, sweetheart."

"Do you know anything?" I asked frantically.

He shook his head. "Not much. She wasn't conscious when they brought her in, and she didn't look good. They said she had a lot of obvious broken bones, but the head trauma was their biggest concern. I'm trying to get any information I can, but unfortunately, we just have to wait." He looked over at my mother. "I've got to finish up with my patient, but I'll come back here when I'm done."

I turned toward Warren and buried my face in his chest and cried. He kissed the top of my head and rubbed my back, but even his magical touch brought little comfort. Adrianne had called me, and I had ignored her.

After a couple of hours in the waiting room with Adrianne's parents and mine, the doctor walked in, hugging a clipboard to his chest. "She's stable," he began. "There was very severe swelling from a head injury, so we placed a monitoring device in her skull to gauge the pressure in her brain cavity. We are giving her medicine to keep her sedated. It will give her body some time to repair itself. The next few hours are very critical. I'm not going to lie. This is very serious." His face was grim. "It will be a miracle if she makes it through the night, but it's still a possibility."

It felt like invisible hands were squeezing and twisting my heart like a dishrag inside my chest. There didn't seem to be enough oxygen in the waiting room anymore. Warren's hand rested on my hip, and I remembered to inhale.

I took a step toward the doctor. "Can we see her?"

He nodded his head but held up his hand. "Once we get her settled and stable in the ICU, two visitors at a time will be allowed in. It will still be a little while before anyone can go back." He sucked in a deep breath. "Please understand she has severe lacerations and bruising on her face. She's intubated, very swollen, and her head is in a stabilizer. It can be a very disturbing sight."

"What else did you find?" Adrianne's mother asked.

The doctor sighed and glanced down at his clipboard. "Besides the brain injury, she has a broken arm, a cracked shoulder blade, three broken ribs, two broken fingers, a broken leg in three places, and more stitches than we could keep track of." He looked up again. "The head trauma is the only thing potentially life-threatening at this point, but she's very banged up."

"Where's the jackass who put her in here?" I nearly shouted at him.

The doctor took a cautious step backward. "The driver of the Jeep was taken into police custody after being treated for minor injuries. That's all I know."

I wished I had Warren's ability to stop a beating heart.

I looked up at my dad. "Do you think she's going to make it?"

He slipped his arm around my shoulders. "Tonight will be the real test," he said. "The odds of her recovery will increase exponentially in the morning."

Tears rolled down my cheeks, and I quickly brushed them away with my sleeve.

I choose to distract myself with anger. "Do you know what happened to Mark Higgins, the driver she was with?"

Dad lowered his voice. "The driver had six stitches above his left eye and a bruised sternum, but you're not supposed to know that. I'm sure he's at the county jail by now."

Anger boiled inside of me.

He squeezed my arm. "I'm going to take your mother home. Are you going to stay here for the night?"

I nodded. "Yeah," I said. "I can't leave."

"I'll stay with her." Warren stood up and offered his hand to my father.

My dad shook it. "I'm glad you're here, son."

I wondered if that would remain true if Mom decided to tell Dad what she had interrupted earlier at my house. I hugged my mother. "Thanks for coming to get me." I dropped my voice to a whisper in her ear. "And I'm really sorry."

She gave me an awkward smile. "Call us if anything changes. Do you want me to bring you some more comfortable clothes?"

Warren stepped forward. "I'll go by the house and get some for her," he said. "Thank you, Mrs. Jordan."

Her smile was even more awkward with him. "Thank you, Warren."

They left, and I sat down beside Gloria. Warren knelt down in front of me. "What do you want from the house? I'm going to go change and grab you some clothes."

I tried to think. "Just some sweats or something," I said. "They are in the tall chest of drawers on the bottom."

He nodded. "Do you need anything else?"

I shook my head and kissed his lips. "No, thank you."

While he was gone, Adrianne's parents were allowed in to see her. When they returned, I was permitted to go in. Adrianne's mom came with me. I froze once I stepped behind the curtain in ICU. There were more tubes going in and out of my best friend than I had ever seen in my life. Her face was so badly injured that I wouldn't have recognized her. Even with the bandaging, I could see they had to partially shave off her beautiful hair.

A doctor stepped in and asked to speak with Mrs. Marx. Before she left, she touched my arm. "Are you all right?" Her eyes were puffy and bloodshot.

I nodded, and she walked out into the hallway with the doctor.

I went to Adrianne's bedside and picked up her left hand. It was unmangled, unlike her right, and still perfectly manicured. I bent down and cried as I grasped her fingers. The machines around us beeped and wheezed, buzzed and clacked. I kissed her nails. "Please fight," I whispered. "Please stay with me."

A moment later, a nurse bustled into the room, and I straightened and wiped my eyes on the back of my sleeve again. "How is she?" I asked.

The small framed woman made some notes on a piece of paper and checked the readout on the machine that was beeping in rhythm with Adrianne's heart. "Her heart rate is increasing. That's a good sign," she said.

I rubbed my best friend's cool fingers as they laid lifeless in my hand. "She's going to beat this." I sniffed. "She's going to come through."

"We're all pulling for her and praying," the nurse said with a sympathetic smile.

Praying, I thought. I had never been much of a praying type of girl, mainly because I had big doubts about a god that could be in control over the entire universe and allow some of the wickedness I had seen and felt in people. If a deity did exist, I wasn't even sure how to pray to him—or her. But for Adrianne, I would try anything. I pressed my eyes closed. *God, if you're listening. I need a favor...*

For a long time, I watched the changing numbers on the machines around the room. I didn't know much about blood pressure, but I knew numbers like 56/40 weren't good. Slowly, the numbers inched up and with each minute increase, I nearly broke out in cheers. When the nurses came in to check her vitals again, I trudged to the waiting room.

Warren was sitting with our little group, slowly swinging the backpack I had carried on our hiking trip between his knees. He stood up when he saw me, and I walked into his arms and buried my face in his chest. "Shh..." he said as I began to sob. He tucked me under his arm and turned me toward the door. "Come on. Let's take a walk."

We stepped out of the waiting room into the hallway. Once we were away from Adrianne's family, he pulled me in close and let me weep in his arms. "She looks so bad," I cried.

He kissed the top of my head. "You heard the doctor. There's still a chance. Don't give up on her yet."

I gathered the fabric of his shirt in my fists and cried until I ran out of tears. When the sobbing subsided he nodded toward the door. "I brought you some clothes and a couple of pillows. Why don't you change and get more comfortable? This is going to be a long night."

I wiped my nose on my sleeve and nodded. I followed him inside, and he handed me the backpack. "Thank you," I said.

He nodded toward the bathroom and nudged my elbow. "Go change."

The single bathroom was empty when I walked in and locked the door. It was the same bathroom where I had changed after bringing Kayleigh Neeland to the hospital. I splashed water on my face before stripping off my sweater and reaching into the bag. I pulled out my blue Victoria's Secret sweatpants and a black S.W.A.T. hoodie I had never even washed.

The next morning, I awoke in a puddle of my own drool on Warren's lap. I had been up and down all night checking on Adrianne but had slept for a couple of hours stretched out across him and three of the plastic chairs in the waiting room.

"Morning," he said as I sat up and wiped the drool off my chin. He was grinning.

If I hadn't been so exhausted, I would have been mortified. "Good morning. Did you sleep at all?" I asked through a yawn.

He gave a weak smile. "A little."

"Have you heard any updates?" I looked down at the time on my phone. It was just after eight in the morning.

He straightened in his seat. "They said she steadily improved overnight and the swelling has decreased significantly. Her mom said you can go and see her whenever you wake up."

"Do you want to come with me?" I asked.

He frowned and shook his head. "It's not a good idea for me to be around critical people. They always seem to get worse."

"Really?" I asked.

He nodded. "Unfortunately," he said. "You go see her, and I'll go get us some breakfast."

He started to get up, but I stopped him and put my arms

around his neck. "I'm so sorry that, once again, our time together hasn't worked out."

He laughed. "Shut up. I'm here. That's all I need. Go see your friend. I'll be here when you get back."

I kissed him and walked toward the ICU.

Mrs. Marx went with me into the ICU room, but stayed to the side so I could get close to Adrianne. I traced my finger along her hand, careful to not disrupt her I.V. "She looks the same."

"They say the worst of it is over," Mrs. Marx said. "The swelling has gone down and her vitals look much better than they did last night."

I let out a deep breath and kissed her hand again. Her fingers flinched under my lips. I sat up and looked at her face. Her eyes were fluttering. Her left eye, which wasn't as swollen as the right, flickered open briefly. "Adrianne?" I leaned down close to her face.

Her mother stepped close to the other side of her bed.

Adrianne's eye flickered again, and I could see a hint of hazel. "Adrianne?" I repeated.

Her fingers slightly curved around mine, and for an instant, she looked at me. I cried again and looked up at her mom. "Gloria, did you see that?"

"I did. Adrianne, can you hear us?" she asked.

Adrianne's fingers bent slightly again.

"She's trying to squeeze my hand," I said. "Come here!"

I stepped aside and let her mother take hold of her fingers. Her eye opened again and she looked at her mother. Gloria began to cry and I covered my mouth with my hands. Another nurse, a male one, came into the room. "What's going on?" he asked.

"She's waking up," I said.

He shook his head and stepped to her bedside. "That's impossible. It's probably nerve endings firing at rand—"

He stopped in the middle of his sentence when he checked her eyes and Adrianne looked right at him. Without thought, I grabbed his shoulder and almost shook his arm from the socket. "Did you see that?" I shouted.

He leaned closer to her. "Adrianne, if you can hear me, I want you to try and blink."

I leaned in close behind him. Adrianne forced her eye closed and then reopened it.

"I'll be damned," he said.

Gloria Marx was about to collapse onto the floor.

The nurse stepped out of the room. "Jamie, call Dr. Wilson. Adrianne Marx is awake."

"Awake?" another voice asked.

"You heard me," he said.

I practically ran to the waiting room. When I went through the door, I slid to a stop so fast I almost lost my footing. Warren—and Nathan—stood up. Nathan looked down at my shirt, raised an eyebrow, and scrunched his mouth over to the side.

My eyes doubled in size as I cautiously moved forward. "Hey," I said. "You're back."

Nathan nodded. "I got in last night. I heard about Adrianne this morning, so I thought I would stop by and see if you were here." He held up a bag from McDonald's. "I brought breakfast."

I smiled and stopped in front of him. "Thanks."

He looked down at the shirt again and back up. His eyes were asking, *Really?*

Warren folded his arms over his chest and nodded toward Nathan. "I filled him in while you were gone."

"Oh my gosh. She opened her eyes. Like, just now while I was in there!" I clapped my hands together. "The nurse said it was impossible, but she did it! She actually did it!"

"That's awesome," Nathan said.

Warren bit his lower lip and looked up at the ceiling.

"What is it?" I asked.

He nodded toward the corner. "Come over here."

"All of us?" Nathan asked.

"Sure. Why not?" Warren said.

We stepped to the empty corner of the room.

I folded my arms across my chest. "What's up?"

Warren ducked his head and lowered his voice. "Do you remember what I said earlier about not wanting to visit her?" His eyes narrowed. "About how I might make her worse?"

I nodded.

"I think this might be one of those situations where you do the opposite," he said.

Nathan's eyes darted with confusion from me to Warren. "Huh?"

"Do you think I'm healing her?" I asked.

Warren shrugged, but his eyes were affirmative.

Nathan held up his hand and stared at me. "Wait. Now you can heal people?"

I turned my palms up.

Nathan pointed at Warren. "Are you saying you make people sick?"

I elbowed him in the side. "Keep your voice down."

"You certainly make me sick," Nathan grumbled.

Warren laughed and I elbowed Nathan again.

Warren shrugged. "I think it's an idea worth exploring."

Nathan shook his head and walked across the room to our seats. "I haven't had enough coffee for this shit."

We followed him, and he handed me a cup of coffee as I plopped down in the seat between them.

"Thanks," I said. The coffee burned my throat. "How are things going with the case?"

Warren passed me a sausage biscuit out of the greasy paper bag.

"Really good," Nathan said. "Search teams are starting to look today in the game lands close to where the abductions happened."

"I hope they find the rest of them," I said. "You guys aren't dragging me through the woods again."

"I thought you did pretty well," Warren said.

"Minus the whining, complaining, and constantly trying to con us into carrying you," Nathan said.

I shot him a glare and pointed my finger at him. "You know, you're pretty hateful considering you'd still be sitting in your office with your thumb up your butt in front of that bulletin board if I hadn't come along. The FBI must think you're a genius for coming up with the hunter thing."

He laughed. "They actually do. They're talking about bringing me on."

I straightened. "Really?"

He crossed his boot over his knee. "Yeah. If we solve this thing, I may be moving again."

"Warren got offered a new job too," I said. "Everyone is trying to run away from me, I think."

Nathan looked across me to Warren. "What's the job?"

"Permanent field training position out in Oregon," he said.

Nathan perked up. "You gonna take it?"

Warren sipped his coffee. "I doubt it."

"It sounds like a good opportunity," Nathan said.

Warren cracked a smile. "For me or for you?"

I jumped in to redirect the conversation before it escalated. "What's Shannon think about the FBI thing?"

"I haven't told her yet." He paused. "She probably won't be too excited since she hated my stories about being on the *S.W.A.T. team*," he said, adding more emphasis to his words than necessary.

I tried to sit back against the seat, but Warren grabbed the back of the sweatshirt I was wearing.

He looked at Nathan, tugging on the hoodie. "This is yours?"

I dropped my head.

Nathan smiled. "It looks good on her, doesn't it?"

Warren slid his hand across my shoulders. "I must have thought so because I picked it out for her *in her bedroom* this morning."

I covered my face with my hands. "Will you two stop it? I'm about to make you both yank out your junk and have a pissing contest right here in the waiting room."

An older couple a few seats down from us turned their wide eyes in our direction. I gave them an apologetic smile.

Nathan got up and stretched his arms. "I'm going to take off anyway. Give Adrianne my best. Keep me posted."

"Thanks for the breakfast, Nathan," I said as he walked across the room.

"No prob," he replied.

"Later, Nate," Warren called.

Nathan gave him the finger before walking out of the room.

Adrianne kept improving throughout the day, particularly when I was in the room with her, so Warren and I went home that evening. I was so tired my brain felt like it was fogged with tear gas. We both fell onto my bed in unison.

I groaned and tugged the comforter over my legs. "I don't think I've ever been so exhausted in all my life."

He flopped back against the pillows and draped his arm across his eyes. "You think you're tired? I've been up since four yesterday."

I rolled over toward him and rested my head on his chest. He wrapped his arm around my back and then shook his head. "Nope. This isn't going to work," he said. "Sit up."

"What?"

He pushed me off of him. "Sit up."

We both sat up in the bed.

"Arms up," he instructed.

I put my arms in the air and he pulled off Nathan's shirt and sent it flying across the room. He pulled me down against his chest. "Now, you can go to sleep," he said.

I laughed and closed my eyes.

CHAPTER SEVENTEEN

I woke up alone again in my bed the next morning. The alarm clock read 8:07 in the morning. Rolling over and sleeping for another hour was a tempting idea, but I wanted to check on Adrianne, and I could smell fresh coffee downstairs. Before sitting up, I grabbed my phone off the nightstand and saw a new message from Adrianne's mom.

She's off the ventilator. Vitals are good.

I closed my eyes and smiled.

Reluctantly, I pushed myself off the bed and shuffled to the bathroom. Warren's toothbrush was in the holder next to mine. With butterflies fluttering in my stomach, I brushed my teeth and then my hair. I applied a light coat of lip gloss before heading downstairs in my sweat pants and sports bra.

Warren looked up from the couch where he was watching television. He was showered and dressed for the day. He put the remote control down on the cushion beside him and smiled. "Good morning, sexy."

I wrapped my arms around his neck from behind. "Am I always going to wake up alone?"

He looked at his watch. "If you always sleep in till eight, most likely."

I shook my head. "I don't like it."

He pulled me around in front of him and down onto his lap. A mischievous grin slowly crept across his chiseled face. "Trust me, I lay there for a very long time before I finally got up. I kept contemplating seriously disrupting your peaceful sleep."

I put my arms around his neck and pulled his ponytail holder out. His black hair fell around his shoulders. "Why didn't you? I would have had no objection." I ran my fingers through his hair which was still slightly damp from the shower.

He squeezed my knee. "Well, I knew you would wake up wondering about how your best friend is doing. Call me sentimental, but I don't want you to be thinking of anything else the first time we are together. That's why I left the bed."

"Oh, that's actually really sweet." I rubbed my nose against his.

He shrugged. "I'm a big softie. What can I say?"

I laughed. "Right."

He rubbed his hand up my thigh. "Get dressed. Let's go check on your friend."

I smiled. "I need a shower. Want to join?"

He dropped his head backward and groaned. "I try to be a good guy with you, and you go and say crap like that."

I pushed myself up. "Fine. Fine," I said. "Give me ten minutes."

"Hey!" He grabbed my arm and pulled me down. He kissed me, then released me. "Now you can go."

I smiled and skipped upstairs.

When we got to the hospital, Gloria Marx and my Dad were talking in the waiting room.

They both stood up when we walked in. "Hey Sloan," she said smiling.

"Hi, Gloria. Hey, Dad. What are you doing here?" I asked as I stepped underneath his outstretched arm.

Dad smiled. "I came by to see how she's doing. I admitted a

patient last night, so I was here this morning anyway. Hi again, Warren."

Warren waved hello.

I looked between Gloria and my dad with wide eyes. "How is she this morning?"

She nodded. "I was just telling your dad she's doing really well. They took her off the ventilator late last night because she kept trying to wake up. So far, so good. They are talking about maybe even moving her out of ICU later today and into critical care."

"Really?" I asked surprised.

"Yep. I swear it's a miracle," she said. "You can go on to see her if you want."

I smiled. "Thanks."

"Gloria, I'm going to go with Sloan if you don't mind," Dad said.

"Of course not. I need to make some quick phone calls," she said.

I looked up at Warren. "Are you going to wait out here?"

He nodded. "Yeah. I'll be here when you get back."

I gave him a quick peck on the lips and walked with my father down the hallway.

When we were out of earshot, Dad leaned down close to me and lowered his voice. "Is it safe to say I can reasonably assume why you were happy Warren wasn't your brother?"

I felt my face turn red. "Yes, I think you can assume correctly." I hoped he wouldn't push the topic any further.

"Well, I do hope you bring him over to the house soon so we can get to know him better. He's kinda fallen out of the sky as far as we're concerned," he said.

"I will, Dad. Soon," I said.

When we got to Adrianne's room, a nurse was changing out one of her I.V. bags. I was amazed at the difference in Adrianne's appearance. A lot of the machines were gone, some of the tubes had been removed, and her cheeks were a more natural pink. "Wow, she looks so much better," I said to my dad.

"Well, with her blood pressure being so low before, and with the drugs they give to keep the pressure on her brain down, it sort of sucks the life out of a person. The pressure in her brain has significantly decreased, so everything in her body is working much better than before. It's a drastic improvement in two days, really. I'm very surprised," he said.

I walked over and touched her hand. She felt much warmer than she had the two days before.

Her eyes opened ever so slightly and she tried to contort her mouth into a smile. "Witch," she whispered.

I laughed. "You almost die and the first thing you say to me is call me a witch?" I asked. "That's some crap."

She wiggled her fingers in my hand.

"How are you feeling?" I asked.

She slightly shook her head and closed her eyes. Tears rolled back onto her pillow. I wiped them away while fighting my own.

"Well, my dad is here and even he can't believe how well you're doing. You're going to be fine, Adrianne. The worst of this is over. Well, maybe not..." I scrunched up my nose. "They screwed up your hair pretty bad. You're going to be pissed."

She tried to laugh, but it was obviously too painful for her.

"Stay," she whispered.

I smiled down at her and lowered my face toward her. "I'm not going anywhere."

Dad stepped over by the bed. "Hi, Adrianne. Sloan is right. You're doing incredibly well. Each day it's going to get better." He patted her leg—the one that wasn't in a full cast. "I'm going to check on you every time I'm at the hospital and make sure they are taking the best care of you."

She didn't respond, but she followed him with her eyes.

He put his hand on my shoulder. "She's going to have a hard

time talking because her throat is really sore from the ventilator, but she's surprisingly coherent."

"Did you hear that? Dad says you're coherent, but you can't talk. That means you have to listen to me and for once keep your mouth shut," I said.

Dad was chuckling to himself. "I'm going to let you girls talk." He leaned over and kissed me on the head. "I love you, Sloan."

"Love you too, Daddy," I said.

When he was gone, I gently sat down on the edge of her bed and held her hand. "You're not going to believe what you did," I said. "I was half naked in my bedroom with Warren—for the very first time, mind you—when my *mother* showed up and barged in on us to tell me your ass was in the hospital. Who's really the witch here?" My eyebrow rose with skepticism.

She tried to smile again.

I folded my arms across my chest. "I really hate you, you know?"

She reached her hand toward my face and I bent to meet her fingertips. "Love," she whispered.

I grasped her hand and kissed it. "I love you, too."

Warren and I left the hospital around lunchtime and went to Papa's and Beer Mexican restaurant to eat. I frowned at him over my fajitas. "I just realized I have to go to work tomorrow. Today is Sunday."

He nodded. "All day long."

I thought it over. "It's impossible for me to take vacation time tomorrow, but I could try and take off toward the end of the week."

"Do what you've got to do, babe. I'll be fine," he said.

"What are you going to do while I'm at work?" I asked.

He sipped his water. "I dunno. I thought about maybe heading up in the mountains and looking around for a few hours. I came a little more prepared with gear this time than I did last weekend."

"You're going to look for the girl who went missing around here?" I asked.

"Maybe," he replied.

"Well, tomorrow I'll probably go see Adrianne over lunch if you want to join me," I said.

"Yeah, we'll see where I'm at when you're ready to go," he said.

I sighed. "I'm glad the worst of this is all over. I hope it is anyway," I said. "I don't know what I would ever do without her."

"I think she's going to be all right," he said. "You actually got her to talk."

"Do you really think I can heal?" I asked.

He nodded. "I think so," he said. "You seem to literally be my better half. Sick people get sicker around me, so it only makes sense they would get better around you."

I dug around with my fork on my fajita skillet looking for another piece of grilled chicken. "I wish I could figure out how to do this stuff on purpose."

"You've got to work at it," he said. "Exercise it till you get better."

"How do I exercise it?" I asked.

"The summoning thing is pretty obvious. You just need to figure out what works and what doesn't," he said. "We could try together."

I pointed my fork at him. "OK. Let me try and summon Mark Higgins, and then you can take him out."

He laughed and pointed at me. "Interesting idea but not exactly what I meant."

"Then what did you mean?" I asked as I bit into a piece of chicken.

"When was a specific time it happened?" he asked.

I thought about it for a second. "The very first time you showed up at my house after I left Nathan's."

He narrowed his eyes at me. "Are you sure that wasn't a coincidence? Because I'm certain I was going there anyway, and I know you didn't call me there on purpose."

I waved a small chunk of a green pepper in his direction. "That seems to be how it happens most of the time. I don't do it on purpose. You didn't feel anything weird?"

He shook his head. "No. I just knew I had to see you."

I shrugged "I don't know, then."

"Have you ever tried to do it on purpose?" he asked.

I nodded. "Sure. I tried for years when I was younger to summon my birth mom," I said. "And maybe a few cute boys."

He rolled his eyes. "But were you serious about it?"

"My birth mom? Absolutely." I shook my head. "I don't think I have to be serious about it. Did I ever tell you about the night I told Adrianne?"

"No," he said.

"I was home from college and we were at this restaurant not too far from here. She was always teasing me because she thought it was funny how people would randomly show up after I had mentioned them. That night, she was begging me to try and summon this guy she was crushing on," I said.

He slid his empty plate across the blue tile tabletop. "What did you do?"

"I pretended I was meditating. I pushed my chair back, crossed my legs, and everything. Then, she started throwing stuff at me and she made me repeat 'Billy Stewart' after her three times."

"And?" he asked.

"And when we walked out of the restaurant, maybe ten minutes later, he drove by. It scared the crap out of both of us because we knew he was supposed to be in a completely different town at work."

He thought for a moment, then tapped his finger on the table. "When I do, *what I do*"—he looked at me with knowing eyes—"it's almost like I speak to them. I see it in my mind before it happens, and I will it on them."

"I did not see Billy Stewart in my mind sitting outside of that Italian joint," I said.

He pointed at me and leaned against the chair next to him. "Maybe not, but I'll bet you wondered what would happen if Adrianne saw him there. I'll bet it crossed your mind what would happen with her if Billy did show up."

I sat back in my chair. "I've never thought about that. That makes sense. I'm sure I probably did."

"I'm also pretty sure your curiosity about me was the same as mine about you that night you were talking to Nate about me," he said. "You wanted to meet me."

"That's true," I said.

"So try to do it now," he said.

"You want me to summon Billy Stewart here? Right now?" I asked.

He shook his head. "No. Try someone else. What's something else you need to do?"

I thought for a moment. "I need to talk to my boss, Mary Travers, about taking the rest of the week off."

He nodded. "That should work."

I pressed my eyes closed and pictured my boss with her mousy brown bob and her smushed face. "Mary Travers."

When I opened my eyes, he was grinning at me.

I laughed and threw a green pepper at him. "You just made me feel like an idiot!"

He laughed. "That was kind of funny." He turned his hand over. "But you never know. It might work."

I rolled my eyes. "Shut up," I said. "Finish your food. I wanna get out of here and actually do something with you today before the week gets crazy."

"I'm trying to figure out if your life is ever not crazy," he teased.

"It's certainly been very crazy lately." I pointed at him. "It's been straight up chaos ever since I met Nathan McNamara."

My phone rang. Warren and I looked at each other.

"If this is my boss, I'm going to go and check myself into the psych ward right now," I said.

He smiled.

I looked down at my phone and then showed Warren. It was Nathan. "I should check myself in anyway," I muttered. I shook my head and answered the phone. "Hey."

"Hey, what are you doing?" he asked.

"Practicing voodoo with Warren." I wiped my mouth with a napkin and then dropped it onto my skillet. "What's up?"

"I wanted to give you a heads up that Mark Higgins, the guy who was driving Adrianne, just bonded out of jail," he said.

My mouth fell open. "Are you serious?"

"Yep."

"How did that happen?" I asked.

"That's how the system works, Sloan. Go to jail, bond out, and wait for your court date," he said.

"That's completely unacceptable!" I slammed my palm down on the table. "I guess I'm going to have to handle it myself!"

"What are you going to do?" he asked, obviously trying to contain his amusement at my outburst.

I pushed my chair away from the table. "I can go find Mark Higgins!" I said and disconnected the call.

"What was that about?" Warren asked.

"Come on," I said. "It's time to go inflict some street justice."

He laughed. "What?"

I shot up out of my chair. "That guy—that creep—who was driving drunk with Adrianne bonded out of jail."

He looked up at me. "What are you going to do about it?"

"I'm going to go find him and kick his ass!"

He laughed and dropped a twenty dollar bill on the table before standing up. He wrapped his hand around mine. "You're so sexy when you're a raving lunatic. Let's go."

I pulled him toward the door and threw it open. A group of Sunday morning churchgoers almost went flying through the parking lot as I stormed outside. When I looked down, I realized that one of the tiny women I had plowed into was my boss.

I stumbled backward into Warren.

"Hi Sloan!" she cheered. "Where are you off to in such a rush? Who's your friend?"

I tried to make my mouth form words but only disjointed syllables came out. "I, uh…the, uh—"

Warren reached around me. "Hi, I'm Warren."

She extended her tiny hand to meet his, smiling brightly. "Hello, Warren. I'm Mary. Sloan and I work together at the county office."

Warren laughed. "No shit?" he said just loud enough for me to hear.

I went into a coughing fit and covered my face with my hands.

Mary grabbed my arm. "Are you OK?"

"I'm fine," I choked out. "I'll see you tomorrow, Mary."

Warren ushered me toward the car. "Well, congratulations, Ms. Jordan, you have mastered your superpower."

"That's crazy!" I jabbed my thumb into the center of my chest. "I'm crazy!"

He held the door to the Challenger open for me and gripped my jaw in his hand. "You're not crazy. You're just not exactly normal."

I huffed and sat down in the car.

He got in and started the engine. "Do you still feel like going and kicking some ass?"

I leaned against the door and covered my eyes with my hand. "No. Just take me home. I need a drink, and I need to lie down."

"I think that's probably a good idea," he said, backing out of the parking space. "I think all the stress and exhaustion is starting to get to you a little bit."

Warren stopped at the grocery store on the way home. He put

the car in park but left the engine running. "I'm going to run in and get some beer and food to make for dinner."

I groaned and sank down in my seat. "I don't cook, Warren."

He winked at me. "I do."

I sighed and rolled my head toward him. "Will you marry me?"

He blinked at me and laughed. "Sloan, you're putting a lot of pressure on me."

I rolled my eyes. "You started it."

When we reached my house, I opened a beer in the driveway.

While he put the groceries in the kitchen, I flopped down on the sofa and put my feet up on the coffee table. I pinched the bridge of my nose and prayed my head would stop hurting.

"You didn't ask your boss for your vacation time," he reminded me.

"Oh, I'm sorry." I smirked. "I was a little bit distracted."

He came into the living room and clinked his beer bottle with mine before sitting down on the coffee table so he could face me. "I think it's pretty cool what you can do," he said as he tipped the bottle up to his lips.

I frowned. "Of course you do. You can kill people."

He laughed. "Think about it. It's a pretty spectacular gift, Sloan."

I shook my head. "Nobody cares about your opinion."

He smiled and leaned toward me. "Why don't you go upstairs, take a nice hot bath, and drink your beer in the tub? Try and clear your head for a little bit. You've had a pretty big weekend all the way around."

I sighed. "What are you going to do?"

He smiled and gave me a gentle peck on the lips. "It's a Sunday in September. I'm going to watch football."

Obediently, I did as he said and went and finished my beer in the hot bath tub. My brain hurt because it was so full of everything that had transpired in the past month. I wasn't sure how much more I could stand. I laid my head against the wall and closed my eyes. *What am I?* I asked over and over again.

Just when I was about to drift off to sleep, there was a gentle knock at the door. I opened my lazy eyes and smiled at Warren who was standing in the doorway.

"Feel better?" he asked.

I nodded. "Much better."

"I think you must have been talking about me..." He slowly crossed the bathroom floor and picked up a towel off the rack. "Because I had this supernatural urge to come up here."

I smiled. "Oh really?"

He nodded his head and smiled. "Yes. It had absolutely nothing to do with the fact that you were wet and naked in the bathtub."

I laughed and reached for the towel he was holding. "Well, I have to get out, so turn around."

He shook his head. "No."

"No?"

"No." His deep tone signaled he wasn't joking.

My heart started to pound in my chest as he towered over me. More than just physically, I was certain Warren had reached heights of experience I had never dreamed of. For me, each romantic encounter left me with a feeling of emptiness, like each lover had been cosmically coerced into my bed. Warren was different. There was no compulsion to his desire. It was raw and genuine and dripping from his eyes as he watched me stand up.

The towel slid from his fingers and fell to the floor as he closed the distance between us. This time, when his lips connected with mine, there was no interruption. There was no holding back. He carried me to my bedroom and covered my body with his own, obliterating every thought of everything else outside of the powerful force of our connection. When it was over, and his sweat was mixed with mine, I was certain of one thing:

I had died in that bed…a couple of times.

CHAPTER EIGHTEEN

Warren was asleep next to me when I woke up the next morning. I was sure it was an occurrence that wouldn't soon be repeated. I smiled and studied the way his silky black hair fell across his perfect face as his muscular arm curled around his pillow. "I feel your eyes on me, Sloan." He didn't even crack a smile.

"I thought you were asleep," I said, tangling my legs with his under the covers.

His lips spread into a thin smile. "I've been thinking of different ways to wake you up since four." His arm slipped under the covers and grasped my bare hip. He pulled my body into his, and his eyes fluttered open.

I pushed his hair off his face. "I'm not sure my legs are going to function today."

He shook his head as his fingers trailed down my spine. "That's OK. You don't need them."

I groaned. "I have to go to work."

He rolled on top of me, his full weight pressing my body into the mattress. "Are you sure?"

"Yes." No.

He pinned my hands over my head and nibbled at the side of my neck. I squirmed underneath him. "I'm going to be late."

"I don't really care."

A half an hour later, I pulled on his t-shirt and my wobbly legs carried me to the bathroom. "What are you going to do today?" I asked as he watched me, smiling, from the bed.

He folded his arms behind his head. "I'm probably going to go scout out the woods and look for that girl from here."

"Leslie Bryson," I said, sticking my toothbrush into my mouth.

"Yep. Maybe I'll meet you at your office and take you out to dinner tonight," he said.

I turned to look at him. My cream colored bed sheet was wound around one of his legs and barely tugged up to his belly-button. I dribbled toothpaste down the front of his shirt and forgot what I was going to say.

He smiled. "Don't go to work."

I groaned and spit in the sink. "I have to." I grabbed the bathroom doorknob. "And I'm never going to get there with you watching me like that." He laughed, and I slammed the door.

Warren had made me a to-go cup of coffee before I left the house, but my travel mug was empty by the time I reached my office. For the first time in my life, I understood why so many people hated Mondays. The weekend hadn't been long enough, and my mind was still at home in bed. The last thing I wanted to do was send out tourism specials for all of Asheville's leaf-enthusiasts. Warren had been right; leaves were stupid.

To add insult to injury, I had an email waiting from the sheriff when I turned on my computer. They were going to have to shut down the public forests in the middle of hunting season, and he would have to make a statement to the press during the five o'clock news hour. That meant I had to make a trip to the jail, and

I had forgotten my Xanax due to Warren's distraction that morning.

Very reluctantly, I left my office and drove to the jail around eleven a.m. Knowing he would be out of the office for the day, I parked in Nathan's parking spot when I pulled into the lot. Anxiety began to pulse through my veins the moment I stepped out of my car.

Ms. Claybrooks wasn't even working at the master control desk to distract me. As I walked down the hallway to the sheriff's office, I nervously wrung my hands and practiced deep breathing exercises. I tried to replay the steamy events of my morning and the night before in my head, but even that wasn't enough to dilute the evil which seemed to envelope me from every direction.

"Are you all right?" Sheriff Davis asked with wide eyes when I walked into his office.

I nodded and sat down across from him. "Just a bit of a headache. I'll be fine."

In record time, I hammered out an apology to the hunters of Western North Carolina. The wildlife game lands would close that day at dusk and would reopen as soon as the area had been thoroughly investigated. I made the necessary phone calls to the media from the sheriff's office, and then I promised to meet him for the broadcast on the front steps of the sheriff's office right after lunch. When he was satisfied with his announcement, I made a bee-line for the exit. My heart rate had to be registering somewhere between cheetah and drumroll.

As I bolted through the final door that would lead to the lobby, I slammed face-first into a green and gold uniform. "Oh, I'm so sorry!" I looked up into the face of Billy Stewart.

He cocked his head to the side and laughed. "Sloan Jordan?"

Billy Stewart was as handsome as he had been when we were kids. He was carrying about twenty more pounds on him and had a few new lines around his eyes, but I could still see why Adrianne had always liked him so much.

Even in the midst of my panic attack, I laughed. "Billy, I was just talking about you over lunch yesterday and here you are!"

"Talking about me?" he asked surprised. "I don't think I've seen you in what? Ten years or more?"

"At least!" I was gripping my chest.

"Are you all right?" he asked.

I nodded. "Yeah, I'm fine," I lied.

"Hey, I heard about your friend Adrianne being in the hospital. That's terrible what happened to her." He crossed his strong arms over his chest. "How's she doing?"

I nodded. "She's getting better every day. I was just on my way to see her."

He raised his eyebrows. "I've been thinking about dropping by there myself. Mind if I tag along?"

Adrianne would kill me if I let Billy Stewart show up with her in the condition she was in, so I smiled. "Sure, but I'm heading out right now though."

He shrugged. "Not a problem. I've got to come back here afterward anyway. Wanna ride on the county's dime?"

I smiled. "Sure." I was desperate to get out of that building as quickly as possible. "How have you been? How's your family?" I asked, begging for conversation to distract me as we crossed the lobby.

He nodded. "Well, my dad passed in '09, and my mom moved to Statesville to be near her sister, but she's doing pretty well."

"Oh, I'm sorry to hear that."

"It was a heart attack. It happened fast and to be honest, he was an asshole anyway," he said. "How about your folks? Your dad still at the hospital?"

I nodded as he held open the door. It was all I could do not to run from the building like my hair was on fire. "Yeah. He's doing a lot of Alzheimer's research these days. Mom and Dad are both doing well."

"That's good to hear," he said. We reached the bottom of the steps and he nodded toward a green truck with the county emblem on the door. "This is me."

I got in the passenger's seat, and he put the files he was carrying in the back seat before getting behind the wheel. I took a series of deep breaths as he pulled away from the curb and gripped the handle on the door to help ease the shaking I couldn't control in my arms.

"What are you doing up this way today?" I asked.

"Had to drop off some paperwork about this search effort they are starting up in the morning."

I nodded. "I was just meeting with the sheriff about it."

He shook his head and chuckled. "There's gonna be a lot of pissed off rednecks 'round here."

He pulled out onto the street and straight into the sunlight. I shielded my eyes as I saw something move out of the corner of my eye. A sharp jab in my thigh caused me to shriek and grab for my leg. As we passed under the shade of an orange oak tree I could see Billy scowling at me. "Why were you talking about me yesterday, Sloan?"

"What?" I asked. I was still trying to inspect my thigh. Whatever it had been had gone straight through my pant leg and into my skin. That's when I saw Billy drop a syringe down between his seat and his door. My brain was scrambling to catch up.

"Why were you talking about me?" he demanded.

"What did you do?" I cried. A wave of dizziness washed over me.

"Don't worry," he said. "Pentobarbital only takes a minute."

"Pentobarbital?" I asked confused.

"Large animal sedative," he explained. "That's one of the perks of being a game warden."

After that, the world swirled out of view.

When I awoke, I was handcuffed to a radiator in a musty cabin with dirty wooden floors. There were holes in the baseboards from small woodland squatters. My head was throbbing and my stomach felt sick. Pain was pulsing through my knees and there was dried blood down my forearms. I looked around at the one room hunting cabin. The sun was low in the sky and casting a warm glow through the chilly room. I had been unconscious for hours.

It appeared as though I was alone, but I knew better. I could sense Billy's presence nearby. On the floor, just out of my reach, the photos of the missing girls were splayed across the floor. My briefcase was open lying next to them.

Oh god. I panicked as the realization of what was happening settled in.

I pressed my eyes closed. "Warren Parish...Nathan McNamara...Warren Parish...Nathan McNamara," I repeated quietly.

"They ain't gonna help you now." Billy stepped inside from the front door with a large hunting knife strapped to his side and his gun on the other hip. He wasn't wearing his uniform anymore. He was in dark camouflage.

"Billy, what are you doing?"

"Waiting for the sun to set. Then I'm going to show you my special place," he said with wild eyes.

"Why are you doing this?"

He smiled as his heavy boots clunked across the wooden planks toward me. "You know, for a minute there, I wondered if you had figured it out. You know, when you said you were talking about me. Then you got into the truck like a damn fool, and I knew better." He laughed and rubbed his calloused palms together. "I guess this is my lucky day."

"What are you going to do with me?" I asked.

He knelt down in front of me and began to count on his fingers. "Well, I'm going to rape you. Then I'm going to kill you.

Then I'll probably rape you some more before I dig you a nice warm hole in the ground."

I shuddered and twisted against my restraints.

He laughed again. "Government steel, honey. You ain't gettin' loose."

"You'll never get away with this," I said. "They're onto you now. Police and volunteers are going to be all over this place tomorrow, and they will find you."

He leaned so close to my face I could smell the rancid chewing tobacco on his hot breath. "I'm heading up the search team. How else are they gonna know where someone might hide a body away from all the tree stands, the deer beds, and the watering holes?"

I thought I might throw up, but I wouldn't give him the satisfaction of seeing me panic.

He leaned over the pile of pictures and took a knee beside them. "You know what's funny about all this?" He started sorting through the photographs. "I was actually lookin' for you the night I killed this one." He spun the picture of Leslie Bryson across the floor toward me.

I looked down at Leslie's face and details started snapping together like building blocks. 2009. Billy Stewart. Chili's Bar and Grill, where Leslie was a waitress, was a block over from Alejandro's. I had summoned Billy that night, and he had been planning to kill me.

He scratched his forehead with dirt-caked fingernails. "Never found you that night, so I chose someone else." A grin, oozing with evil, spread across his lips. "But I've found you now."

I shook my head. "No. You screwed up taking me. You finally made a stupid mistake. Detective McNamara is already searching this area, and you'd better believe he's keeping a close eye on me. If I go missing, he'll burn the forest to hunt you down."

He grabbed me by my hair and pulled till I screamed. "He won't burn it before you're nothing but a pile of body parts," he said, showering my face with spit. He shoved me toward the floor, and I hit my head on the radiator.

He crossed the room and picked up a small box off the wooden table. He flipped it open as he walked toward me. I scrambled away from him as he produced another syringe. "Don't worry," he said. "This will make you woozy for a little bit, and then you'll sleep till we get there."

He slid the needle carefully into a vein in my arm and pressed down on the plunger. Then he tucked the needle back into the box and walked away.

I looked to where my hands were cuffed. My mom's older sister had a radiator like it when I was a kid. Even then, Aunt Joan's was so old that it hadn't worked in years. I wasn't sure how old the rusty piece of metal was, but I was sure it wasn't as strong as the handcuffs. I pulled and tugged and pounded the edge of the handcuffs into the radiator bars but nothing cracked. The cuffs were biting into the sensitive crevices between the bones in my wrists, and my thumbs and pinky fingers were going numb.

He laughed on the other side of the room. "Good luck with that. You're not the first bitch that's tried to break that thing."

I slumped against the radiator. My scalp felt warm and sticky with blood against the cold metal. The chill seeped into my skin, making my body tingle.

"Warren, where are you?" I cried, barely above a whisper.

"Oh, are you praying? Are you calling out for help?" Billy whimpered, teasing me. "It's OK, Sloan. It will all be over soon."

When I awoke again, it felt like I was being drawn and quartered, only I was being dragged, literally, by my arms across the rough terrain of the mountain. I didn't need to be able to see to know that my body was bloody and broken. My legs screamed like the skin was being peeled away with a jigsaw. Something was shoved into my mouth that I couldn't expel because of the strong tape that was stretched tight across my lips. It was almost completely dark, and I knew if I didn't put up a fight soon, I was going to quickly run out of chances.

Desperate, I scrambled to get my feet under me. My bare and lacerated toes tried to fight for a foothold into the cold, hard earth beneath my feet. Billy spun around and backhanded me across the face. "Calm the hell down, you dumb whore! You're making this a lot worse for yourself!"

I tried to claw at him, but my fingers couldn't find his skin.

Wrecked with exhaustion and agony, the fight left my arms. Billy continued to drag me about a hundred more feet over dirt, rocks, and tree roots that stuck out of the ground like tire spikes. I thought of the day in the woods when I had wanted Warren or Nathan to carry me. I remembered the terrified look on Nathan's face when Warren produced the jawbone from the dirt. I remembered trying to imagine Warren singing along with Dionne Warwick. *It's funny the things that flash through your mind when you know you're about to die.* I swear I could hear Warren singing...

Billy stopped walking. Billy heard Warren singing too. I hadn't imagined it. Nathan and Warren had already found the 'special place' where Billy was planning to hide my body along with Leslie Bryson's corpse.

"What was that?" I heard Nathan's voice say. "I heard movement up there."

I tried to look around, and for a split second I thought I could see a light flash up in the distance. Billy knelt down and grabbed me by my right arm and my right thigh and hoisted me over his shoulder like a lame sheep. He was turning around and heading back the way we came.

He was retreating because Warren and Nathan were really there!

I tried to struggle, but I was dangling upside down. Then I saw it. Billy's hunting knife was just within my grasp. He was moving too quickly and with too much panic to notice when my fingers unsnapped the leather that was holding it. With the nerve damage in my hands it was difficult to hold onto the knife, but somehow I managed to cut him in the side deep enough to make him yelp with pain and stumble.

It was enough to cause a stir of leaves in the woods behind us. "Who's there?" I heard Nathan shout.

Flashlights were going wild through the trees. I looked up to see salvation coming. There was just enough daylight for me to make out two figures rushing toward us as Billy tried to run. I stabbed at him again. This time, he dumped me off his shoulder and made a run for it. I felt my ribs crash into the unearthed roots of a large tree and thorns tore through the flesh I had left along my right thigh.

I rolled over enough to see Billy lunge for the driver's side door of his truck. As he yanked it open, Warren fired a bullet into the door spinning Billy around and slamming him face-first into the dirt.

Warren cautiously approached as Billy reoriented and tried to get to his knees. "Get your hands up!" he ordered with a voice so dark and menacing that it seemed to add to the darkness of the forest.

Billy began to rise up slowly as Nathan shined his flashlight in my direction. His eyes locked on me and fear flashed through him. "Sloan!" he shouted.

Distracted by the sound of my name, Warren looked away for a split second. I couldn't even scream when I saw Billy raise his gun and fire wildly into the air. The gun fired again and Nathan dove in front of me. His airborne body seemed to explode in a different direction and land just out of my reach.

Behind him, Warren was down on one knee when he fired twice, sending Billy Stewart flying backward through the air.

I scrambled toward Nathan and used both cuffed hands to roll him onto his back. "Sloan," he sputtered, splattering my face with blood. His eyes were terrified.

I couldn't even scream.

"Nate, you all right?" Warren yelled as he approached Billy cautiously. "I need your 'cuffs. This guy's not dead. Sloan, can you hear me?"

I tried to scream but couldn't.

I yanked Nathan's shirt up and found a bloody exit wound a few inches below his collarbone. I pressed my hands to it and looked desperately around for Warren.

He had his knee pressed into Billy's throat as he unloaded Billy's gun. "Nathan!" he yelled again. Finally, when he had no other choice, Warren reached into Billy's truck and pulled the keys out of the ignition. He locked the doors and slammed it closed. Then he shot Billy again in the foot before running across the road.

When he reached me, visible panic washed over him. "Holy shit!" he yelled as he dropped down next to me. My eyes begged him to help Nathan first, but instead, he peeled off the sticky tape that covered my mouth. I fought to spit out the wad of fabric that I was beginning to suck down my windpipe.

"Help him, Warren! He's been shot. In the back or the side. I'm not sure," I screamed.

"Back, near my ribs," Nathan sputtered.

"We've got to move you to the road," Warren said as he grabbed Nathan under his armpits. Nathan tried to help push with his feet, but he was having a hard time breathing.

When we made it to more level ground, Warren produced a knife and cut Nathan's shirt away. He rolled him until he found the bloody hole in Nathan's back. "Sloan, get me that tape," he instructed.

I grabbed Nathan's flashlight and scrambled to the grass. I found the discarded scrap of duct tape and carried it to Warren. He was shredding Nathan's shirt with his knife. "Nate, I need you to exhale all the way." He handed me a strip of fabric. "Sloan, wad this up and seal off that hole in the front the best you can."

The hole in the front of Nathan's chest was producing foamy, gurgling blood. I looked into Nathan's eyes and he nodded. "Do it," he whispered. Blood was drizzling out of the corners of his mouth.

"Don't you die on me," I threatened.

"Exhale," Warren told him.

When he had, Warren covered the fabric with tape. Then, he did the same thing on his back. "It's hit your lung, man," he said. "We've got to get you out of here."

"Really, Warren? No shit," Nathan gurgled.

I scowled. "This is not the time for a smart mouth, Nathan McNamara."

Warren searched for Nathan's handcuff keys, then finally freed my hands. I couldn't feel my fingers at all. "Are you OK?" he asked me.

I wiped mud and sticky wet blood off my face. "The game warden. It's him. It's Billy Stewart. He's the killer."

Warren's head jerked with recognition. "Billy Stewart?"

I nodded furiously. "Yes!"

"Other than the obvious, did he hurt you?" he asked.

I shook my head.

Billy was attempting to crawl away from the truck when Warren and I carried Nathan over. "Do you want me to shoot you again?" Warren shouted. Of course Billy kept going.

Warren unlocked the truck and we carefully laid Nathan across the back seat. Then he looked over at me. "I'm going to need your help with the game warden."

I nodded.

Billy had made it to the side of the road, leaving a thick trail of blood behind him. Warren kicked him in the side, toppling him over onto his back. He coughed up blood, spewing it in my direction as I painfully knelt down next to him. My ribs and every inch of my torn skin were screaming with pain.

Warren put his muddy boot down on Billy's throat.

I wanted to smack him across the face, but I couldn't feel my fingers. "OK, asshole. It's truth time," I said.

He gasped. "I'm dying here."

I put my knee square on the center of one of the bloody holes in his chest, making him squirm in agony. "I certainly hope so," I hissed. "But right now, you're going to talk and tell me the truth."

"I'm not telling you shit!" He gurgled and spat blood on me.

Warren kicked him in the face.

"Warren, can you tell how many victims this guy has on him?" I asked looking up to where Warren stood over us both.

Warren studied Billy's face for a moment before finally looking at me. "Twelve."

We had only been aware of ten missing girls, not twelve. "We know about the ones between here and Raleigh. Where are the others?" I pressed my knee harder into Billy's chest.

"Toccoa, Georgia," he whispered.

I looked at Warren. "Think that's it?"

He nodded. Warren's eyes were fierce and his jaw was set. "Should we let him bleed out?" he asked.

I struggled to my feet. "No. I don't want to take any chances. Finish him."

Billy began to scramble as I turned toward the truck and Warren leaned down close to him.

There was a loud crack of lightning, but I didn't even flinch.

CHAPTER NINETEEN

Warren folded down the front passenger's seat of Billy's truck, and I sat on top of it as we navigated our way down the obscure mountain access road. I held pressure against Nathan's chest. His breathing was shallow and uneven. His face was pale and he was sweating, but he was alive.

"Sloan, are you OK?" His voice was weak and raspy.

I shivered with the release of adrenaline through my veins. My chin had begun to quiver with shock. I did my best to force a smile. "I'm not as bad as you."

"Would you mind filling me in on what the hell just happened?" he struggled to ask.

"That was the game warden. He's your serial killer." I pointed out the window where we had left Billy Stewart's body lying by the road. "He kidnapped me this afternoon. What were you guys doing up here?"

Nathan coughed. "Warren called me and—"

"Let me do the talking, Nate," Warren interrupted, looking over his shoulder. "I found another body up here today. I called Nate, and he met me at the bottom of the mountain. We hiked in together and had just gotten here when we heard someone coming up behind us. Surprise, surprise. It turns out it was you and the serial killer."

"How did he kidnap you?" Nathan wheezed.

"He's an old friend of Adrianne's. We all went to high school together," I explained. "I ran into him at the jail today and invited him to come with me to see her. He offered to drive because he said he had to come back to the sheriff's office after lunch."

"You went with him willingly?" Warren asked surprised. "Could you not feel how dark he was? That dude was exactly what I imagined a serial killer would feel like."

I shuddered with a sickening chill. "I ran into him at the jail, so I really didn't notice. I was already mid-panic attack, and I wanted to get out of there as fast as possible."

"But you knew him before, right? Didn't he freak you out before?" Nathan asked.

I shook my head. "No. I mean, we were kids then."

"Before he committed his first murder," Warren said almost to himself.

I nodded. "It had to have been. I'm pretty sure Adrianne told me he went to NC State to study forestry after he graduated from our high school."

"In Raleigh," Nathan wheezed.

I looked down at him. "I told you NC State was terrible."

He pointed at me with a blood-stained frown. "Hey!"

Warren glanced back at me. "But you told me yesterday you saw him when you were in college. You didn't sense the evil then?"

I thought back to the night with Adrianne at Alejandro's. "I only saw his truck from a distance."

"Damn," Warren said.

"Anyway, once we were in the truck, he injected me with some kind of animal tranquilizer. Check in the door pocket next to you, Warren. I'll bet it's still there," I said.

Warren flipped on the light in the cab and searched between the door and his seat. He steered the truck with one hand as he carefully reached down and picked up a long, metal syringe. He flinched just looking at it.

"I passed out in the passenger's seat and when I woke up, I was chained to a radiator in an old cabin somewhere up in the woods," I said. "I was there for hours."

"He was waiting till dark when the woods were cleared, just like Warren said he would," Nathan said. "He was going to bury you there with Leslie Bryson."

"He was going to do a lot more than that." I thought I might vomit.

"You're sure you're all right?" Warren asked again. He reached back to touch my shoulder.

"Oh, I'm very far from all right considering I was just nearly raped and murdered." Another chill shot down my spine. "I'm sure my ribs are broken, and I doubt I'll be wearing shorts this summer."

"You've got to get checked out," he insisted.

I nodded. "I will." I looked at Nathan. "He said there were twelve girls altogether and that the other two are buried in Toccoa, Georgia."

"A team from Hickory found Colleen Webster just outside of Statesville today," he said.

"His mother lives in Statesville," I told him.

He nodded. "Is he dead?" Nathan asked.

"I'm pretty sure he bled out before we left," I lied.

He sighed and closed his eyes. "Good."

After a moment, I looked at Warren. "Weren't you wondering why you hadn't heard from me?" I asked.

"Well, when I got off the mountain, I called but got your voicemail. I assumed you were busy. Then I hiked up here with Nate and didn't have cell service," he said. "Honestly, I wasn't worried about you. I was afraid you were going to be mad at me for being gone all day."

"Well, I am a little mad at you." I pouted. "I was kidnapped and you weren't even worried."

"I was worried about you," Nathan croaked and winked up at me.

Warren and I would have laughed if it hadn't been so serious.

"We do have a problem," Nathan said.

"How to explain me being there...again?" Warren asked.

"Yep."

"Maybe we'll luck out and Raleigh and Asheville won't connect the dots?" I offered.

Nathan shook his head.

"No babe. This is going to be big," Warren said.

My shoulders sank. "The West Coast is sounding pretty good about now."

Warren smiled over his shoulder at me. "We'll figure it out. We are going to have to tell them I was in those woods last week on purpose."

We rode for a while in silence. My hands felt each breath that Nathan struggled to take. I knew he was going to live, but I knew it was because of me that he almost didn't. If I had been right when I suggested to Warren that I might have a neutralizing effect on people's hatred of him, then the same had to be true for me. That night, Nathan McNamara dove in front of a bullet to save me. I wasn't sure how much truer love could get than that. Nathan rested his hand on top of mine and closed his eyes.

Part of Nathan's lung had collapsed by the time we got to the hospital, so they took him immediately into surgery. I also got to see the extent of my injuries when I was rolled into triage. Apparently when I got out of the car at the emergency room, everyone thought I was the patient. I looked a bit like something out of a zombie movie. Warren stayed with me the whole time, and the hospital staff called my parents.

The majority of the sheriff's office was waiting when we arrived at the hospital. That seemed to be standard protocol whenever a detective calls in his own 'officer down' distress over the radio. The sheriff himself walked into my triage room with his hands on his hips.

"Miss Jordan, do we have you on the wrong payroll list? You keep showing up at my crime scenes," he said.

I raised an eyebrow and settled against my hospital pillow. "If I am on the wrong payroll, you certainly don't pay me enough, Sheriff."

He laughed and shook his head. "I was worried when you didn't show up for the press conference today, but I would never have imagined this would be the reason."

"Well, I was really worried about all the disappointed hunters in the area, so I decided to speed the case along," I said with a smile.

He rolled his eyes. "Well, mission accomplished."

"Did your guys go up to Pisgah?" I asked.

He nodded. "We're up there, the state is up there, and the feds. You're going to have a lot of work to do when you get out of here."

I groaned. "Well, I have nerve damage in my hands from being thrown around in handcuffs, so there may not be a whole lot of typing in my future for a while. I may have to dictate your news stories."

"What else did the doctors say, if you don't mind me asking?" he asked.

"I have a concussion, two broken ribs, and I'm missing enough skin on my legs from being dragged that they asked if I had been pulled behind a car."

He cringed with sympathy.

"I keep trying to figure out if this is workman's comp related since I was kidnapped from work by an officer of the state and bludgeoned half to death," I said.

He laughed. "Well, I think, at the very least, the county can afford you some time off."

I shook my head. "I'm already working on the press release in my head. I'll get someone else to type it."

The sheriff noticed Warren in the corner. "You must be the big hero."

"Sheriff Davis, this is my boyfriend, Warren," I said.

They shook hands and Warren smiled. "I just happened to be at the right place at the right time."

The sheriff cocked his eyebrow. "That seems to be happening around you a lot these days."

Warren shrugged. "McNamara is a friend of Sloan's, and he told me the disappearances might be related. Because of my background in human tracking with the military, he asked for my help. Yesterday, we decided to scope out some similar places to where I found that girl last weekend. Everything else is all a really lucky coincidence."

"I'll say. It's a huge lucky coincidence," he said. "I'm sure we'll be talking with each other some more."

Warren nodded. "Whatever you need, sir."

The sheriff pointed at me. "You get to feeling better, Sloan." He turned to leave, but stopped in the doorway. "And please try and stay out of trouble."

When he had gone, Warren stretched out on the bed beside me. "How are you feeling?"

"Like an MMA champ," I said.

He shook his head and laughed. "I wouldn't say 'champ' exactly." He traced his fingers along my arm. "Seriously, how are you doing?"

I rolled my face toward him. "I'm going to have nightmares for a while. He was going to kill me. If you and Nathan hadn't been there, I would be lying next to Leslie Bryson's bones right now."

He rested his forehead against mine. "But we *were* there, and you're not buried in the woods. Thank God." He pressed his lips to my temple.

I shuddered remembering the feeling of being dragged along that wooded path. "Thank God," I agreed.

Across the room, a shimmer of light reflected off of my discarded clothes that were laying on the table near the door. Kayleigh's angel pin had somehow survived the ordeal in much better condition than the bedraggled blouse it was still attached to. A thought that I couldn't quite piece together rolled around in my brain. Perhaps it was the morphine.

"Warren, can I ask you a serious question?"

He sat up a little and looked at me with concern. "Of course. What?"

"Do you think we will ever figure out what we are? Why we can do the things we do?" I dropped my head back and stared at the fluorescent lights above.

He reclined against my pillow and rolled his head toward mine. "The answer is out there somewhere. Maybe someday we'll find it. I think we're off to a pretty good start."

I blew out a deep sigh. "Can I ask you something else?"

"Anything," he whispered and closed his eyes.

I cut my eyes at him. "Were you really singing 'That's What Friends are For?' with Nathan in the woods?"

He burst out laughing and planted a kiss on my lips.

CHAPTER TWENTY

Two weeks later, I was sitting on Warren's lap with my heavily bandaged legs resting on the edge of Adrianne's hospital bed. We were sharing a tub of popcorn. Nathan was on the other side of the bed popping Skittles into his mouth. Adrianne was wearing a hat and sitting up as she slurped on some purple jello.

"Oh, this is it!" I squealed. I reached for the television remote on Adrianne's bed but winced with pain from my ribcage and drew my hand back

Warren shook his head. "Please let me do it." He picked up the remote and turned up the volume.

Shannon Green's face appeared on the television set. She was dressed in a bright yellow suit with freshly whitened teeth and enough hairspray to set the city ablaze.

Adrianne scrunched up her nose. "What's going on with her hair?"

"I was afraid she might get too close to the stage lighting and blow us all up." Nathan laughed gingerly, still with a bit of rasp to his voice.

Shannon smiled at the television screen and began her monologue.

"Some are calling it the luckiest break in criminal history. Others are calling it nothing short of a miracle. I am Shannon Green with WKNC News coming to you from our studio with an exclusive interview with two people at the center of one of the most fascinating crime cases in our state's history. We are here with Detective Nathan McNamara and Buncombe County Public Information Officer, Sloan Jordan."

I leaned into Warren. "I love this part."

The camera panned to Nathan, who carefully shifted toward Shannon in his seat. He was wearing a suit. "Thank you for having us, Shannon. We are delighted to be here," he said and smiled at the camera.

We all laughed and Nathan launched a red Skittle at my head. "Shut up!"

"Oh, it gets better," I assured them.

Shannon folded her hands over her knee. "Twelve girls have gone missing in North Carolina and Georgia. Gone without a trace. One of the first of them was your sister, Nathan, and she disappeared almost thirteen years ago. How is it, that such an unlikely pair could solve a case that has had police and investigators across the nation puzzled for well over a decade?" she asked.

Nathan smiled at the camera again. "Well, Shannon, Miss Jordan and I met by chance on another case recently where she brought some very valuable insight and opinions to the..."

Warren squeezed my thigh. "My girl? Opinionated? No..."

I tried to clamp my hand over Warren's mouth. "Shhh…"

"She is actually the one who found the link between the disappearances and the hunting season." Nathan smiled at the camera again.

"Why do you keep smiling like that?" Adrianne asked. "You look like a demented Ken doll."

We all laughed again.

Shannon forced a smile on screen. "You two must have been spending an awful lot of time together to be able to come up with such an elaborate conclusion." Her voice was squeaky and more high-pitched than normal.

The camera moved to me. "Over the course of a few weeks, Detective McNamara and I did spend almost every waking hour together."

Nathan shook his head. "You're mean, Sloan."

I smiled at Warren and then looked back at the television.

"We did a lot of traveling and interviewing people. We employed the help of a friend who was able to track and locate the bodies that were found in Raleigh and ultimately the one that was found here in Asheville. That discovery also led to the demise of the killer himself," I explained.

Shannon leaned forward in her chair toward me on screen. "I believe the question of the century is, how is it that you came by the information that led to the discovery of the first two bodies in Raleigh? What caused you to look in the exact spot where the bodies had been overlooked for so many years?"

On screen I turned and smiled at Nathan (who then turned and smiled at the camera) before I continued. "We did a very thorough process of elimination of different areas, and I guess there was a bit of a woman's intuition at play, Shannon."

Warren shifted to look at me. "A 'woman's intuition'? Did you really just say that?"

I laughed. "I couldn't exactly say my boyfriend is somewhat of a cadaver dog, now could I?"

"What about this mystery hero that located three of the girls without any aid from standard search equipment?" Shannon asked me.

I smiled. "Well, he has wished to remain anonymous, but I can tell you he is a bit of a bad(BLEEP) who has had the best tracking training and experience in the world."

Adrianne reached over and nudged my arm. "Check you out, Sloan! You got bleeped out on television!"

I laughed and squeezed her hand.

"Sloan, this was a particularly terrifying ordeal for you as you were almost the next victim. Is it true you were kidnapped and tortured before the assailant was apprehended?" She was smiling a little bit too much for the words she was saying.

"Would you say we actually 'apprehended' him?" Warren asked.

I giggled. "Shh…I'm on TV!"

"I was actually taken from the sheriff's office building by someone I believed I knew fairly well. I trusted him and it almost got me killed. I think it should be a good reminder that we can never be too careful, ladies," I said directly into the camera.

Nathan was shaking his head on the other side of the hospital bed. "Just like a publicist to squeeze in a good public service announcement."

"Hey! I could be saving lives!"

He laughed and dumped the rest of the bag of Skittles into his mouth.

"After being held for over six hours, I was taken into the woods where Detective McNamara and our other companion had already discovered the remains of Leslie Bryson. They were still on the scene, and they were able to stop Game Warden William Stewart and save my life," I said.

"Detective, this is when you were shot during the struggle?" Shannon asked.

Nathan smiled at the camera.

We all laughed.

"Yes. I was shot in the back while I was attempting to shield Ms. Jordan from gunfire," he said.

Adrianne pointed to the television. "Look at her face!"

Shannon's mouth was smiling, but her eyes could have been burning holes in Nathan's skull. I was a little surprised his head wasn't smoking.

I held up my hand in suspense. "Oh, wait for it."

Shannon leaned forward in her seat toward Nathan. "Does it hurt, Detective? Does it hurt very badly?"

We all howled in laughter at the television.

"Does it hurt very badly?" Warren mimicked.

Nathan shook his head. "You guys suck."

"It could have been a lot worse. Thank you for asking," he said.

"Sloan, what are your plans for the future now? Do you plan on getting involved with any more crime solving mysteries?" she asked me.

I laughed. "No, Shannon. I think I'm going to try and stick with writing the news instead of living it."

"Fantastic. Well, we are thankful this nightmare is over for everyone, and we appreciate you both taking the time to talk with us here. I am Shannon Green with WKNC, Six O'clock News."

I held up my hands. "Wait, wait!"

The camera panned to Nathan. "Stay safe, Asheville," he said with a smile—and a wink—into the camera.

The room erupted into hysterics again.

"'Stay safe, Asheville'? What the hell is that about?" Warren laughed.

"Personally, I like the wink," Adrianne said, doing her best to wink at him.

Nathan got up, flinching slightly with pain and slammed his candy wrapper in the trash. "I hate you all."

"I think you've missed your calling in show business, man," Warren teased.

"Hey, Warren, I hear American Idol is doing auditions soon!" Nathan fired back.

I laughed and kissed Warren on the forehead.

When the laughter died down, Adrianne adjusted the incline of her bed. "Do you guys think anyone bought that bullshit?"

Nathan sat down and shook his head. "Not a chance."

"I've already had a call from the CIA and the Pentagon," Warren grumbled.

I kissed Warren again, this time on the lips. "We can always run to Mexico."

"I think that's a wonderful idea." He kissed me again.

Nathan groaned. "I'm getting out of here before I start puking like Sloan with a migraine."

I laughed and stood up carefully. I grabbed Warren's hand for support as the blood rushed down to my throbbing legs. "Come on, guys. Let's get out of here," I said.

We paused at Adrianne's bedside to say our goodbyes for the

night. She reached for my hand. "So have you two decided if you are going to use your powers for good or evil?" she asked.

I smiled down at her. "I still plan on using them for evil when I get my hands on Mark Higgins."

She laughed.

I slowly leaned over and kissed her on the forehead. "I love you, friend. I'll come by tomorrow."

She squeezed my hand. "I love you, too."

I turned toward Warren and Nathan. "You boys ready to go?"

"Yep. Lead the way. Bye, Adrianne," Warren said.

Nathan waved. "See you later, girl."

She smiled.

Warren draped his arm over my shoulders as they walked—and I limped—down the hallway.

Nathan looked at Warren when we got on the elevator. "So, the Pentagon? Really?"

Warren nodded and pressed the button for the first floor. "Yeah," he said. "Apparently they want to fly me up to Washington sometime, maybe next week. They didn't tell me much more about it."

I looked up at him. "Do I get to come?"

He tensed and gave a doubtful smile. "I don't think it's a 'bring a friend' deal."

I gave him a sheepish smile. "But I'm a celebrity now."

Nathan smirked looking up to watch the floors countdown. "Yes, I'm sure Hollywood will be calling for the movie rights any day now."

The door to the elevator opened.

Mark Higgins was holding a bouquet of bright yellow daisies.

With one punch, I knocked two shiny, veneered front teeth to the floor.

BOOK TWO

The Siren

IN STORES NOW

All the missing victims of North Carolina's deadliest serial killer have been found, all except Rachel Smith. When the FBI produces a photo proving Rachel is alive and well in Texas, one case is closed but another one is opened. Either this is a case of mistaken identity or there are more people than just Sloan Jordan and Warren Parish who seem to walk the earth without a soul.

Along with Detective Nathan McNamara, Sloan and Warren travel south to find Rachel and solve the biggest mystery of all: determining who—or what—they really are.

TURN THE PAGE TO START READING

THANK YOU FOR READING!

Please consider leaving a review! Reviews help indie authors like me find new readers and get advertising. If you enjoyed this book, please tell your friends!

REVIEW IT NOW

Want more of your favorite detective?

THE DETECTIVE

A Nathan McNamara Story

Here's a FREE GIFT for you!

Download The Detective at

www.thesoulsummoner.com

THE SIREN

ELICIA HYDER
SOUL SUMMONER BOOK 2
THE
SIREN
A SLOAN JORDAN STORY

THE SIREN

WHOMP WHOMP WHOMP WHOMP WHOMP. CLACK, CLACK. EEEENG! EEEENG! EEEENG!

"This is a test. This is only a test of the Emergency Broadcast System." I was practicing my best radio announcer's voice.

"Sloan, stop talking," my father said through his microphone. "And please, lie still."

Lying still was becoming increasingly more difficult with each second that passed. I had been trapped inside the deafening MRI machine for more than twenty minutes. My father had insisted on the test after my last hemiplegic migraine, but I knew its results would be as useless as the last two CT scans he had ordered. There was nothing wrong with my brain, and there was nothing wrong with me...except it seemed I had the power to read and control people's souls. That, however, had nothing to do with my migraines that I was aware of.

The trigger for my latest headache was the same as the others: Warren Parish had left town. He and I seemed to be bound together by an electrifying force, and when we were apart, paralyzing migraines were the penalty.

The MRI was going to be inconclusive.

When the machine stopped whirring and knocking like the inside of a drag racer's engine, I wiggled my feet from side to side. "Are we done yet?"

"All done," Dad said. The MRI table slid slowly out of the electronic cave I had been confined to.

My father was fascinated and terribly worried by my new development of headaches, but I knew telling him the truth wouldn't help. My adoptive parents were incredibly loving and supportive, but they were also medical professionals who believed everything had a scientific explanation. Being that my father was a geriatric physician who specialized in dementia, I knew what his diagnosis would be—mental instability.

Dad walked into the room as I sat up on the table and adjusted my twisted gown. Even in his fifties, he was still movie-star handsome with the brightest blue eyes I'd ever seen. He was looking down at a sheet of paper in his hand. "You can get dressed."

I held the back of my gown closed while I stood up. "What did the test show? Is it all sawdust and rocks up there?"

Dad rolled his eyes. "Nothing stood out to me, but I'm going to have a friend of mine in neurology look over it to be sure."

I put my hand on his arm and looked up at him. "Dad, I'm fine."

He kissed my forehead. "I can't be too careful with you. You're the only Sloan I've got." He started toward the door. "Do you want to grab lunch before you head to work? I have another hour or so before my first patient of the afternoon."

I looked at the clock on the wall. I had told my boss that I would be in around noon, and it was already after eleven. "Will you be terribly heartbroken if I skip lunch this time? I want to pop in and check on Adrianne before I go to the office, if that's OK."

He smiled. "Of course. Give her my love, and tell her I'll drop in to see her sometime this week," he said. "I'll see you at dinner tonight?"

I nodded. "I'll be there."

"Will Warren be joining us?" he called as I shuffled toward the door in my socks.

I looked back and shrugged. "I'm not sure. He's flying in from D.C. sometime today, but I can't remember when his flight lands. I'll let Mom know if he gets here in time."

"All right, sweetheart. We'll see you later," he said.

Adrianne Marx, my best friend, had been a patient at the hospital for almost three weeks since the guy she was dating decided to drive drunk and flip his Jeep into a highway guard rail. I had knocked out his front teeth in return and none of us had seen him since.

When I got to her room, she was reading a trashy tabloid magazine and munching on potato chips. Her hair was starting to regrow from where they had to shave it, and aside from the pink scars left by the stitches, her face looked almost back to normal.

I rapped my knuckles against the open door. "Knock, knock."

She looked up and smiled. "Hey, weirdo." She shifted against her mound of pillows as I crossed in front of her feet and plopped down in the chair by her bed. "What are you doing here?"

"I had an MRI upstairs. I thought I would swing by and say hello before I went to work."

She sat up in her bed. "An MRI? I thought you just had a few broken bones and some stitches."

Barely two weeks before, Warren and I had helped Detective Nathan McNamara take down a serial killer who had been murdering women across the state of North Carolina for over a decade. Billy Stewart had drugged me, beaten me, and then dragged me to his Bundy-style, secret body-stashing spot where he planned on raping and burying me in the woods. Thanks to Warren's ability to track down dead bodies and Nathan's protective instincts, I walked away with only a few broken ribs, nerve damage in my hands, and enough gashes on my arms and legs to potentially keep me in pants for the rest of my life.

I shook my head. "Dad wanted the MRI because he's worried about my migraines. I had another really bad one on Sunday."

Her head tilted to the side. "So Warren is gone?"

"Yeah. He had to go to Washington for a meeting at the Pentagon."

She folded the open end of her bag of chips and laid it on the bedside table. "That sounds alarming. What do they want with him?"

I shrugged. "I'm sure they want to know how he tracked down those missing girls."

Her eyes widened. "I wonder how he's going to explain that."

I laughed, though I was more worried than amused. "I don't know, but I don't think telling them he can *feel death* is going to cut it."

"Probably not," she agreed. "When he left, did you puke all over the detective again?"

Heat rose in my cheeks at either the embarrassing memory of my last migraine or at the simple thought of Nathan McNamara. I wasn't sure which. My endocrine system had been thoroughly confused since Warren and Nathan came to town. "No. I was with my parents, and I didn't puke on anyone this time."

"How is Nathan?" she asked.

I leaned against the armrest. "I guess he's doing OK. I haven't seen him in a few days. This week he's in Greensboro looking for Billy's last victim on our list who hasn't been found."

"Which one is she?" she asked.

"Rachel Smith. She was reported missing by her co-workers in 2008. She didn't have any known relatives, so her case went cold pretty fast. She was a social worker," I said.

Adrianne shook her head. "That's so sad."

"Let's talk about something else, please." I was desperate to change the subject. Talking about the whole case still made me feel squeamish.

She nodded. "OK. How's the boy drama?"

"Oh, it's still drama." I sighed. "Warren finished moving his stuff into my house this week. He put his furniture in storage over in West Asheville, but his clothes and his many weapons are at my house. My guest room looks like a freaking armory."

She looked at me sideways. "Are you planning on living together, like long term?"

I laughed and shrugged my shoulders. "I haven't planned anything with Warren up until this point, and life hasn't exactly allowed for a lot of forethought and decision-making. I don't know what we're doing."

She raised an eyebrow. "What does Nathan think about it?"

I sat back in my seat. "I have no idea. It's not like we have heart-to-heart discussions on the subject. He still comes by the house and my office all the time, so I guess it hasn't fazed him too much."

"Is he still dating Shannon?" she asked.

The muscles tensed in my jaw at the mention of Nathan's girlfriend because if I had a nemesis, Shannon Green would be it. But that bitterness was rooted a lot deeper than in just her relationship with Nathan. His presence only added fuel to embers that had been smoldering for over a decade.

I rolled my eyes. "I guess they're still together, but you would never know it. He's always around, and she's never with him, and he doesn't talk about her."

Adrianne held out her hands. "Why is he with her?"

"I've been asking the same thing for a while now."

"What does Warren say about Nathan showing up all the time?" she asked.

"He doesn't say much. They actually spend more time together than Nathan and I do these days. Warren's been helping recover the missing victims, and aside from their constant ping-ponging of insults back and forth, they've actually become pretty good friends. They love to hate each other."

"I've noticed," she said. "To be honest, I kind of feel bad for

Nate. He's crazy about you, and then Warren showed up and it was over with you guys before it even got started."

I nodded. "I know. Warren came into town like a hurricane." I chewed on my pinky nail. "Wanna hear a secret?"

She scooted forward in her bed. "Of course."

I pointed a warning finger at her. "Do you promise to take it to the grave?"

She crossed her heart. "I swear."

I lowered my voice. "I keep thinking about that night in the woods when Nathan dove in front of that bullet for me. He could have died trying to save me. That's love on a whole different level."

"Are you having second thoughts about you and Warren?" she asked.

I shook my head. "No. That's what makes it so hard. I genuinely care about them both, but it's too different with Warren for there to even be a competition. He's like gravity or oxygen. I can't *not* be with him."

"You guys are really intense," she said.

I tapped my finger against my forehead. "Intense enough for migraines." I laughed. "Enough about my supernatural soap opera. How are you doing?"

"I'm doing OK. I started physical therapy yesterday, which sucked more than you could ever imagine," she said with a groan. "They are talking like I'll be able to go home maybe tomorrow or the next day."

"That's awesome," I said.

She nodded. "Yeah. Everyone is pretty shocked at how fast I've recovered. Most of the nurses didn't think I would live, much less be walking out of here anytime soon." She eyed me suspiciously from the bed. "I'm pretty sure I have you to thank for that."

I shrugged. "Who knows?"

"Sloan, you're the only one I remember being here during the beginning of all this. I remember you being in my room when I still couldn't even talk," she said. "It was like I could feel you right here next to me."

"Really?" I asked, surprised.

She smiled. "Yeah. I think Warren is on to something. I think you healed me."

"Well, I wouldn't say 'healed' necessarily." I laughed. "Have you seen your hair today?"

She threw a pillow at me. "Shut up."

"So, what are you going to do when you get out of here? Go to your apartment?" I asked.

She shook her head. "Not for a while. I can't get up and down the stairs yet. I'll probably stay with my parents till I'm fully recuperated."

"What about work?" I asked.

She shrugged. "They're holding my booth at the salon, but it will probably be a while before I can be on my feet all day again."

I leaned forward and put my hand on her broken leg.

"Are you putting your voodoo on me?" she asked with a smile.

I winked at her. "It can't hurt."

★ Want leaked chapters of new books?

★ Want the first look at what's coming soon?

★ Want to win some awesome swag and prizes?

Join HYDERNATION, the official fan club of Elicia Hyder, for all that and more!

Join on Facebook

Join on EliciaHyder.com

OFFICIAL MERCHANDISE

Want Nathan's SWAT hoodie?

Want to start your own patch collection?

We've got you covered!

www.eliciahyder.com/shop

ALSO BY ELICIA HYDER

Be brave. Be strong. Be badass.

Roll into the exciting world of women's flat track roller derby, where the women are the heroes, and the men will make you weak in the kneepads.

A brand new romantic comedy series from Author Elicia Hyder.

ALSO BY ELICIA HYDER

The Bed She Made

2015 Watty Award Winner for Best New Adult Romance

During her wild and crazy teenage years, Journey Durant's father warned her that someday she'd have to lie in the bed she made. But she didn't believe him until her ex-boyfriend is released from prison and he threatens to bring her troubled past home with him

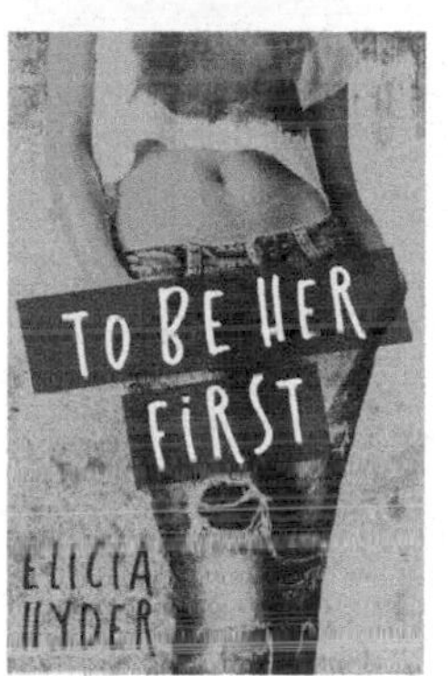

To Be Her First

The Young Adult Prequel to The Bed She Made

At sixteen, Journey Durant hasn't yet experienced her first anything. No first boyfriend. No first date. No first kiss. But that's all about to change. Two boys at West Emerson High are vying for her attention: the MVP quarterback and the school's reigning bad boy.

ABOUT THE AUTHOR

In the dawning age of scrunchies and 'Hammer Pants', a small-town musician with big-city talent found out she was expecting her third child a staggering eleven years after her last one. From that moment on, Susie Waldrop referred to her daughter Elicia as a 'blessing' which is loosely translated as an accident, albeit a pleasant one.

In true youngest-sibling fashion, Elicia lived up to the birth order standard by being fun-loving, outgoing, self-centered, and rebellious throughout her formative years. She excelled academically–a feat her sister attributes to her being the only child who was breastfed–but abandoned her studies to live in a tent in the national forest with her dogs: a Rottweiler named Bodhisattva and a Pit Bull named Sativa. The ensuing months were very hazy.

In the late 90's, during a stint in rehab, Elicia was approached by a prophet who said, "Someday you will write a book."

She was right.

Now a firm believer in the prophetic word, Elicia Hyder is a full-time writer and freelance editor living in central Florida with her husband and five children. Eventually she did make it to college, and she studied literature and creative writing at the American Military University.

Her debut novel, **The Bed She Made**, is very loosely based on the stranger-than-fiction events of her life.

www.eliciahyder.com
elicia@eliciahyder.com

Made in the USA
Monee, IL
23 May 2020